# DWARFIN' DONE

# DWARFIN' DONE

## DWARF BOUNTY HUNTER™ BOOK TWELVE

MARTHA CARR

MICHAEL ANDERLE

DISRUPTIVE IMAGINATION®

Version 1.00, September 2021
ebook ISBN: 978-1-68500-413-2
Paperback ISBN: 978-1-68500-414-9

## THE DWARFIN' DONE TEAM

**Thanks to our JIT Team:**

Jeff Goode
Zacc Pelter
Dorothy Lloyd
Diane L. Smith
Peter Manis
Jackey Hankard Brodic
Dave Hicks

*If We've missed anyone, please let us know!*

**Editor**
SkyHunter Editing Team

# CHAPTER ONE

"So." Charlie rubbed his hands together and grinned like a lunatic as he gazed around the room. "Who wants to go first?"

The five humans inside the Summer Dayz Salon in Chico, California, cast wary glances at one another before they looked at Johnny Walker and Lisa Breyer for an explanation.

The bounty hunter glanced at the ceiling and shook his head.

"For what?" The woman seated front and center among the others brushed her dark bangs out of her eyes and regarded Charlie in confusion.

He chuckled and gestured toward her. "Introductions, what else? Come on. A party's not a party if people don't get to know each other a little. Hey, don't make me break the nametags out."

"It ain't that kinda party, Charlie," Johnny grumbled.

"Sure smells like a party." Luther sniffed around the cleared floor of the salon. Both hounds stopped beside the folding banquet table and raised their noses toward the cheap, thin plastic tablecloth and all the snacks laid out on trays. "I love the smell of parties."

Rex snorted and nudged his brother aside so he could get a

better sniff. "Can we even say it's a party, bro? No one's touched these."

"Yeah. Hey, Johnny. Who's gonna eat all these—"

Their master snapped his fingers and the hounds sat immediately and thumped their tails against the tile floor.

The humans gathered to await the special guest of the hour—Bronson Harford, the shifter heir—looked completely lost.

"No chocolate-chip cookies for hounds," Lisa muttered and approached the table to shoo the hounds away subtly. "Go on. Get out of here."

"Jeez, okay."

Luther whined. "No party, then. You know why? 'Cause you're a party pooper, Lisa."

She pressed her lips together to hold a laugh back and folded her arms.

"We aren't the ones who need to start with introductions," the woman with bangs commented as she pulled her gaze away from the dejected hounds to look at Charlie. "You told me over the phone you'd explain everything when we got here."

The biker dwarf spread his arms in protest. "I didn't tell you anything."

"That was me." Johnny nodded and glanced at his black field watch. "I imagine it takes a while to get here from San Fran."

Lisa sidled up to her partner and leaned toward him to mutter through the side of his mouth, "Do you honestly think Bronson went all the way home?"

"Well, he ain't here yet so I suppose he could have gone anywhere." He grimaced and cleared his throat. "All right. Y'all are here to meet—"

"Bronson Harford." A man in his late twenties with neatly cropped hair and huge, round, thick-framed glasses sipped on the same plastic cup of iced tea he'd nursed for the last half-hour. "We know why we're here. But Megan's asking for an explanation."

"Because he needs it," the bounty hunter replied. "Y'all wanna make this whole meet and greet official, right?"

"It won't be official if he doesn't arrive." Another woman with bleached blonde hair and a flawlessly deep tan stood from the salon chair and pointed at the door. "He was supposed to be here fifteen minutes ago."

"And he's comin'."

"Even you don't look so sure of that," the man with the glasses added.

The half-dozen humans responded with a muddled cacophony of agreement, questions, resistant claims, and a few eye rolls. Two more stood from their chairs to follow the blonde toward the front door.

With an exasperated glance at Lisa, Johnny let the protests draw out as long as was necessary.

*Two second cousins and the rest of 'em all however-many-times removed. I assumed folks out here would still care about family as much as we do in the South.*

"I'm not interested in being messed around like this," the blonde woman stated and shook her head. "This is already emotional enough."

"You know what? I recognize you." A balding man in his mid-thirties pointed at Johnny. "You're the dwarf from that show. The bounty hunter."

He glared at him. "That ain't got nothin' to do with this—"

"Wait, are you filming this?" Megan's eyes widened. "Are we part of one of your…uh, bounty hunts or something?"

"Trust me, darlin'. The five of y'all ain't anywhere near my top twenty of how to lure a bounty in —"

"Johnny, that's not helping," Lisa whispered harshly.

"Hell, they're the ones tossin' accusations around."

"You'd better have us sign a waiver," the balding man added as he headed dejectedly toward the refreshments table. "We might as well get something out of this."

"I'm out." The blonde stormed across the salon. "This was a waste of time. I knew it was too good to be—"

"Okay, okay." Charlie leapt in front of her with both hands raised. "Wait a second."

She straightened and glared at him in disapproval. "Please get out of my way."

"Yeah, let her leave," Luther said. "More snacks for us."

"Hey, guy." Rex looked at the balding man and the giant stack of cookies he built quickly on a napkin in one hand. "Don't worry about dropping crumbs. I got you."

"Everyone hold on!" the biker dwarf shouted. The salon quieted instantly and he gave their human guests a pert smile before he nodded at the blonde woman he'd prevented from reaching the door. "What's your name?"

She scowled and tried to brush past him.

"Whoa, whoa. Hey, I'm not trying anything here." He raised both hands in front of him. "Honest. Listen, I'm Charlie. That's Lisa and—"

"Johnny," Megan interrupted and leaned forward in her chair. "We know your names. And it looks like you guys are wasting our time for no conceivable reason."

"Sure, okay." Charlie chuckled. "Maybe it looks that way. But hey, here's something you don't know, all right? Johnny's my baby cousin."

The bounty hunter snorted and folded his arms.

"Well, he's not a baby anymore but we're family." He gave his cousin a crooked smile and a wink before he returned his attention to the humans who stared at him in disbelief. "Family's important. And yeah, I'm older, but that doesn't always mean I know better."

*Damn straight.* Johnny raised an eyebrow. *What the hell is he goin' on about?*

"Which one of you here is the oldest?" the shifter dwarf continued.

The humans shared more confused looks but nodded and shrugged before someone responded with, "Tina."

"Okay, Tina. Which one of you is Tina?"

"Me," the blonde replied and continued to glare at him with her arms folded. "And I've had it up to here with this stupid—"

"Wow. You're the oldest?" Charlie studied her for a long moment and grinned. "I honestly would have pegged it on the dude near the cookies losing his hair but hey. Good for you."

"Charlie," Lisa warned but Tina simply tried to brush past him again.

"Wait, wait. It's a compliment." He darted in front of the impatient woman. "Forget everything I said, huh? I'm only trying to make a point."

"So am I."

"I get it. I do. You're thinking we set this whole situation up for some crazy reason we aren't willing to tell you, right? But here's the thing."

Tina looked over her shoulder at the rest of her blood relations, all of whom returned her gaze with complete cluelessness. With exaggerated patience, she rolled her eyes and gave him a sliver more of her attention.

The shifter dwarf sighed. "Family's a big deal, okay? Trust me, I know. And it's not always pretty either. Take me and Johnny, for example."

The bounty hunter grunted. "Or not."

His cousin laughed and scratched the shaved side of his mohawked head. "See? Me and him? We've been through serious crap together. Yeah, and most of it was crap I got us into or tried to pull on him simply because I could. But he's still here. If me and my cousin could go fifty years without talking to each other, you guys can go another fifteen…twenty minutes to finally meet the guy you're waiting for. Right?"

"Fifty years?" The balding man chewed on his cookies and looked from one dwarf to the other. "How old are you?"

"Well, Johnny's pushing a hundred—"

The bounty hunter scowled at his cousin. "Ain't there somewhere else you gotta be right now?"

"Come on, 'coz. He's not even here yet and I'm not done talking."

Lisa caught her partner's arm to hold him back when he lurched toward the other dwarf. She leaned toward his ear again and muttered, "Let him keep going. I think he might be onto something."

"Yeah, like pinnin' me as pushin' a damn century."

"Well, compared to human lifespans, he's not wrong."

He frowned at her and shook his head.

*That's how it's gonna be, huh? Both of 'em crackin' jokes now with me as the damn punchline.*

Against his inclination, he held himself in check a little longer to see what other useless crap would come out of Charlie's mouth.

Besides, Lisa might have been right because the humans gathered in the salon were now focused intently on the next story too.

*They ain't any less clueless-lookin' but at least he has their attention.*

"Okay. Tina?" The shifter dwarf smiled at the blonde woman in front of him before he gestured toward her empty chair. "Do you mind taking a seat? It's only for a little longer. And if I can't convince you it's a good idea, you can waltz right on out of here like you wanted. Does that sound good?"

Tina looked at a scowling Johnny and an encouragingly smiling Lisa before she sighed and shrugged. "Okay, but only a little longer."

"Thank you." Charlie rubbed his hands together and scanned the wide-eyed human faces in front of him. "So like I said, me and my cousin have been through hard times—together and apart. And if anyone knows what all of you are going through right now, it's Johnny."

The bounty hunter raised his eyebrows.

*Where the hell is he goin' with this?*

"That's what I mean about introductions." Charlie chuckled self-consciously. "I guess we should have started there. And I'm not only talking about me and my blood relations either. Lisa here's part of the family too." He stepped toward her with his arm outstretched in her direction. "The way I heard it, these two hated each other when they met."

She laughed reflexively and covered it quickly with a hand. Johnny closed his eyes.

"Two completely different professionals with completely different jobs were forced to work together and forced to make it work. And lemme tell ya, being forced to hang out with Johnny Walker isn't exactly a walk in the park."

The balding man crammed more cookies into his mouth, chuckled, and turned to face Charlie. The other humans responded with small smiles and knowing nods.

"See? You know what I'm talking about. Family gets hard." The shifter dwarf grinned. "Even before you even know you are family. And look at them now, huh? This unlikely pair over here found each other and decided they'd stick around."

Rex sniggered. "Not for much longer if Johnny kills you, dude."

"Hey, Charlie." Luther licked the cookie crumbs from around the human man's feet. "You should tell them about what Johnny and Lisa do when they're—"

Johnny snapped his fingers. "Hush up."

"We think it's funny."

"Yeah, to each their own, Johnny."

Charlie ignored the hounds' side comments and jumped into his impromptu speech with both feet. Now that he was on a roll with at least a semi-captivated audience, he wouldn't stop.

"These two"—he wagged a finger at Johnny and Lisa—"found a way to make it work. They started their own business and learned how to do this family thing their way, you know? And don't ask me what she sees in him 'cause I don't have a damn clue."

The three men chuckled and Megan and Tina studied the bounty hunter with the same mix of surprise and interest he'd received from women everywhere for his entire adult life.

Lisa bit her bottom lip to hide a smile and bumped her shoulder against his. "It's not his business anyway," she whispered.

"There ain't a damn part of this that is." Johnny growled his displeasure.

"Okay, I'll give you this much," the man with the glasses said before he took another small sip of iced tea. "You can tell a story. But seriously, what does this have to do with why you called us all here to talk to someone we've never met? We didn't even know Bronson existed until a few days ago."

"Yeah, I hear ya." Charlie gave the man an uncharacteristically businesslike nod. "Why would you guys want anything to do with a guy you don't know? Hell, it's all hearsay anyway, right? Three strangers call you and say you have an additional cousin waiting in the wings. And yeah, it might be hard to think about what your life's gonna be like knowing you have even more family out there. You're merely going about your business, doing your thing, knowing how you fit into the world, and bam! An instant extra, am I right?"

The salon fell silent at that last punchline and he grinned at his audience for another five seconds before he clicked his tongue. "Fine. Maybe that one didn't strike home like I thought it would. Okay, Johnny knows what I'm talking about, right, 'coz?"

The bounty hunter sniffed. "Nope."

"Aw, come on. You had the same thing—an instant extra."

When his cousin gave no other response but a blank stare, he scoffed. "Your kid, man. I mean the one you got now."

"Dammit, Charlie. I ain't talkin' about my—"

"Yeah, yeah. I got it. Listen, people." The shifter dwarf addressed his audience again. "This guy didn't think he'd ever have any more family than he was already stuck with. But you know what? It happened, and not only Lisa either. Johnny took in a kid, a little girl without anyone else in the world and nowhere else to go. And they're doing fine." He gestured expansively. "See? Family."

Johnny shook his head slowly and stared at his cousin.

*This dwarf's lost his damn mind.*

"That's why we're here," Charlie continued and looked from one pair of wide, thoroughly confused eyes to the next. "Family. You guys are all related and as soon as we add one more to the mix...well, you'll have one more."

"That's why we're here," the bald man said and frowned at his pile of cookies. "I think."

"So why are you here?" Tina asked. "This isn't your family. Did someone pay you for this or—"

"What? No." The biker dwarf laughed and paced the salon. "That's my whole point. Are we going way out of our way to set this little reunion up and give you guys a chance to meet for real and in person? Definitely. This isn't generally what we do."

"We don't do anythin'," Johnny muttered.

Lisa nudged his arm.

"Hey, listen. I know what it's like to go through life feeling like there isn't anyone who has my back." Charlie swallowed. "Floating around, always on the road, and disconnected. And I went through all that knowing I had family and knowing exactly where they were. I merely didn't reach out." He turned briefly toward his cousin and shrugged. "But reaching out and getting kicked to the curb is better than doing nothing."

*Uh-uh. This ain't the time to get mushy on me in public. What the hell am I supposed to do with that?*

The shifter dwarf cleared his throat. "Anyway, that's why we're here. To help all of you but mostly to help Bronson. I'm not gonna go into all the gory details of why or how but trust me. He needs it. Maybe you guys will get something out of it too. I don't know."

The humans shifted in their chairs, looked at each other, ran fingers through their hair, or shrugged.

"And he wants it too, right?" Megan asked. "I assume he does if he sent you guys to find us and call us all here first."

Johnny grimaced and stepped forward. "Now, that ain't—"

"Yeah, for sure." Charlie nodded and waved him away again. "Bronson wants to meet you. It's hard to guess how he'll react but this was his idea. You guys aren't gonna let him down, right?"

The bounty hunter glared at his cousin, clenched his hands into fists, and barely registered the hums of agreement and hesitant consent rising from the humans.

*Dammit, Charlie. You have a lifetime of lies up your damn sleeves and you went with that?*

Tina sighed heavily. "You're right. It's the least we can do."

Charlie grinned. "Awesome."

"But I don't have time to sit here for another hour doing absolutely nothing. So if he's not here soon—"

"Oh, he'll be here. Trust me, Bronson wouldn't miss this for the world." The shifter dwarf slapped one fist into his opposite hand and nodded. "So now that we got all that out of the way, where's the music in this place, huh? We should get some tunes playing. Come on, people. It's a party! And hey, bonus points for anyone who can get Johnny to dance."

With a small chuckle, Megan stood to plug her phone into the sound system and upbeat jazz music filled the salon. Her cousins and extended family stood to get snacks and refill their drinks, and Charlie joined the balding cookie-eater quickly to launch into an explosively animated story about when he and Johnny were kids.

"Wow." Lisa gave the bounty hunter's arm a reassuring squeeze. "Look at that. You weren't kidding when you said he could work a room."

"Uh-huh. With a load of bullshit. Look at him. Tellin' strangers about our days under three feet tall." Johnny scowled. "How much do you wanna bet he ain't even tellin' it right?"

She laughed and patted his shoulder. "If it keeps them here long enough for Bronson to arrive, let him have a little fun."

"At my expense?"

"It's for a good cause, right?"

He grunted and shook his head. "Family my ass. This ain't the reunion he's makin' it out to be."

"But they don't know that." She smiled at the humans, leaned toward her partner, and lowered her voice to barely above a whisper. "And if this goes the way we want it to, it's the first step to stopping this shifter war before anyone else gets hurt."

"First steps gotta be taken first, darlin'. I ain't entirely sure Bronson's gonna take to this little bit of charity the way you're hopin'."

"And if he doesn't, we're prepared for that. Do you want a drink?"

Johnny clicked his tongue and turned to scan the refreshments table. "Fine. Where's my whiskey?"

"It's not that kind of party, Johnny." She gave him a quick peck on the cheek and slipped past him toward the table. "So iced tea's gonna have to do."

The bounty hunter turned to peer through the front door of the salon at the crowded parking lot and the empty street beyond.

*This ain't the kinda party any of us are fixin' to have. If Bronson doesn't arrive soon, Plan B's screwed too.*

11

# CHAPTER TWO

"Aw, now—" Johnny closed the door to the salon's restroom and frowned. "That ain't a damn party favor, Charlie. It's a broom."

His cousin whooped heartily when the balding man bent back dangerously far to shimmy beneath the broom. "All right, Doug. I didn't think you could move like that, buddy."

The others burst out laughing.

"Who let him do this?" The bounty hunter strode toward Lisa and stuck a thumb out at the five humans playing ridiculous party games while the shifter dwarf egged them on. "I step away for two damn minutes and he's already turned the place into a circus."

"Don't tell me you've never danced the Limbo before." She raised an eyebrow and his scowl made her smile falter a little. "Right. I forgot who I'm talking to. They're only trying to loosen up."

"It ain't this kinda party either, darlin'."

"You're right. But Megan suggested it. I think it started as a joke but Charlie ran with it."

"Uh-huh. And now he can run his ass out behind the buildin'."

"It's her shop, Johnny." Lisa chuckled as the hounds pranced around the legs of the next person to shimmy under the broom being used as a Limbo bar. "At least they're doing something fun to kill the time while we wait for Bronson."

"This ain't the way to do it. If he walks in here and sees a group of grown-ass strangers throwin' a birthday party for a six-year-old when there ain't any kids around, Bronson won't even get out of his car."

"But they're still here." She folded her arms and gave him a coy smile. "You know, I might even go so far as to say that if we didn't have Charlie here, this whole plan of ours would have gone up in smoke...oh..." She looked at her watch. "Half an hour ago."

"Are you sayin' I can't keep almost half a dozen humans locked in a salon all on my own?"

"That wasn't a challenge. And we're not locking anyone up. Not now, anyway."

"Johnny!" Charlie's laugh boomed and he waved his cousin toward him. The broomstick in his other hand wobbled and almost smacked the top of Tina's head before she could finish her Limbo round. "Get over here. Come on. I bet you can go real low, 'coz."

"Of all the stupid—" Johnny scowled at the ceiling. "I can't believe this is what it turned into."

"It's only to pass the time." Lisa patted his shoulder. "I have no idea how much longer this will work, but for now, it's—"

"Johnny." Luther whipped his head up and scurried to face the front door before he uttered a low chuff. "A car."

"Yeah, Johnny. Someone's here." Rex sniffed the air and yipped. "It sure smells like him, Johnny."

"I don't see anythin'." The bounty hunter peered through the glass front door. "Y'all better not be—"

"It's him!" Luther barked sharply and his brother echoed the alarm.

"Murderer alert, Johnny!"

"Party's over, right?"

Charlie glanced at the hounds and looked at his cousin before he turned to face the door. A dark Bentley slowed in front of the entrance to the parking lot and began to turn toward the building.

"Y'all could smell him in his car all the way down the road?"

"He stinks, Johnny."

"Yeah, all the weird shifters do. Not in a good way either."

"And he had his windows down until, like, five seconds ago."

"All right." He snapped his fingers. "To me, boys."

The hounds raced between dancing legs and laughing humans to skitter across the floor toward their master. "Want us to get out there first, Johnny?"

"Yeah, we'll be the welcome wagon."

"Welcome waggin', bro." Luther spun in a quick circle after his tail and both hounds laughed.

"Hey, he's got a tail too. It's perfect!"

"Hush." Johnny snapped his fingers again and the hounds sat.

"I think this is it, people," Charlie shouted as he lowered the broom. "Hey, can we turn the music down?"

Megan took the broom from him and propped it against the wall while her extended family put two and two together. Lisa went to the phone on the counter and turned the music down to a barely-there volume before she took her place with Johnny a little inside the front door.

"That's him?" Doug asked and tilted his head.

"Oh, yeah." Charlie glanced at the Bentley as it finally rolled to a stop outside, pulled his phone from his pocket, and tapped the screen. "Hey, I gotta hit the john. You got this, 'coz?"

Johnny grunted but said nothing.

*Sure. Party games weren't part of the plan but now, he's tryin' to play it all off as casual.*

"Why don't you all sit?" Lisa suggested and gestured toward the chairs. "It might make him feel a little more comfortable than if we're all standing around, right?"

With muttered agreement and quick searches around the room, the five humans hurried to their seats. A thick, heavy silence permeated the salon again as the bathroom door shut behind Charlie.

"Yeesh." Luther's tail thumped against the floor as the only sound now. "Talk about a buzzkill."

"To you, bro, everything's a buzzkill."

"Quiet," Johnny muttered.

The driver's door of the Bentley opened and Bronson Harford stepped slowly out of his car. Johnny leaned sideways beside the door to get another look at the young shifter, who studied the front of the salon.

*You've already come this far, bud. It ain't the time to get cold feet now.*

"He looks a little lost." Megan started to rise from her chair again. "Maybe I should go out to meet him—"

"That's all right." The bounty hunter raised a hand to stop her. "Y'all sit tight. Givin' him a little space is the best thing right now."

"Oh. Right." The woman nodded quickly, frowned, and sank into her chair again. "That makes sense."

*He's gotta come in all on his own. His choice. Sure, he ain't got a clue why he's here, but still.*

Lisa nodded. "This is it."

"It's only the beginnin', darlin'."

"Yeah, fingers crossed."

Rex and Luther snuck forward toward the bottom edge of the door and sniffed furiously. "He's right outside, Johnny."

"Want us to go for the ankles or the throat?"

Their master had barely enough time to grasp both their collars and haul them back again before the door swung inward and the bell tied to the handle jingled and clicked against the glass pane.

Everyone in the room held a collective breath as Bronson

stepped halfway through the doorway. He paused when he noticed the five humans seated in salon chairs, the banquet table laden with snacks and drinks on one side of the room, and the napkins and half-empty plastic cups scattered across the counters.

"Oh, I'm…sorry." He cleared his throat. "I didn't mean to interrupt—"

"All good, man." The man with the glasses nodded and waved him forward. "Come on in."

"Thanks." Bronson stepped fully through the door but his hand still rested on the edge to keep it propped open. "This is Summer Dayz Salon, right?"

Tina smiled. "The one and only."

"You know, I'm supposed to meet someone here but I think I might have been given the wrong address—"

"Nope." Johnny shoved the door away from himself to close it and startled the newcomer enough to make him step aside quickly. The bell jingled again and the bounty hunter turned the giant deadbolt on the inside of the door as he gave their new arrival a smug nod. "This is the place, all right."

The young shifter stared at him and put the rest of the pieces together on his own when he noticed Lisa and hounds standing beside the dwarf. "What is this?"

"We're only comin' at it from a different angle, son." Johnny cocked his head toward the silently waiting humans. "I tell you what, though. It took you long enough to get here. I thought you were more the punctual type."

"No." Bronson thrust a finger in his face, snarled, and leaned toward him. "I'm done with you. Agnes should have listened to me in that club. I told her you'd simply reappear but she said you were finished. I can't believe—"

"I know it's a surprise," Lisa interjected softly, "but we're not here to hurt you."

"I'm not an idiot. You two had better be on the other side of the country tomorrow because when I—" He stopped in surprise when he tried to jerk the door open again as he hadn't realized it was locked. "What? Dammit. Come on."

"Take a load off, huh?" Johnny slid in front of the door and pressed his back against it. "Stay awhile."

"You're insane."

"Hell, you're the one tryin' to open locked doors."

Bronson snarled and lurched toward him. "If you don't get out of my way right now, dwarf, you'll—"

"He'll have to explain to everyone here why you didn't agree to stay," Lisa added firmly and raised her eyebrows.

Johnny smirked.

*Way to play it close to the belt, darlin'. He ain't gonna risk his name and his face goin' public with the news that the Harford heir attacked a couple of magicals in a damn hair salon.*

"I don't even know these people." Bronson growled in irritation. "Quit trying to screw around with me."

"Bronson?"

The shifter froze when he heard his name from the other side of the room. Johnny wiggled his eyebrows, and Bronson turned slowly.

Megan had finally stood from her chair and no one had tried to stop her this time. She met the young shifter's gaze and nodded with a warm, welcoming, reassuring smile as she took a hesitant step forward.

*If that smile doesn't get him, I have no clue what will.*

Johnny darted Lisa a "let's see how this goes" look before he folded his arms.

"It is Bronson, right?" Megan added.

The young shifter straightened and frowned as he tried to shake his confusion off. "I'm sorry. I'm usually good with remembering faces. Have we...met somewhere?"

"No." She gestured toward the five other extended family

members seated behind her, all of whom had adopted the same knowing, accepting smiles. "But that's why we're here."

"Listen, ma'am, I'm…" He cleared his throat. "I was mistaken. I shouldn't have—"

"That's it." Doug snapped his fingers and wagged a finger at the shifter. "I got it. Wow, this is insane. He looks exactly like Grandpa Harry, doesn't he?"

"Oh, you're right." Tina pushed to her feet and tilted her head to study Bronson's face. "The frown's a little off, though."

"He gets that from Great Aunt Lou," the man with the glasses added and the humans responded with light, hesitant chuckles. "At least that's the part I always remember in all her pictures." He looked at his cousins, stepped forward, and extended his hand. "I'm Mike."

"Bronson Harford." The shifter took the man's hand hesitantly for a brief shake.

"Yeah, man. We know."

"It's hard to believe we're seeing you in the flesh right now." The man in a cream-colored linen suit and a blue-and-green polka-dotted bowtie stood to approach the newcomer too. "Tommy. I…uh, well, Mike's my first cousin. I'm very sure that makes us…what? Twice removed?"

"Man, no one knows how all those extra branches on the family tree work," Doug said as he left his post beside the snack table. "The point is it's all the same tree, right?"

Megan's smile widened as she focused curiously on the young shifter. "I know it's not exactly the most polite thing to ask, but… well, I can't help it. How old are you, Bronson?"

His eyebrows drew together in a deeper frown as he gazed from one human face to the next. "Twenty-five."

"Wow." She widened her eyes. "After all this time, no one bothered to tell us. I wonder if they even knew."

Bronson swallowed thickly. "Knew what?"

"Knew about you."

# CHAPTER THREE

Johnny watched the exchange from his position in front of the door and gauged the tension that dissipated quickly in the room.

*There we go. It's all startin' to come together, ain't it, bud?*

Lisa smiled cautiously at him but stayed where she was. Now that they'd brought this family meeting together, it wasn't their place to get involved.

The hounds were amazingly quiet as Rex gnawed on a forepaw and Luther dipped his head between his legs for a good canine licking.

"Sorry." Bronson chuckled half-heartedly in his attempt to hide his confusion. "I have no idea what you're talking about."

"That's cool." Mike nodded. "It's a lot to take in, for sure. Hey, if you're not ready to open this particular Pandora's Box right now—"

"Don't call it that." Tina scoffed and smacked her cousin's arm with the back of a hand. "It makes it sound awful."

"He knows what I meant."

"No, I…" The young shifter shook his head furiously and took a step back. "I honestly don't. All this? It's… It's hard to—" His voice broke before he stopped himself and sniffed.

Johnny tugged his beard and squinted.

*All right. Gettin' all choked up's a good start.*

Bronson shook his head. "I don't know any of you and I have no idea why you're here. What is this?"

The bounty hunter took one step forward away from the door. "This right here—"

With a violent hiss of warning, the young shifter spun and glared at him. "I didn't ask you."

Lisa moved toward him and low growls rose from both hounds' throats, but Johnny held a hand up to stop all three of them. "It's the secret you ain't willin' to spill, son." He gestured toward the humans. "The one I doubt even your old man knows."

"I don't see how it's any business of yours." Bronson growled and fixed him with a hard stare. "And you had the nerve to—" His anger was instantly replaced by realization. "Wait, my father told me about a meeting here. Does he know about—"

"He doesn't know anything," Lisa interjected. "We merely asked him to get you here because we knew you wouldn't listen to us. We also knew this was something you needed to see for yourself."

Tears welled in the shifter's wide eyes. He tried to snarl at her too but it faded almost instantly as he blinked to hold back the tears. After a moment, he turned slowly to the humans who watched him with empathetic smiles and nodded encouragingly.

The partners shared another glance before Johnny grunted and looked away.

*I assume the high emotions are keepin' these folks from realizin' Charlie lied to their faces through his damn teeth. Bronson had no idea but he sure does now.*

"I need—" The young shifter choked back another emotion-hardened swallow and tried to compose himself as he lowered his head. "I need someone to tell me what's going on."

"We're your family, Bronson," Megan said.

"My…" He shook his head. "I don't have any other family. Not anyone who's still alive."

"I know. It's a little weird to take in, right?" Smiling, Mike removed his thick-framed glasses to clean them with the hem of his shirt. "That was the first thought that went through my head when your friend called us."

"That dwarf is not my friend."

Doug chuckled. "Well, maybe he should be after this, huh? It must have been fairly hard to find us all." He leaned sideways to peer around Bronson at Johnny. "Hey, by the way, how did you find us?"

The bounty hunter spread his arms in a deprecating gesture. "It's part of the job description."

"I still don't—" Bronson shook his head. "How are we related exactly?"

"Well, um…" Doug glanced at the ceiling. "See, it's…"

"Complicated," Mike finished.

Tommy scoffed. "You guys seriously didn't try to work this out on your own before we got here?"

"I didn't think there was much to work out, honestly. I simply showed up."

"Men." Tina rolled her eyes and stepped forward past all of them to get Bronson's attention. "My grandmother—and Megan's grandmother too—was Lou McCarthy. Her sister, Carol Shriver, was your grandmother."

"That's not possible." Bronson shook his head. "My grand-mothers were Madelaine Harford and Cecilia Appleman."

"Right. Of course." Megan nodded sympathetically and touched the young shifter's arm. "The grandmothers you knew."

"Richard and Carol Shriver only had one child," Tina contin-ued. "Helice—"

"No." Bronson stepped away again and shook his head. "This is…I can't…"

"Her parents died when she was very young and Helice, your mother, went to—"

"Stop." With his fists clenched at his sides, the shifter looked desperately at each of the faces of his distant cousins, who stared at him in return. "You have no idea what you're talking about."

"Hey, man," Mike said gently, "we're not trying to drop bombs on you here, okay? If you need a little more time to process this, we get it. I guess we all assumed you already knew."

"He knows his mother was adopted." Lisa stepped forward and watched Bronson warily. "Everyone knows. That part's public record and easy enough to find if you know where to look. After all, Helice and Jasper Harford did found The Appleman House."

The young shifter thrust a finger at her and his hand shook. "Stop."

"That ain't the secret," Johnny added. "Which we worked out a little too late before you and your girl Agnes gave us the slip."

"That has nothing to do with this." Bronson snarled in protest.

"It's a story with a happy endin', I'll give you that. A little girl adopted by a nice shifter family with a kid of their own, all willin' to take her in and give her a new life—a better one."

"Shifters." Megan raised her eyebrows quickly in surprise. "I don't think we realized that part."

"There's nothing to realize," the young man snapped, although the vitriol in his voice had softened again when he addressed his human cousin. "None of this was supposed to happen."

"How did we not know that?" Tommy asked and looked from Johnny to Lisa and back again. "That Helice was adopted by shifters. It's not like it matters, though. I think magic's fantastic."

The bounty hunter snorted. "Yeah, a real kick in the pants."

Lisa glanced warningly at her partner before she smiled at the five humans and their shifter cousin. "Back then, magic hadn't been revealed yet. No one declared out in the open what they were, shifters especially."

"So no one knew." Doug shrugged. "Fair enough."

"But they have to know now, right?" Tina nodded at Bronson. "If you're a shifter too—which is great, by the way, and no judgment—you got that from your dad."

"No." Bronson swallowed. "Harfords don't marry humans."

Tommy gave him a crooked smile mixed with a playful grimace. "Well, it kinda sounds like someone already broke that rule."

"You're wrong. Again, none of you have any idea what you're talking about."

"It's okay, Bronson." Megan grinned and rubbed his arm. "You don't have to explain anything. The past is behind us, right? We could all be angry that our parents and grandparents never told us about your mom and that we had another aunt or second cousin out there, even if she was adopted. Honestly, I'm merely glad we found each other."

"Yeah, and it's awesome we have a shifter cousin." Doug clapped Bronson on the opposite shoulder with a laugh. "You seem like a cool dude."

The shifter wrinkled his nose. "You don't know anything about me."

"So why don't you tell us?" Tina walked briskly toward the snack table. "Iced tea or…Diet Coke?"

Lisa stifled a laugh at that.

Johnny shook his head.

*I send Charlie out to do one simple damn job and he can't even bring back the fully-loaded pop.*

"I, uh…" Bronson shrugged. "Tea's fine. Thank you."

"That's right, my man!" Mike gave his newly discovered cousin a playful punch in the shoulder. "Hey, let's turn the music up, huh? We have a lot to talk about."

"I'm on it." Megan moved to where her phone was still plugged into the sound system. As she turned the music up and changed it to something a little more lively than the previous jazz instrumentals, she called over her shoulder, "So what do you do, Bronson? I mean, for a living."

"Oh, yeah." Doug nodded vigorously and shoved another cookie into his mouth. "That's gotta be good, right?"

"It is what it is." The young shifter shrugged and accepted the plastic cup of iced tea from Tina like he was moving through a dream. "I recently took over the family business."

"No kidding? What's the business?"

"Charity, mostly."

"Ha." Tommy pointed at him. "Now that's something you got from your mom, right?"

"Everyone loves a charitable guy." Mike lifted his plastic cup in a toast. "I bet you know that better than anyone, huh?"

Bronson replied with a small, weak smile and raised his cup slowly halfway before he drank.

Lisa sidled slowly toward her partner and leaned toward him to mutter, "It looks like it's going fairly well."

"What a thing looks like ain't always what it is, darlin'." He lowered his head. "Especially on this case."

"True. Still, I'd say a smile from Bronson, even a confused one, is a step in the right direction. He needs this although I don't think he knows how much."

"Naw, he knows." Johnny shrugged and glanced at the young shifter. "But goin' after somethin' like this on his own would mean he couldn't keep hidin' from the truth. Hell, he wants to."

"Then it's a good thing he has Johnny Walker Investigations to force him into it, huh?"

He darted her a sidelong glance and smirked. "Is that what we do now? Force folks into gettin' what they want?"

She smiled in response. "Hey, if it works. To be honest, I can't help wondering if it will work." She nodded toward Bronson surrounded by his newfound human family. "Do we still think this is enough to pull him out of his…uh, you know?"

*His murderous rage and thirst for vengeance? Yeah, we'd be idiots to bring all that up right now.*

"It's hard to tell just yet, darlin'." Johnny folded his arms. "But if I had to say one way or the other, I reckon I'd—"

"What?" Bronson looked up sharply from his cup to stare at Tina with wide eyes.

The blonde woman grinned and shrugged one shoulder. "You know, are you seeing anyone? If there's no one special right now, that's okay. You have an entire family business to run, right?"

"Aw, come on." Doug elbowed the young shifter in the side, completely oblivious to how rigid he had become. "A good-looking guy like him? I bet he has women lining up across San Francisco simply to—"

"No." Bronson's voice had dropped into a low growl as he stared blankly across the salon. "There is no one."

"Oh, okay. That's cool, man. You have plenty of time to—"

The red plastic cup in Bronson's hand popped as he clenched his fist around it, and the rest of his iced tea spilled over the side and spattered the floor. The humans stepped away to avoid the mess and stared at him.

Lisa grimaced. "You were saying?"

"Shit." Johnny gritted his teeth. "We should have told 'em not to mention relationships."

# CHAPTER FOUR

"Hey. Whoa." Mike leaned toward his shifter cousin and stared at the crumpled cup. "Are you okay, man?"

Bronson hissed a breath and in the mirrors lining the walls of the salon, the two partners had a clear view of his eyes flashing silver before he snarled and threw the destroyed cup on the floor. "This was a mistake."

The humans all backed away in surprise. Megan was the first to recover from seeing a shifter on the verge of losing control. "Wait a minute. Bronson."

She hurried after him but he didn't stop. Johnny and Lisa had left their positions at the door, which gave the enraged shifter direct access without interception. He didn't bother with the lock this time either and when he shoved against the door with both hands and a furious snarl, the hinges shrieked and bent before the lock and the door's metal frame burst apart.

"Holy shit!" Luther leapt to his feet and yipped. "Now it's a party, Johnny."

Rex scrambled in front of his brother to head for the door. "Didn't know we were gonna start breaking things."

"Hey!" Megan stared at the damage to her establishment. "There's no reason to break doors—"

"Yeah, we'll pay for the damage," Lisa said quickly before she raced outside after Bronson.

Johnny scowled at the back of her head as he stormed onto the sidewalk.

*Every damn time. Someone else breaks something and I gotta be the one to pay for it. That ain't how to run a business.*

"Bronson, wait." Lisa jogged toward the driver's door of the Bentley, which the shifter had barely jerked open before she pressed her hand against the frame to close it again. "Take a second to think about this, okay?"

His eyes widened as he glared at her and tried not to unleash his freshly returned rage on the half-Light Elf who tried to stop him. "Get your hand off my car."

"This ain't the way to do it, Bronson," Johnny added. "You can't run away from this. We know you been keepin' this secret your whole life and now, it's out and in your face. But that ain't a reason to—"

"How much is my father paying you for this?" the young shifter roared. "To corner me out here and make me think those...those humans are my family?"

"He ain't paid us a dime." The bounty hunter stopped beside his partner and folded his arms, although his hand itched to grasp an explosive disk on the utility belt he now wished he'd kept on. "Jasper has no clue who those folks are in there or even why we asked him to send you here."

Lisa nodded. "All he knows is that we called in a favor and he was glad to help us without getting any of the details."

"A favor?" Bronson laughed bitterly. "For what?"

Johnny shook his head. "That's private information, son—"

"Don't call me that!" With a thud and squeal of dented metal, Bronson almost drove his fist through the side of the Bentley. "Do you think you know what I need? You have no clue what you're doing. And your shitty attempt to...to make me forget who I am didn't work. You lose!"

"Lose?" The dwarf lunged at him and drove his back against the dented side of the car with both fists buried in the young man's shirt. "You listen here, boy. This ain't a goddamn game!"

The hounds barked madly and howled as they skittered wildly across the asphalt. "Get him, Johnny."

"Yeah, show him what you're made of." Luther stopped and cocked his head. "Wait, what is Johnny made of?"

"Shifters are dead," Johnny snarled as he thumped Bronson against the car again. "Hundreds of 'em. And I tell you what, I have half a mind to let you join 'em right now."

"But he won't," Lisa interjected hastily, stared at the young shifter, and hoped her partner was lucid enough to get the hint. "That's why we're here. Because none of us want any more bloodshed, right?"

"Why—" Bronson grimaced and ripped the dwarf's hands away from his shirt. "Why should I listen to anything you have to say? This doesn't have anything to do with you."

Johnny thrust a condemning finger at the shifter's face and roared, "Well, you'd best believe what we're tellin' ya—" Lisa's hand brushed the back of his shoulder and made him catch a breath before he took two steps out of Bronson's personal space, followed by another deep breath. "You'd best believe we mean everythin' we're tellin' you right now, Bronson. None of us want a war."

"Yeah, so much so that you set this whole elaborate scheme up simply to throw me off."

"Most things ain't the way they seem, Bronson." The dwarf rolled his shoulders back. "And I mean most things, especially those drivin' you to do the wrong damn thing for what you think are the right reasons."

"I have no idea what that's supposed to mean." The shifter

reached for the door handle. "If you stand in my way this time, I will run you over."

"Maybe you don't know what it means," Lisa added hastily, "but you do have more to fight for now. Right?"

Bronson paused and glared at his reflection in the Bentley's darkly tinted window. He didn't say anything either but at least she'd caught his attention.

"That's right." She nodded and stepped slowly toward him. "You have more to fight for. And it's a good reason to do the right thing. Those people in there are your family—"

"I have a family."

"Uh-huh, sure." Johnny shrugged. "A pops who don't know left from right outside the foundation and y'all's estate and a murderin' uncle who ain't even yours by blood. He knows what your mama was, doesn't he?"

"I don't have to listen to this—"

"He knows what happened to her—his own sister—and he's still killin' transformed shifters he thinks ain't fit to stick around if they ain't a part of his plan."

"Johnny, please..." Lisa held a hand up to silence him. "Hold on."

"It's all right there in front of him and the kid still won't open his damn eyes!"

She ignored him and focused intently on the young man hunched over his car and still at war with himself over the entire situation. "Bronson, listen to me. Meeting relatives you didn't know you had doesn't make Jasper or Langley or anyone else less than your family. But those people in there? They care about you."

"They have no idea who I am."

"They don't have to. They care about you simply because you're family. Not because you're taking over the foundation for your dad or you're Langley's nephew, or because you're Tyro—"

"Or a goddamn vigilante-gone-bad tryin' to get some kinda warped justice for his murdered girlfriend," Johnny snapped.

Lisa glared at her partner but couldn't risk spending any more time cleaning up after his outbursts. "We know you want to do the right thing, Bronson. We know all this—the skirmishes, the wars, the violence—is not what you truly want. That's why we put this whole thing together—to remind you. We're not here with weapons and handcuffs, okay?"

The bounty hunter snorted. "We sure as hell could have, I'll tell you that."

"Think about it." She rested her hand on the tortured shifter's arm and he flinched a little at her touch but continued to glare at his reflection. "The transformed you're trying to blame for all your pain have families too. Families exactly like yours. Humans who aren't a part of this world but care about them just the same. And yes, if you continue down this road, it will affect so many more than merely the shifters from both factions. You know that."

Bronson was trembling now but he still didn't move.

*Well, hell. If I'd known it was this easy to talk some sense into the kid from the beginnin', I would have saved us all a couple of weeks of torture.*

"They're still waiting for you inside," Lisa said gently. "If you want to go back in and—"

"Shut up!" With another furious snarl, Bronson whirled toward her and shoved her away with both hands. She stumbled and shifted her hand to her pistol in the shoulder holster that wasn't there.

"Whoa, whoa! Hey!" Rex crouched and snarled. "That's our Light Elf, asshole."

Luther snapped at the shifter's ankle. "Yeah, asshole. No one touches our two-legs."

His eyes flashed silver as he clenched both fists but the impending shift was knocked out of him when Johnny charged with a low oath and swung an uppercut into his gut. He grasped the young man's collar again and thumped him against the car.

"We were playin' nice, boy." He growled in Bronson's face. "But you lay a finger on her one more time, even for half a second, and I'll show you what losin' looks like."

"Johnny, I'm fine," Lisa said breathlessly. "I'm not hurt. It's okay."

"Uh-huh." The bounty hunter jerked his head toward the young shifter's face and widened his eyes. "I'm only makin' real sure we understand each other, darlin'."

Bronson didn't react but he didn't fight back either.

With a curt nod, Johnny shoved him against the car again and released his collar before he stepped back and gestured warningly. "It looks like you have some serious contemplatin' to get to. That's fine but it doesn't mean we ain't watchin'—"

"I know what I'm doing!" Bronson lurched away from the car and punched him in the jaw.

"Hey!" Lisa summoned an orb of golden light energy in one hand and tried to keep it hidden from view. It wasn't something that would go down well in the middle of a parking lot in broad daylight. "This is not the way you want to handle this."

Johnny grunted rubbed his jaw. "What the hell? You call this knowin' what you're doin'?"

"No." The shifter's eyes flashed silver again. "I'm making up for a mistake I shouldn't have made."

"Like punchin' me in the face. You're damn right you sh—"

Bronson swung his other fist into the opposite side of his face and the bounty hunter reeled.

"Bronson, stop it." Lisa hissed a sharp breath. "This is your last warning."

"Hell, forget the last one." Johnny shook his head vigorously and wiggled his jaw. "He done used 'em all up."

"Uh-oh." Luther sniggered. "Johnny's mad now, shifter."

Rex barked twice. "Yeah, you better run."

"You want a fight?" The dwarf spread his arms in a challenging gesture. "It's the best way to work out a few issues. Let's go."

"Johnny, this is not why we're here," Lisa protested.

"Hell, I ain't here to get my face beat either. Let's go!"

The young shifter snarled and leapt toward him. His eyes flashed again and he drew back for another swing.

The broken door at the front of the salon banged against the wall, followed by a high-pitched laugh that made everyone in the parking lot stop and turn to look.

Charlie strutted onto the sidewalk with his arms spread expansively. "Bronson! You made it. Whew, lemme tell ya, buddy. Burritos and a sloppy joe for lunch? Not a good idea. Sorry I missed the welcome."

Bronson snarled. "What's he doing here?"

Johnny cocked his head. "I thought it might help havin' another transformed around—make you feel a little more like you fit in. You know, since you've been killin' off all your own kinda shifters during the last few months—"

"I am nothing like them!" Bronson bellowed. "I would never do what they did to me. What they did to Addison—"

"That's exactly what you're doing," Lisa said firmly. "It's the same thing. And so many people are left behind wondering why their loved ones are gone because of something they had no control over."

"You don't see any of them killin' shifters under a piss-poor fake name, do ya?" Johnny added.

"It's not the same." The young man growled with suppressed fury. "And I have to finish what I—"

"Hey!" Charlie shouted again from the doorway. "You aren't going anywhere, right? I thought you were gonna stick around and party with the fam."

Bronson gritted his teeth and charged toward the front of the salon, but he stopped when he saw Tina, Doug, Megan, Mike, and

Tommy all crowded around the doorway behind the biker dwarf. They stared at him with wide eyes, confused and hurt and undoubtedly a little scared that their newest cousin would try to beat up the magicals who'd brought them together for a good reason.

"Maybe..." Megan stepped toward the sidewalk. "Maybe we can help?"

After he drew in a shuddering gasp, Bronson spun and staggered toward his car.

"You oughtta stay," Johnny told him.

"We can help you too," Lisa added. "It starts with making only one different choice, Bronson—"

"Get out of my way." He strode past her and could have torn the driver's door off his Bentley if he'd been any more enraged.

"Whoa, whoa. Hold up." Charlie raced toward the car and slapped both hands on the hood. "Come on, man. You can't run away now that—"

Bronson slammed the door shut and the shifter dwarf leapt away from the hood when the Bentley's engine revved violently. The Harford heir ground the gear into reverse and accelerated across the parking lot. Thick plumes of smoke rose from the tires when the car skidded in a jerky circle before it fishtailed toward the side street.

Five seconds later, the young shifter and his car disappeared from view.

# CHAPTER FIVE

"Aw, man…" Luther's ears and tail drooped together. "I thought we were at least gonna have a little fun with him, Johnny."

"Yeah, why didn't you fight him? That was fun when he was a wolf."

"To fight him wasn't the point, boys," Johnny grumbled. "And I'm sure that ain't what he wants either."

"Wait." Luther sat to scratch behind one ear. "I thought the point was always to have fun."

"Would have been fun, Johnny."

Their master snapped his fingers. "That's enough."

Lisa waved away the thick exhaust smoke as she approached her partner, and they both stared down the road where Bronson had disappeared. "Well…I guess it went better than it could have. How's your face?"

She took his chin and turned his head gingerly from side to side. Johnny scowled at her while she studied him. "That's the last damn time I'm leavin' my gear in the car."

"We agreed it was better to be unarmed for this. You know, so he didn't get the wrong idea."

"It looks like he got the wrong idea anyway, right?" Charlie commented as he walked toward them. When the bounty hunter turned to face him, his cousin winced. "That's probably gonna leave a mark, 'coz."

"What the hell are you talkin' about? You can't see a damn thing through my beard."

"I don't have to." He clapped a hand on Johnny's shoulder and nodded. "You only get that look in your eyes when someone hit you hard enough to make you wanna kill them."

He shrugged off the attentions of his two companions, grunted belligerently, and strode across the parking lot toward the front of the shop. "Sorry, folks. It didn't work out the way we wanted but he'll come around."

"Is he…" Doug scratched his head. "Is he okay?"

"I tell you what, any fella who throws a punch like that will be fine."

"I wish there was something we could do," Megan added.

"Naw. Nothin' right now. Except let me pay for your busted door. Charlie."

"Yeah."

Johnny turned and gestured impatiently. "Where is she?"

"Oh! Ha." The biker dwarf sniggered. "I got caught up in watching the show and I almost forgot."

He stuck two fingers between his lips and blew an ear-splitting whistle.

"Ah! What the—" Rex whimpered and pawed at his ear. "That's as bad as the hound-gun, Johnny."

Luther barked sharply. "Don't ever do that again or I'll eat your boots."

Charlie chuckled before he shouted, "He's gone!"

Soft footsteps approached from the side of the building and a moment later, a shifter woman wearing black jeans and a black long-sleeved shirt stepped into the parking lot to join them. She scanned the area, then the faces of Johnny and his team. "I assume he didn't take the bait."

"It wasn't bait." Lisa frowned. "It was real. He merely didn't want it to be."

"Are you sure he didn't run because he smelled me here?" the woman asked.

Charlie scoffed. "Please. It's hard enough for me to tell the difference. All he smelled was another transformed on the lot and probably on his car and as far as he knows, I'm the only one."

Rex snorted and shook his head. "Yeah, and you all stink."

"Serious stink," Luther added.

"Like someone burned Johnny's workshop with crazy magic."

Johnny snapped his fingers. "Now that's blasphemy. Hush up."

The shifter woman folded her arms and raised an eyebrow. "Fine. He won't be able to tell the difference. Do you think it'll work?"

"Are you kiddin' me?" The bounty hunter tilted his head to give her a condescending sidelong glance. "There ain't a damn thing I made that don't work exactly the way it's meant to."

She shook her head and tried to hide a smile. "I'm not talking about the tracking device I put on his car. I'm talking about what happens after."

"Uh-huh."

Lisa shrugged. "I guess all we can do now is wait and hope this first part loosened him up enough."

"I don't know." Charlie squinted and scratched his head. "One mention of a girlfriend and the guy completely lost it. If you take a dude as broken as Bronson Harford and drop enough surprises on him, I guess there are only two ways it could go."

"Right." The half-Light Elf took a deep breath and nodded. "He either comes to his senses and recognizes that he's been going about this the wrong way or—"

"Or he doubles down and goes in the complete opposite direction," the shifter woman finished. "It's hard to imagine anything worse than the damage Tyro's already caused but I think you were right back there."

"Of course I was." Johnny studied her for a long moment. "Which part are you talkin' about?"

"The part where this war grows way beyond two shifter factions."

The parking lot fell silent as they all let the severity of that potential and seriously major problem sink in. Luther sniffed along the edge of the sidewalk and stopped in front of the shifter woman's black boots for a fierce investigation. He snorted violently, shook his head, and trotted away from her. "Come on, lady. Can't you freaky shifters find a way to cover that stink? You're killing me."

She looked slowly at him with hardly any expression at all. "Trust me, dog. If I were killing you, you'd know."

Rex sniggered. "That hound? No way. He'd tell you to stop tickling him before he asked for snacks afterward."

"That's right, lady. I'm that fierce." Luther barked once at her.

"Bro, you're that dumb."

"Ha. Thanks, Rex. You always got my back—wait. Hey. Take that back."

"It's the truth."

"Boys." Johnny snapped his fingers and Rex sat immediately before Luther barreled into him with a snarl. "Aw, hell."

The hounds resolved the issue with a five-second scuffle of snapping teeth, low growls, and a few sharp yips before they reached canine agreement and instantly changed course toward the salon's front door.

"Yeah, yeah. You're right. Time for snacks. Hey, two-legs. You got any leftover cookies in here?"

"They can't hear you, bro."

"Doesn't mean they can't hear me, know what I'm saying?"

When Johnny gave up trying to get the hounds' attention and turned to face his cobbled-together team, he found the shifter woman staring at him. "Do you have somethin' to say, darlin'?"

"Your dogs talk too much."

"Oh, he already knows that," Charlie interjected with a chuckle. "He can hear them too. Did you realize that part already?"

"It doesn't matter now anyhow, Charlie." Johnny glared at him. "But thanks for dishin' out information that ain't yours to dish. And here's another piece for ya." He pointed at the shifter woman and raised an eyebrow. "I'm the only magical who gets to complain about my hounds, understand?"

She laughed wryly. "Sure."

"I'd better help them clean up in there," Lisa said before she moved to the salon's broken door. "And keep Rex and Luther from killing themselves with chocolate chips as the murder weapon."

"I'll come with you." Charlie grinned at the shifter woman and gave her a thumbs-up. "Way to go. Excellent espionage. Good job not getting caught."

As he followed Lisa inside, the shifter woman frowned at him in confusion. "Is he like that all the time or is he merely having an off-day?"

"Charlie?" Johnny shrugged. "By now, I think he's lost more than his fair share of brain cells. But he ain't dead."

"Whatever. I'll tell the others to stand by."

"Uh-huh." He watched her pull out a thin, sleek-looking phone unlike any he'd seen before.

*That's gotta be Coalition gear. No way Azure the warlord has access to someone who can make anything like that.*

"Do these…others know what to expect?" he asked.

"That was the plan all along, isn't it?"

"I'm simply double-checkin'. Which one are you, by the way?"

The woman finished sending her typed message and looked slowly at him as she slipped the thin phone into her back pocket. "Dee."

"Dee. Have we met before?"

"If you count knocking out your entire team, tying you up,

and throwing you in a magic-proof cell at our headquarters, then yeah. I guess we've met."

Johnny snorted. "That's right. My bad. All y'all transformed resistance fighters look the same these days."

Dee cracked a smile and folded her arms. "I feel the same way about dwarves."

"Yeah, well, I'm the only Johnny Walker. You ain't forgettin' my face after we help y'all end a war before it starts."

"We'll see."

# CHAPTER SIX

Bronson Harford paced across the large, richly decorated living room of his apartment on the third floor of the Harford estate. The table in his breakfast nook lay in half a dozen pieces beside the bay window. Shattered glass was strewn across the floor beside the two expensive standing lamps he'd hurled across the room in his rage. Broken dishes and spilled food coated the marble of the kitchen countertops and floor.

He snarled, ignored the mess around him completely, and clutched two huge fistfuls of his hair.

*It shouldn't take this long for him to get back to me. How hard is it to pick up the phone and reply to a single—*

His phone buzzed loudly on the countertop beside an uncovered tray of half-eaten roast chicken.

"Finally!" The young shifter leapt across the living room to get to his phone and didn't even bother to look at the caller ID before he answered immediately. "It's been two days and you—"

"Yes, it has, son," Jasper said flatly on the other line. "I'm glad you finally answered your phone."

*I'm not.*

Bronson jerked the phone away from his ear to see the number for his father's direct line illuminated on the screen.

*It had to be Dad and not Langley, didn't it?*

"What do you want?"

Jasper sighed. "I want to give you your space, Bronson. If that's what you truly want. But I'm concerned about—"

"It's not what I want, Dad. It's what I need. And if I need anything else, I'll call you." With a growl, he stabbed his phone screen to end the call and shoved the rest of the uneaten chicken off the counter. The serving tray clattered noisily on the marble floor with the meal.

*I can't talk to him. Not now. He sent those morons to make me think I'd found my family and now he wants to have a chat about it?*

With a bitter laugh, he whirled and barely managed to not hurl his phone across the room too.

*He knows about Mom. He has to. But for how long? Of course he wouldn't tell me. Me—his son and his damn* successor. *And this whole time, he said nothing.*

"You left me in the dark!" Bronson bellowed and kicked the toppled silver tray across the floor until it came to a violent stop against the front door of his apartment.

Breathing heavily, he stared at it and considered placing his phone on the counter so he wouldn't end up breaking that too.

*If he knows she wasn't born a shifter and was one of them, that's one thing. He can't find out anything else about what I've done and what I'm still doing.*

He spun and pounded both fists on the kitchen counter. It was only pure luck that he didn't shatter his phone in the process.

"He'll disown me. Cut me off and I'll lose everything."

With a scowl, he pulled up his Uncle Langley's cell number and furiously typed the fifth message in the last forty-eight hours.

*Dammit, Langley. This is important! And if you can't see that by now, you're as bad as the rest of them.*

Sending a text like that to his uncle under the overpowering influence of his rage wasn't generally a part of Bronson Harford's character. He was so tired of being ignored, overlooked, and treated like a child. Acting like one now didn't make him feel any better, though.

*I deserve respect!*

He thumped his fist on the countertop again before he stormed around the granite island toward the opposite wall of the kitchen.

"They all think they can simply move me across the board like a fucking pawn, don't they? Bronson, do this. Go there. Bring the target back. Call the governor. Don't forget your place." With a bitter laugh, he snatched up the half-empty bottle of Beluga Noble Gold—his third in the last two days—and poured himself a sloppy vodka on the rocks. He tossed it back and grimaced.

"It's never gonna stop. I won't get out from under this until they are gone. All of them."

He poured another drink and spilled at least half of it over the side and onto the counter.

*I'd be fine if they all simply disappeared.*

That thought made him stop.

*No. Not all of them. Mom should still be here. Addison should still—*

His throat constricted and the freshly refilled rocks glass almost toppled off the counter when he went to pick it up again.

"Addison…"

Tears welled in Bronson's eyes and he blinked them away slowly before he downed yet another stiff drink.

*Too many lies and too much hiding. I have to get out of here.*

That thought gave him the nudge he needed to move out of his stupor. He ran a hand through his disheveled hair, snarled, and stormed across the kitchen again to snatch his keys off the counter. When he headed to the door of his apartment, he had only one place in mind. He didn't even pause to think before he took the entire bottle of vodka off the counter to take with him on the road.

---

A sober person would have made the trip from Sausalito to Sacramento in close to two hours. With his Bentley and a bottle of Beluga Noble Gold, Bronson Harford made it in under an hour and a half. He couldn't remember the last time he'd been in the city for anything that wasn't a direct mission for Kaiser and his never-ending crusade.

*No. I don't want to remember the last time. I can't.*

His attempt to ignore the memories of Addison's funeral service—complete with an empty casket for a body that had never been found—seemed impossible as he drove through the heart of Sacramento. It didn't stop him from driving the old route he'd taken so many times that he could practically do it blindfolded.

Doing it with a heavy buzz was as easy, and he didn't even realize where he was going until he turned onto the street and slowed the Bentley to a crawl.

More memories flooded through him—meeting Carter and Megan Taylor, warm invitations to step inside for dinner, barbeques on the back porch during long summer nights, and Christmas around a blazing fire.

*I shouldn't be here. It won't solve anything.*

The Bentley crawled with aching slowness past the home of Addison's parents and Bronson gazed at the front door with glistening, bloodshot eyes.

*They're in there, living their lives without her and I can't even stop to say hi. Or to say I'm sorry and tell them I'm trying to fix it.*

The tears burned in his eyes again and in a fit of guilt and shame, he pushed hard on the accelerator and raced down the street, simply to get away. No matter what he did or how hard he tried, he couldn't fix any of this. Now, every two-bit magical with a chip on their shoulder was popping out of the woodwork.

*Trying to tell me what to do. Me—Bronson Harford. I'm not a damn puppet!*

The young shifter had lost count of how many times he'd taken long pulls from the bottle of vodka nestled beside him on the passenger seat. It was enough to give him courage, though, to do what he hadn't been able to bring himself to do yet.

He'd only been to this cemetery once a few months before when the empty casket had been lowered into the ground and the headstone with Addison Taylor's name on it had marked the seal on her final resting place. At least as far as the rest of the world was concerned.

It was the closest Bronson could get to her now and he parked the Bentley neatly enough between the lines in the parking lot before he snatched his trusty bottle up and walked through the entrance gates.

As he staggered down the main walkway, he snarled and wiped his eyes angrily with the back of a rough hand. All the gravesites blurred together. He couldn't read a single name on the headstones he passed, not even those as freshly engraved as the one he was looking for. Still, he didn't need to look for her name.

He would never forget where they hadn't buried her and where her parents hadn't had the closure they'd hoped to find through a funeral. He recalled it vividly even though he hadn't come to visit since the hole was dug and filled in again on top of nothing but glossy, expensive wood and silk lining.

*They should have chosen somewhere more private. Even if she was in there, she doesn't deserve to be surrounded by strangers.*

Addison's parents had graciously accepted the Harford family's offer to pay for their daughter's funeral and burial expenses but they'd drawn the line at them choosing a site. Even for an empty grave.

Through his tears, he forced himself to focus on the giant A and T on the headstone before he fell to his knees at the foot of the grave. Below her name was an epitaph that cut him to the core—*Beloved daughter and friend. She will never be lost.*

*She is lost and she was so much more than a daughter and a friend. Addison was mine. She was everything.*

A low moan escaped him as he hunched over his knees in the warm, dry dirt beneath the baking California sun. Bronson muffled it with another long swig of booze and swayed.

"I can't…"

When he looked at the headstone again and noticed the fresh bouquet of brightly colored flowers resting at its base, what little remained of his composure completely snapped.

"I'm so sorry," he whispered. "I should have done something. I should have stepped in and taken you out of there when I had the chance. I never meant—"

A strangled sob escaped him and the almost empty bottle slipped from his fingers before he landed in the browning grass with a dull thud.

"I miss you so much, babe. Every single day. I can't get…can't get my head straight. It's all a mess. Everything." The tears fell freely now and as he leaned even farther over his bent knees, the dam of his emotions finally broke. He sobbed at the foot of his fiancée's grave and said all the things he hadn't dared to say out loud since the night he'd lost her.

"I've done so many horrible things trying to make this right, baby. I thought I could fix it. I've been trying so hard to…to keep my heart out of it. To not let it eat me up. I know you'd tell me to let it go and forgive them but how am I supposed to do that, huh?"

Two small blackbirds fluttered from the tree behind him and swooped low over the cemetery before they vanished into the clear blue sky.

"I can't forgive them. Those bastards took you from me and

I'm the only one who can do anything about it. And now…now I have this secret that's about to be blown wide open. The only secret I never told you because Mom made me promise to not tell anyone and to not talk about it out loud ever. Jesus, that was the last thing she said to me before she died and I can't even forgive her—"

Another sob escaped him and he could barely lift his head to wipe away the tears, the sweat, and the wetness around his nose and mouth. Somewhere nearby, the rustle of a small animal, maybe a rabbit, rose through the otherwise silent cemetery, but Bronson couldn't be bothered to look around. He was buried too deeply in his grief, drunkenness, and the weight of everything on his shoulders.

"I couldn't tell you, Addy. I couldn't. A…a deadly secret. That's what she said. But she was already dying so it's only deadly for me. If anyone else finds out about what I've done—"

His voice broke at the end and he doubled over his knees and tried to fight the unending sobs that built up under his dwindling courage.

A twig snapped behind him.

"It sounds like you might want to start with trying to forgive yourself first."

Bronson spun on his knees and with a trembling hand, barely stopped himself from falling back. His anger boiled up again with a snarl. "What kind of heartless—"

All the curses and insults and indignation at being caught there in his current state—at the grave of his fiancée—disappeared the second he saw the woman who'd spoken.

"What—"

"Bronson." Addison spread her arms slowly and gave him a small, weak smile. Her gaze darted toward the empty liquor bottle on the ground beside him and she lowered her head. "I know this is—"

"Get away from me." He scrambled across the grass in a drunken crabwalk. "Who the hell are you? Who sent you?"

"Babe, it's me."

She looked exactly like his Addison—maybe a little thinner and rougher around the edges but exactly like her.

*That's impossible. Why am I even comparing them? This isn't her!*

The fake Addison stepped forward toward the foot of the real Addison's empty grave and Bronson snarled. "Don't. Don't come any closer."

"Okay." She raised both hands, widened her eyes, and stopped where she was. "Okay. I know you probably have so many questions right now—"

"Get out!" He stabbed a finger at the entrance to the cemetery. "This is a sick joke. You're not her."

"Bronson—"

"Leave me alone!"

"Will you at least give me a chance to explain?"

"No!" He slapped a hand on top of the gravestone and hauled himself to his feet. Stupidly, he had to steady himself with both hands after that because the entire world was spinning. "You're not real. This isn't happening. That's what this is. I'm...I'm hallucinating."

"I promise you I'm right here."

"Yeah, that's it." Relatively sure he wouldn't fall if he let go of the gravestone, he turned to pace in a stumbling, swerving line behind her grave. "I'm finally insane. Ha. That makes so much sense. Who wouldn't go insane if they were in my...my shoes?"

With a heavy scowl, he spun to pace in the other direction and almost lost his footing.

*Fine. It's fine. I'm only a deranged shifter hallucinating my dead girlfriend. I can work with that. Shit, maybe I should have gone to that therapist Dad recommended.*

"Bronson."

"No. No, no, no."

"Look at me."

He stopped pacing and slowly did what his hallucination had told him to do.

*Yep. Utterly crazy. Talking to the voices in my head and doing what they say. God, she looks so real.*

Addison took another cautious step forward. "It's me. I'm truly here and no, you're not crazy."

"That's what crazy people tell themselves," he whispered and his eyes bulged in disbelief. "There's no way you're real. I watched you…I watched you die."

"You watched me get shot and fall into the bay." Her small smile had completely faded now, replaced by a sympathetic frown, and her lips pressed tightly together. "It's not your fault, Bronson. There was no way you could have known—"

"No. Stop." He spun fully toward her and pointed with a condemning finger. "I'm not listening to you. I need…I need another drink."

"Bronson."

"That'll make all this go away. I have to—"

"Bronson, you have to stop. This isn't how I wanted this to go either but we need to talk. Come here." Addison moved toward him but he leapt away.

"I won't go anywhere with anyone. This is my life even if I'm hallucinating."

"Please."

"Stop telling me what to do!" He snarled, fueled by his rage without any thought about how stupid it was to charge a figment of his imagination and his grief.

Bronson lunged toward her with outstretched hands. His eyes flashed silver and the tingle of an oncoming shift prickled beneath the surface of his skin but his foot snagged on an uneven lump of soil and he pitched forward with a cry.

As drunk as he was, he couldn't react in time to stop his face from hitting the dirt first. His arms were pinned awkwardly beneath him and he was vaguely conscious of a dull ache although he wasn't sure what part of him hurt.

"Whoa, hey." Addison moved cautiously toward him. "Are you all right?"

With a low groan, he stared at the black combat boots that stepped closer across the grass.

*She would never wear those. There's no way this is real.*

"I'm..." He panted as his eyelids fluttered and sagged closed. "I'm not..."

The sentence faded into a sigh and he passed out completely beside Addison Taylor's grave.

For a moment, she stared at him, then dropped into a crouch beside the unconscious Harford heir and reached out tentatively to touch his shoulder. He didn't stir.

"Bronson? Can you—"

A loud, stuttering snore interrupted her and even when she shook him gently, she couldn't rouse the inebriated man drunk on grief and hard liquor.

"Shit." She removed her hand and tapped her fingers against her lips. "This certainly wasn't part of the plan."

It took her another minute crouched there and staring at her grieving fiancé before she could finally bring herself to brush the blades of dry, brown grass off the side of his cheek.

*He truly doesn't believe I'm here. And I can't convince him of anything while he's like this.*

Addison stood, pulled her phone from her back pocket, and scrolled through her contacts to find Johnny Walker's number. She paused before she dialed it.

*Maybe they drove him to this point with that family reunion or he would have gotten here all on his own. Johnny and Lisa will only make it worse when he's like this. It's time for Plan B.*

She pulled Dee's number up instead and made the call.

# CHAPTER SEVEN

When Bronson woke, he immediately wished he hadn't. His head pounded fiercely and a sharp pain seared behind his eyelids with every beat of his pulse.

*What did I do?*

The foggy memory of his drunken tirade at the cemetery returned slowly. The booze, the crying, and his drunken confession at the foot of a grave that didn't even hold the remains of the one he'd been talking to.

"Addison." He broke into a fit of dry, wheezing coughs when that single word seemed to burn his throat raw.

*Jesus, I hallucinated her and then I passed out like an idiot. I need to get home. I need to—*

He tried to roll over and push himself off the ground but his wrists were bound behind his back.

*What the hell?*

A few weak tugs against the restraints convinced him he wouldn't be able to free himself. After a moment, he noticed how cold the ground felt against his cheek—not the warm, brittle grass of the cemetery but smooth concrete.

His eyes fluttered open and he realized he was in complete

darkness. Somewhere behind him, the slow, steady drip of water that plinked into a shallow pool seemed incredibly loud.

"Hello? Is—" He cleared his throat. "Is anyone here? Hello? Hey!"

The young shifter struggled to free his bound wrists but his efforts accomplished nothing except to make his pounding headache flare again with renewed strength.

*How did I get here? I don't even know where here is. Where's my car? What time is it?*

Bronson tried to glance at his watch but was reminded yet again of his inability to move.

"Hey! Whoever you are, I know you can hear me. My name is Bronson Harford and when my father finds out what you've done, he'll destroy you. Let me go."

A single footstep broke the silence in the cold, dark room.

He froze and finally remembered how to use his senses. Cautiously, he closed his eyes and sniffed the air.

*Shifters—transformed. Shit. How did they find me?*

With a low growl, Bronson readied himself to shift. While he felt the blaze of his transformation race through him with a fierce tingle, nothing happened.

*No, no, no. This isn't possible. This can't be happening.*

"Listen." He grunted and tried to push into a seated position but couldn't get his body to move the way he wanted it to. "If this is some kind of kidnapping for ransom, you'll get whatever you want. Call my father Jasper Harford. He's in Sausalito at the Harford Est—"

"Stop talking." The man's voice was a low growl laced with a very clear warning.

"So you're standing right there next to me, huh?" The young shifter swallowed. "Again, we can make this easy for both of us. My father—"

"Your father has nothing to do with this," a woman replied

from the opposite side of the room. "You're the one who will pay for your crimes."

"My…my crimes?"

*They can't know. That's impossible. Unless that idiot dwarf told someone who Tyro is. I didn't think he was that stupid.*

He replied with a weak chuckle. "My crimes. I don't know what you're talking about. Look, my family runs the Harford Foundation, okay? We're a charity. We send underprivileged kids to college with full scholarships. I don't…whatever you think I did, I'm telling you that you have the wrong guy."

"No we don't," another man said. "We know exactly who you are."

A dark-red light bloomed in the darkness on Bronson's left. Two more rose on his right accompanied by the overpowering scent of intensely strong magic and burning plastic. He thought he saw eyes glinting behind those low-glowing lights but he couldn't move his head enough to be sure.

"Then you know I'm someone you don't want to mess with," he muttered.

"That's where you're wrong." A fourth red light bloomed into existence in front of Bronson's face and he lurched away as far as he could with his wrists still bound.

This light was brighter and cast enough of a glow to illuminate the woman's face. Her features were sharp and gaunt-looking with all the lines of shadow and she'd pulled her hair severely into a tight, slick bun on the top of her head. Her eyes glinted at him from within two large circles of thick, smudged black makeup.

*She makes this look like some kind of Special Ops and not a kidnapping.*

He couldn't be sure in the red light and from his useless angle, but he thought those eyes were blue. They held him almost in a trance and he couldn't for the life of him think of what to say before he blurted, "What is this?"

"This is your moment to atone." The transformed woman in front of him drew away from the red light she'd produced and leaned closer.

"I already told you, I don't—"

"And to shut up while I tell you how this will play out."

Bronson swallowed and couldn't stop staring at the haunting eyes lined by so much darkness.

"I know the secrets you've been keeping," she continued and leaned even closer. "All of them."

"I don't—"

She hissed a warning and he flinched before he snapped his mouth closed.

"Whatever you think is still hidden, I can promise you it isn't hidden from me. But the only secret of yours I'm interested in is the one that affects what me and my army do next. The secret that decides where we all go from here."

"Your...army?" the young shifter whispered.

The woman's lips twitched into a devious sneer. "You're starting to get the point now."

"No, I'm not. No one has an army." He scowled and shook his head as much as he could while lying on the concrete. "Who are you?"

"You can call me Azure." She drew away from him enough to prop one foot on the floor before she draped a forearm over her thigh and leaned forward slightly again. "Does that ring a bell?"

"No. And I'm good with names."

*This crazy transformed thinks she can scare me into whatever she wants? That is not gonna happen. And I thought I was crazy.*

Bronson would have laughed at that if he wasn't sure it would only exacerbate the massive headache that made it impossible to think of a way out of this.

"I'm sure you are." With a slow sigh, Azure pushed to her feet and stepped back. The faintly glowing red light traveled beside her until she'd stepped into the shadows of her own making again. The other three lights around the room dimmed with hers. "Trust me, when we're through with you, you'll never forget the name."

"Probably not." He tried to sit again but gave up. "You don't seem to recognize mine either. Which is unfortunate for you because when my father sends his men out to look for me, you're—"

"I don't care who your father is," Azure snapped. "And the name you gave me isn't who you are."

"What?"

*No. She can't know.*

"Here's the deal." Her eyes widened briefly in the darkness. "You will tell me everything you know about Kaiser's organization and his plans. I need everything—his strengths and weaknesses and how he thinks when he's trying so hard to keep his little enterprise running smoothly."

Bronson scoffed but it sounded fake even to his ears. "I don't know anyone who calls himself Kaiser. What, do you think I can simply pull all that information out of thin air?"

"If that's what you want to call it."

"Even if I did know, you kidnapped me, tied me up, and locked me in this...wherever we are. Why would I help you?"

Azure sighed again and cocked her head. "Like I said. I know all your secrets, Tyro."

That jolt of realization struck him like a physical blow. Maybe he'd physically recoiled at the mention of the name from a stranger who knew who he was, but his mind reeled and focused somewhere else completely.

*She knows. They all know. And if she has an army and is looking for Kaiser... Shit, how did I let this happen?*

"So you have nothing to say, huh?" Azure sneered.

The young shifter pressed his lips together and stared at the glint in light eyes beneath the soft red light.

*I'll get out of this. I'll think of something but for now, I don't tell her anything.*

"That's fine." The terrifying transformed woman brought the red light in front of her at chest level to transform her face into a horrendous mask of shadows. "I think we can help you loosen your tongue a little."

Immediately, the four red lights blazed brighter and crackled with sharpened intensity. Azure spread her arms and the light divided between her hands to race up her wrists and arms. He could only see a fraction of one of the shifter men beside him but the same sparking, electric sizzle of magic was unmistakable.

Four shifters—four transformed shifters—surrounded him and cast magic. It was impossible.

But that wasn't the worst of it. What truly chilled him was that even with an agonizing hangover and his wrists bound behind his back to somehow dampen his ability to shift, he recognized the magic.

*That's exactly what Agnes can do. Shit. If these psychos have learned how to harness the blood witch's magic, we're all screwed.*

# CHAPTER EIGHT

Johnny pressed the gas pedal of their rental SUV to the floor and tightened his grasp on the steering wheel. "I can't believe we're doin' this—again."

In the passenger seat, Lisa clutched the handle above her door and grimaced. "What? You mean you driving like a lunatic and me hoping you don't kill us?"

"He's not gonna kill us," Luther said from the back. "That doesn't even make sense."

"Yeah, he knows what he's doing," Rex added. "Right, Johnny?"

The car went over a small pothole in the road that made it bounce and jerk dangerously at such high speeds. The hounds yelped and skittered across the back seat.

"Yeah." His partner fought to catch her breath. "I can't believe we're doing this again either."

"I ain't talkin' about my drivin', darlin'."

"Then what are you—" They hit another bump and she gasped. "What are you talking about?"

"I'm talkin' about drivin' my ass across this part of the country every couple of damn days—one I ain't keen on seein' as much as I've seen it already. All because we gotta keep tabs on these damn shifters who can't stick to a plan and see it through."

"Pissed at the shifters." Rex snorted. "Makes sense."

Luther chuckled. "Hey, good thing the pirate dwarf's out there on his deathmobile and not in here with us. Right, Johnny? You'd probably try to kill him too."

The bounty hunter gritted his teeth and stared at the straight Nevada highway that stretched seemingly forever in front of them. "For once, I ain't talkin' about my damn cousin."

"If he's driving over these potholes like you are, Johnny, it wouldn't surprise me to see him sprawled across the desert in the next few miles."

"There's nothin' wrong with my drivin'." He grimaced so hard, his upper lip peeled away from his teeth. "And it's impossible to focus on it with everyone naggin' me about every little thing."

Lisa turned her head slowly to fix him with a wide-eyed stare. "Excuse me?"

Johnny growled, released one hand from the steering wheel, and thumped it down again. "You know what I mean."

"Uh-huh. And I know you didn't seriously mean to say I'm nagging you."

"Yep. Sorry."

"Okay. I guess this isn't exactly the time for elaborate apologies." She sighed and turned her attention to the road. "Listen, I'm as angry as you are about the whole thing—"

He snorted. "Is that right?"

"Johnny."

"Sorry. Again."

Luther sniggered. "Two sorry's in two minutes? Bro, that's a new record."

"Keep talking and he'll probably throw you out the window," Rex whispered. "Without saying sorry."

Johnny ignored them in an attempt to keep his temper under control and Lisa shook her head.

"Yes. I'm as angry as you are because we've been on this case together from the beginning. Exactly like all the others."

"Hell, darlin', I know that—"

"You know what?" She thumped the side of her fist onto her thigh. "Forget angry. I'm pissed."

"Now you're makin' it sound personal."

"It feels personal, Johnny." She pressed her lips together tightly and glared at the shimmering heat waves that rose from the highway. "I thought we had an understanding."

"Wait—you're pissed at me?"

"No, we're talking about Addison."

"Right." The bounty hunter sniffed and gave her a sidelong glance from behind his black sunglasses. "Do you feel like elaboratin' on—"

"Okay, yeah. She lied to us, thought we were spies for Kaiser, knocked us out, and locked us in a magic-proof room for days so she could run around playing warlord. But Fiona helped us smooth all that over."

"Uh-huh."

*Where have I heard that rundown of our not-so-fun run-in before?*

"So we let bygones be bygones," his partner continued and her voice grew louder by the second. "And I had a talk to Addison myself—alone. We agreed that she'd stick to the plan and do what she had to do to make things right."

"Did she give you a promise to not drag Bronson out to the middle of the desert by the tail?"

She glanced condescendingly at him. "Seriously?"

He shrugged. "Sorry."

"We shouldn't have had to get into specifics like that anyway, you know? How hard is it to follow one very simple, very detailed plan? No one else needs the specifics of what not to do."

He cleared his throat. "I wouldn't go so far as to say all that—"

"Please. I wasn't talking about you or Charlie or any of the other Walker dwarves I haven't met yet."

*All right. She's pissed. It's time to keep your damn mouth shut, Johnny.*

"And Addison's smart," Lisa continued and gestured wildly with her hands as the only real outlet for her frustration. "She has to be if she's put together an entire army of transformed shifters to stand up and fight back. But come on. She was only supposed to talk to Bronson once she tracked his car to a safe location. That's it. And now she goes and does something like this? Behind our backs? Without giving us so much as a, 'Hey, by the way, I decided to change things up a little?'"

The SUV fell silent and she turned toward Johnny with another of her pressuring looks. "Seriously? You don't have anything to say to that?"

"Uh...I assumed that was all rhetorical."

"No, Johnny. We're having a conversation."

*Huh. So now it's all right to open my mouth. Fine.*

"Well, she did find him. And she must have talked to him."

She scoffed. "Right before she completely went against what we'd agreed."

"What can I say, darlin'? We have no clue what kinda words they exchanged when she found him. But hell, shit between couples sometimes gets heated from time to time."

*Like now, for instance. And I have no idea why.*

"Yes. That happens." She sighed heavily. "But I've never kidnapped you when things got heated."

The bounty hunter couldn't fully muffle a grunted chuckle. "You ain't ever died and come back as a warlord either."

"Well, I..." Lisa stopped, tilted her head, and dropped it back against the headrest. "Huh. Touché."

*I'm willin' to call that one a win for now and leave it at that.*

After another five minutes during which they barreled down the highway in silence, she asked, "So how are we supposed to fix this mess?"

"Between two hotheaded second-generation transformed

shifters who were fixin' to get hitched until one of 'em had to die and come back from the dead so they could spill the rest of their secrets to each other?" Johnny clicked his tongue. "It's one hell of a question, darlin'."

"But you do have a plan, right?"

"You know the plan. We get in there, stop whatever Addison's tryin' to do with her fiancé who's grievin' over nothin', and get our plan back on track. At least they're together now. This had better be the last time I gotta haul ass across the desert to keep young idiots in line."

Lisa smiled. "They are young."

"Uh-huh. They'll learn."

After they turned off the highway onto what could barely be called a nondescript road in the desert sand and another interminably long stretch of racing across the nothingness, Johnny finally slowed the SUV. Huge dust clouds curled behind the vehicle as they approached the entrance gates to the same private facility they'd escaped from only days before. "All right. Gettin' outta this place was easy enough. Gettin' in oughtta be a walk in the park."

"Oh, good. Charlie made it here first."

The shifter dwarf sat astride his bright orange Harley with the engine still idling. He looked over his shoulder at the approaching SUV and nodded before he said something to the large, overbearing shifter in dark sunglasses who manned the entrance.

"What's he gone and done this time?" Johnny muttered. "They have visitors. It's time to open the damn gates."

Lisa lifted a finger slowly to point indirectly at the guard. "I don't think this is about Charlie."

"What? Why not?"

When she nodded at the guard, Johnny took a better look at

the guy and brought the SUV to a complete stop a few yards behind his cousin's bike.

"Shit."

"He won't be happy to see us here again," she commented.

"Happy ain't got nothin' to do with it. I'll handle this." Johnny shoved the gearshift into park and left the engine on as he exited the car.

The hounds panted loudly in the back seat and Luther licked his muzzle. "Oh, wait. Hey, hey, hey. We know that guy."

"Whoa, you're right."

Lisa stared at the Walker dwarves and shook her head. "Seriously? They think it's a good idea to talk to the shifter they threw out of a stolen SUV in the middle of the desert. Yeah, that guy doesn't want to talk."

"Hey, don't worry about us, Lisa," Luther responded.

"We'll stay right here."

She leapt out of the passenger door and hurried toward the gate, where Johnny and Charlie were already in a standoff with the transformed shifter guard.

"You're standin' here lookin' at us tryin' to get inside." The bounty hunter gestured impatiently. "Did you forget how to do your job?"

The huge shifter folded his arms and lowered his head, his eyes completely hidden by his dark sunglasses. "My job is to make sure only the people who are supposed to be here are let through."

"Then open the damn gates."

The guard grinned broadly. "Payback's a bitch, huh?"

"It ain't supposed to be twice." Johnny stepped toward the guy and pointed a finger in his face. "I kicked you outta that damn car 'cause you didn't know what was good for ya. Are you fixin' to end up the same way?"

"We're not in a car this time, dwarf. And none of you will step foot on this base."

"Fine." He lowered his hand to his utility belt—which he'd refused to leave off his person again—and brushed his fingers against the hilt of his knife. "If you wanna go at this the hard way, that's on you."

"Whoa, whoa. Hold on a second." Charlie stepped in front of his cousin and raised a hand to stop him from launching into an unplanned attack. "Hey, man. What's your name?"

"Bill."

"Bill. Cool. You recognize me, right?"

The shifter regarded him impassively. "I wish I didn't."

"Well, that's— Whatever. Listen. We've been working with Azure. We're on your team, okay? And we know she's inside so let us in. It's not like there's anything in there we haven't seen before, right?"

"Then there's no reason for you to go in again."

Charlie scoffed and stepped toward the man before he plastered a sheepish grin on his face. "Come on, Bill. Transformed to transformed, huh? We have to get on this base because a few things are going down inside that compound that we should have been a part of by now."

Bill lowered his sunglasses slowly over the bridge of his nose and leaned toward him. "We're not on the same team."

"Hey, man. I'm not the one who threw you out of the car, okay? I tried to stop him—"

"The answer's no, pal. Get back in the vehicle and turn around."

"Goddammit," Johnny grumbled. "There ain't no time for holdin' a grudge when we're tryin' to stop a damn war."

Lisa cleared her throat. "This is a private facility, isn't it?"

The dwarves turned slowly toward her in confusion. Bill merely grunted.

"If I had to guess, I'd say it's something left from either CIA or FBI," she continued. "You know, before the Coalition got their hands on it to lend it to Azure. From what I already know about how your leader works, I have a feeling she's running a few things in this facility that haven't been approved by the Coalition."

"Lady, do you have a point?"

She scowled at him. "My point is that none of you, including Azure, would find it very much fun if the FBI were involved. They might not know what you guys are up to out here, but I can promise you they won't appreciate—"

Bill threw his head back and bellowed with laughter.

Lisa placed her hands on her hips and ignored the perturbed glances from both Walker dwarves.

Johnny growled and turned to their guard with a grudge. "What the hell's so funny?"

"You think—ha! She's...she's making threats like she has any pull with the feds."

"I do," Lisa stated firmly.

Bill's laughter finally died into a low chuckle and he whipped his sunglasses off to scrutinize her with derision. "Not anymore, sweetheart. Do you think we don't have access to personnel files in this place? Even inactive ones?"

She pressed her lips together and didn't say a word.

*Well, damn. Azure's army got their gear from the Coalition and access to all the shit we ain't made public.* Johnny gritted his teeth. *This guy ain't bluffin'.*

"We have to get inside, man," Charlie added. "It's kinda one of those life-and-death things, you know?"

"Sure." The guard shrugged. "Get out of here and I'll let you idiots live. Same thing you did to me—"

"That's it." Johnny drew his knife and flicked it open. "I ain't standin' here arguin' with this brainless ass while the guy we're supposed to be settin' on the right path is holed up in that compound gettin' the shit beat outta him."

Bill tossed his sunglasses into the sand beside him, spread his arms again, and grinned. "Bring it, pal."

Rex's sharp bark came from the back seat of the SUV. "Hey, Bill! Hey, remember us?"

"We're back..."

With more sharp yips, the hounds scrambled over the center console to race through the open driver's door toward the gates.

The transformed shifter grew rigid and his eyes widened as they bounded across the sand. "You brought your dogs?"

Johnny nodded. "I bring 'em everywhere. Why? Did you miss 'em?"

"I hate those dogs." Bill stepped back without looking away from Rex and Luther who skittered to a halt beside their master.

"Don't worry, Johnny."

"Yeah, we got this."

Rex barked once and snarled. "Johnny says we're getting inside, shifter. So we're getting inside."

Luther lowered his head and his hackles rose as he uttered a low growl. "We can chase you this time. You'd better scram."

"Get those things on a leash." Bill stabbed a finger at the hounds and backed away again. "I mean it. You can't let them run all over the place."

The bounty hunter grinned. "Watch me."

Luther lunged toward the shifter and snapped his jaws. "Better listen to him, Bill."

"Or not," Rex added. "It's been a while since we've chased someone as big as you. Think we can catch him, Luther?"

"Definitely."

"Shit." With wide eyes, the guard scurried across the sand toward the gate tower and thrust his hand through the open window. A low beep and the whirring of machinery filled the air as the gates opened slowly. "There. I opened the gates, okay? Now keep those dogs away from me."

Rex cackled maniacally. "How's he gonna do that, huh?"

"Yeah. No leashes."

With matching growls, the hounds leapt after the terrified

shifter, who almost fell flat on his face before he scrambled into the gate tower and slammed the door shut behind him.

"Take that!" Luther jumped up against the wall and snarled through the window. Bill cried out and staggered back against the short table behind him.

"We'll be watching you, Bill. Better do what Johnny says next time."

Laughing, the hounds spun, trotted calmly toward their master, and panted with their tongues hanging from their mouths.

"Look at that." The bounty hunter waved at the terrified guard and turned to get back into the SUV. "Good work, boys."

"Guess we figured out one good thing about how much these shifters stink, Johnny."

Luther stopped to sniff a patch of sand that looked like every other patch and his tail wagged furiously. "Covers up hound pretty well. He never even smelled us coming."

"We should get moving before he changes his mind," Lisa suggested. Bill scowled at them through the window of the gate tower but remained mostly focused on the hounds' calm retreat.

"Do you think we can sic the hounds on the rest of the transformed who don't want us where we're goin'?"

"No, I'm very sure that was a one-time thing."

# CHAPTER NINE

By the time they reached the front of Azure's base, three transformed had stepped through the front door into the bright
sunlight.

"I guess our friend Bill called ahead."

"It looks like it." Lisa opened her door and paused. "Can we
please try to not hurt them? That's the whole point of this."

"If they're smart enough to get outta our way, darlin', sure. I
ain't gonna hurt 'em. Much."

Charlie stepped off his bike and slapped huge clouds of red-
brown sand off his riding leathers before he dusted it out of his
mohawk. "Roads. How hard is that to do, huh?"

A shifter man with his black shirtsleeves rolled to his elbows
stepped forward and frowned at the newcomers. "I thought Bill
was pulling some kinda prank when he said you idiots came
back."

"The only idiots here are those standin' in our way." Johnny
drew his knife but didn't open it yet. "We're lookin' for Azure."

"She's not taking visitors." A transformed woman with short,
spiky hair shrugged. "However you guys got in here, you need to
turn and go out."

Charlie scoffed. "How do you know she's not taking visitors, huh? You saw us here. We're all on the same team."

"We haven't been authorized to let anyone inside." The third shifter stood beside the door with his arms folded. "So we won't."

"All right, I know y'all are tryin' to play badass military here but you ain't got a clue what you're talkin' about."

"Want us to tear their legs off, Johnny?" Luther asked.

"Hey, yeah." Rex snarled at the shifters and walked toward them. "It'll hurt even worse if we leave a little piece still hanging on."

The shifter woman snarled. "I'd like to see you try, doggy."

"This is ridiculous." Lisa pulled her phone out to call Addison directly but it went straight to voicemail without ringing once. "We need to hurry. Come on."

She stormed toward the front door and the third shifter stepped forward to block her path. "We said no, lady."

"Well, you aren't the one giving orders around here and I don't take orders anyway." She skirted him and reached for the door handle but he shoved her away.

"Hey!" Johnny shouted, and finally flicked his blade out. "Watch yourself, asshole."

Once she'd regained her balance in the sand, Lisa rolled her eyes. "What is it with shifters thinking they can push me around this week?"

"You don't belong here. Get back in your car—"

"We don't' have time for this!" She summoned a massive orb of golden light energy and blasted it into the shifter's chest. He catapulted back six feet before he landed on the sand with a thump and a grunt of surprise.

No one said a word.

She sighed in exasperation. "Sorry."

The other two transformed snarled and lunged at the dwarves. Johnny slashed his knife at the shifter woman, who leapt away to avoid being sliced. Luther darted behind her at the perfect moment and she stumbled over his legs before she landed hard on her rear.

The final shifter leapt at Charlie, who scuttled behind his Harley to put something between them and raised his hands. "Hey, hey. Whoa. We're only trying to get inside and don't need to fight about this."

With a snarl, the man shoved the motorcycle over in a puff of dust.

The biker dwarf's jaw dropped as he backed away from his fallen ride and pointed at the shifter. "Well, now we certainly need to fight about this."

"Charlie, let's go!" Lisa shouted.

"Did you see what he did? Did you *see* what he did?"

"Dammit, Charlie. Come on." Johnny and the hounds raced toward the open door where she waited for them.

"You're trespassing!" the shifter shouted. "You can't go in—"

The shifter dwarf delivered a crushing sucker punch to the man's jaw and he crumpled beside the motorcycle. "Watch us."

Once he reached the others, Lisa took a final look at the transformed who began to pick themselves up slowly before she let the door close again. "Why doesn't anyone believe us when we say we're here to help?"

"Shifters ain't used to gettin' help from anyone. Especially transformed shifters." The bounty hunter glanced down the first branching hallway as they hurried through the compound. "I thought you said we were tryin' to *not* hurt 'em."

She shrugged. "I got annoyed."

"No kidding." Charlie scoffed. "Me too."

"Coming up on the left, Johnny." Luther panted and licked his muzzle.

"That's where she has Bronson? All right."

"Wait." Rex yipped sharply. "No, no, no. That's not—"

Two more of Azure's soldiers emerged around the corner as Johnny headed that way. "Hey! What are you—"

The bounty hunter shoved the closest man so he stumbled into his companion and they both collided with the wall.

"Well, is it this damn hallway or not?"

Luther sniffed the air. "I only meant shifters were coming, Johnny."

"Bronson's down this way," Rex added before he moved forward again.

"Oh, for the love of—" With a grimace, he hurried after his partner and cousin to follow the hounds' trail through the compound.

Another transformed woman in all black and carrying a massive crate in her arms stepped through an open doorway as they passed. "Who are you?"

"We're looking for Azure," Charlie replied. "Do you know where we can find her?"

"Who let you in?"

He rolled his eyes and jogged to catch up with the others. "No one wants to answer the actual question these days."

"It might be 'cause you ain't askin' the right—"

An alarm blared with an obnoxious shriek and red lights pulsed slowly on the hallway ceiling.

"Seriously?" Charlie spread his arms in irritation. "They set the fire alarm off on us?"

Lisa shook her head slowly and her frown deepened. "She never told the rest of her army who we are or that we're here to help them."

"It's too late for that now, darlin'. You can hurt her later."

"What? I'm not—" With a frustrated growl, she quickened her pace to catch up with the Walker dwarves.

Shouts erupted from the various corridors they passed and transformed shifters raced to intercept the perceived intruders. One of them grasped Lisa's wrist and she whirled to swing her forearm into his elbow to release his hold before she landed a swift kick in his gut. "Sorry!"

Azure's soldiers darted around corners to catch them and Johnny and Charlie held them off with quick strikes while they still had the element of surprise—a glancing punch to the face, an elbow to the throat or solar plexus, and a sweep of the foot to knock their would-be attackers off their feet.

Charlie laughed after the last shifter twice his size doubled over with both hands clamped to his crotch. "Is this how you handle the real cases, Johnny?"

"This is a real case. Shut up."

"Yeah, but I'm talking about the undercover stuff or whatever. The FBI stuff. Boy, if I knew it was this easy to—" A snarling transformed whipped the door open as he passed and lunged forward. Charlie slapped him in the face, caught hold of his shirt collar, and shoved him back into the room before he grasped the handle and slammed the door shut. "How easy it is to waltz into a place and take everyone out like this. Maybe I should have been a bounty hunter."

"The hell you should have." His cousin glanced down the next branching hallway at the half-dozen confused shifters who walked swiftly out of a room at the end of the hall. He yanked an explosive disk from his belt and thumbed the button before he lobbed it carelessly into the air. "Y'all stay back."

In their confusion, the ragtag soldiers paused to watch the disk before it clattered on the floor and the bounty hunter walked on.

"It's never this easy."

"Because they don't know who we are," Lisa added. "And again, we're trying to not—"

The disk exploded with a bang and elicited several startled, angry shouts and snarls from the group of shifters penned in the hall.

"Johnny!" she shouted.

Her partner turned with a shrug. "I told 'em to stay back. It sounds like they listened."

She gaped at him in disbelief and gestured dramatically. "No bombs in the building."

"Yeah, all right." He shook his head and turned to follow Charlie.

"Up here, Johnny," Rex called.

"Yeah, we found him all right." Luther barked. "Turn here, and he's right—hey!" With a yelp, Luther skittered away from the insanely muscular shifter woman who tried to clamp her hands around him. "What is wrong with you, lady? You don't sneak up on a hound and start grabbing whatever you want."

"Johnny!" Rex raced out of the hall where they'd smelled Bronson, his eyes wide as he skidded across the linoleum floor. "Johnny, Johnny, Johnny, make it go away!"

A shifter man who wore what looked like a black beret darted after the hound and swiped a long silver pole at Rex, who barely managed to escape before he thumped against the wall. At the end of the pole, a black noose sparked with electric-blue light.

"Holy shit," Luther muttered. "He's trying to take you to the pound, bro."

"Not if he takes you first."

Both hounds darted around the shifter and snapped at his heels as he whirled and tried to swipe at them.

"Are you kiddin' me?" Johnny scowled and stormed toward the shifter. "Y'all ain't learned the first time how to get a couple of coonhounds to settle?"

"Huh?" The guy with the pole stopped and looked up in time to see the bounty hunter's fist swing toward his face.

The magi-tech dog-catcher clanked to the floor and its wielder staggered against the wall and slid down it in a daze.

"Next time, try layin' out a couple of steaks." Johnny tsked at the guy before he hurried down the hall. Both hounds burst into uproarious laughter.

"You sure showed him, Johnny."

"Yeah, he'll never put a steak out again—wait…"

71

"Which door, boys?" He stopped in the middle of the hallway to scan the three nondescript doors in front of him.

"The one at the end, Johnny."

"He's in there."

"Him and a group of stinky shifters."

Lisa rounded the corner and frowned at Charlie, who loomed over the fallen guard and brandished the sparking end of the dog-catcher in his face.

"Do you think you'd like this to tighten around your neck?"

"Charlie." She patted his shoulder as she passed him. "Put it down."

"Fine." He threw the pole down the opposite hallway and shuffled disappointedly toward his cousin, who was about to open the door at the end of the hallway.

When it opened, the bounty hunter scowled. "What the—"

The metallic click of firearms being drawn was unmistakable. He glared at the four transformed in the room, all of whom aimed weapons at him, and raised both hands slowly as he backed away.

Lisa stopped. "What's going on?"

The shifters squeezed through the door and fanned out to train their weapons on the entire team who had breached the compound. None of them were Addison or Bronson.

"Wrong door, boys," Johnny grumbled.

The hounds stopped at the far end of the hall and stared at their master. "Yeah, we know it's the wrong door, Johnny."

Rex snorted. "Why did you open that one?"

"Because you told me he was there," he retorted through the side of his mouth.

"Uh…no we didn't."

"We said the door at the end of the hall, Johnny. They're right down here. Come on."

*I have four pissed-off transformed soldiers fixin' to pump us all full of holes and my damn hounds are arguin' semantics.*

"Oh, come on." Charlie's shoulders slumped as he raised his hands too in half-hearted surrender. "Why did you have to bring guns into this? We were having fun."

"We're here to escort you out." The woman carrying the biggest automatic rifle of them all swung the end of the barrel briefly toward the main hall in the direction from which the team had come. "It's time to get moving."

"All right, all right." The bounty hunter nodded and stepped toward Lisa. "This is all a misunderstandin', folks. We're friends and I can prove it. Here. Lemme show ya what I'm talkin' about."

The shifters glanced at each other in confusion before a short man with more cargo pockets than a single outfit should ever have jerked his chin at him. "So prove it."

"Uh-huh." Johnny lowered one hand slowly.

Lisa glanced at his belt and nudged him with her elbow. "Don't you dare."

"I'm reachin' for my phone, darlin'." He widened his eyes at her. "Where I said I have proof that we're cleared to be here and ain't fixin' to...uh, do whatever these folks with guns think we're fixin' to do."

"Oh. Right."

Johnny withdrew his phone, looked at the shifters who glowered in response, then pressed one button and pulled up the only name on his mind.

*If droppin' Azure's name ain't gettin' us through this, I know a crazy redhead who might finish the job.*

He raised his phone so the transformed soldiers could see the screen and the name displayed on it—Fiona Damascus. "Do y'all recognize the name?"

They looked at each other and shifted uncomfortably from one foot to the other. "Azure's Coalition contact," one of them muttered.

*Christ, even they don't know who Fiona is.*

"Uh-huh." Johnny nodded. "She and I go back a long time and

she always answers my calls. Now, I have the woman's number on speed dial, understand? Don't make me use it."

The hallway was completely silent before Charlie sniggered and shook his head.

The shifters, however, didn't seem to think his threat was so funny—or a threat, for that matter.

"She's the one who came here to break them out the first time."

"And they were stupid enough to come back."

"Yeah, but do you want Fiona to come back? The woman's insane."

"She's training us."

"She's still insane."

"That probably isn't even her number."

"He pulled it up with one click. Why would he save a fake number in his phone?"

The deliberation continued like this for at least another two minutes and Johnny scratched his cheek through his wiry red beard before he turned to meet Lisa's gaze. She raised her eyebrows and shook her head.

*These bozos need a good kick in the pants. Their guns are pointin' at our faces while they try to decide that I ain't lyin'.*

After another thirty seconds, he'd run out of patience. "All right. Y'all're a little slow today, so I'm gonna—"

"Don't." The guy with too many pockets glanced fearfully at him before he lowered his firearm. "Don't call her."

The others lowered their weapons too and relaxed their warning stances.

"Well, all right, then." The bounty hunter slipped his phone into his pocket and nodded. "I'm glad to see y'all have some sense in your heads after all."

"Where's Azure?" Lisa asked.

The shifter woman's large rifle now dangled from her hand

and its barrel almost scraped the floor. She nodded toward the end of the hall and frowned at the hounds who stood with their tails straight in the air and their tongues lolling from panting mouths. "Turn right at the end of the hall. First door on your left."

"Now that's more like it," Johnny said with a fake smile that was more of a grimace.

His partner drew a deep breath. "Do we need a key or access code or anything?"

With a snort, the shifter woman studied her disdainfully for a moment before she walked into the room she and her fellow soldiers had previously occupied. The others followed her and the door clicked shut two seconds before the blaring alarm and the pulsing red lights overhead cut off completely.

"I guess that helps." Lisa glanced at the ceiling. "It was still rude to not answer my question."

"It doesn't matter whether we need it or not, darlin'." Johnny turned to head down the hall and Rex and Luther wagged their tails before they scurried around the corner. "We're gettin' in now."

Charlie joined them. "You know, out of all the times I've had a gun pointed in my face, that was the weirdest."

Lisa pressed her lips together to hide a smile. "But it's a very big milestone for Johnny."

Her partner grunted. "What makes you think that, darlin'?"

"I think that's the first time you've ever entered a hostile location and had weapons pointed at you without blowing anything up."

"I lobbed a disk down the hall a few minutes ago."

"Okay, fine. I meant without blowing any*one* up."

"Huh." He grinned as they neared the end of the hall and the branching corridor. "It might still happen before we're done here. But I'm more interested in what the hell Fiona did to these transformed to make 'em so afraid of a phone call."

"That woman's freaky enough without having to do anything," Charlie said. "And I don't mean in a good way."

"I'm sure you can imagine it, Johnny. You've seen her in action, right?"

The bounty hunter stopped before he turned down the hall where the hounds now sat dutifully in front of the actual door they wanted. "Uh…not exactly."

"Not exactly what?"

"I ain't seen Fiona in action, darlin'." He shrugged. "I've heard stories, though—the kind that makes a guy not wanna see it up close and personal."

"Oh, great. And we signed off on letting her mentor our kid."

"That's got nothin'—"

"Hurry up, Johnny," Rex muttered as he stood and backed away from the door. "Come on."

Luther sniffed at the bottom of the door before he bounded away. "Yeah, you wanna get in here quick. Like right now."

"What's up, boys?"

"It smells like those stinky shifters are about to—"

A loud crack came from the other side of the door, followed by a man's cry of surprise and most likely pain.

*Dammit, she's gonna break her fiancé before we have a chance to fix him.*

# CHAPTER TEN

They didn't need a key or an access code to open the door behind which they expected to find Azure and her soldiers torturing and maiming a seriously confused Bronson Harford. Johnny grasped the handle, jerked it down, and opened the door half an inch before it banged into something solid on the other side.

The something solid uttered a yelp of surprise. "Seriously? We told you we'd be out when we're done—"

"And I'm tellin' y'all we're comin' in." The bounty hunter shoved his shoulder against the door and the shifter who stood on the other side was knocked away to stumble into a pile of something that clanked and clattered noisily to the floor. Johnny threw the door open the rest of the way and paused.

The light from the hallway illuminated enough to seriously confuse the team. A wide-eyed Bronson lay on his side in the center of the room, his wrists bound behind his back, and three dark figures illuminated themselves with crackling red trans-formed-shifter magic that wasn't supposed to exist.

"What the hell do you think you're doing?" Addison snarled.

"Hey, there you are."

"You can't simply walk in here. We're in the middle of—what are you doing?"

Johnny lurched forward into the room and slapped his hand against the wall to find the light switch.

All four shifters snuffed their magic out the second the bright light turned on and Bronson clenched his eyes shut against the glare and curled into himself.

With a hand on the doorframe, the bounty hunter took one sweeping look of the six-by-six-foot space and laughed. "You gotta be kiddin' me. This is where you chose to torture a prisoner for information?"

Addison—fully done up as her Azure persona—lurched from where she crouched in front of Bronson and spun with a hiss. "This has nothing to do with you."

He laughed again. "It's a damn broom closet."

"And he had no idea until you arrived and turned the lights on."

"Seriously?" Charlie poked his head around the corner of the open doorway and looked around. "There's nothing even remotely intimidating about a broom closet. It brings back a few good memories from high school, though."

"I don't believe this," Bronson muttered. He tried to sit but was either too weak or too shocked to manage it so he snarled at Johnny instead. "Jesus Christ, you people show up everywhere. And now you're with her?"

"I can promise you this much, son, she ain't payin' us a dime and neither is your old man."

"She kidnapped me. And her little thugs are—"

"Get out!" Addison roared.

The sound was deafening in such a small space and the bounty hunter stuck a pinky in his ear to wiggle it a little before he pointed at Addison's accomplices. "Y'all heard your fearless leader." He couldn't help but snigger. "It's time to come on outta the closet."

"That's not what I said."

"That's what we're sayin'. Let's go."

"They don't take orders from you, Johnny." She stepped toward him. "They listen to me."

"And you're the one sayin' get out. I'm merely repeatin' the message."

Lisa stepped toward the open door and cleared her throat. When the transformed leader met her gaze, her eyes widened. "You should do what he said. He has Fiona Damascus on speed dial."

Her partner looked over his shoulder at her. "That's my line."

It seemed that was all they needed to say to get Azure's three right-hand shifter lieutenants moving. Two of them stepped around Bronson's prone form without giving him so much as a second glance. The third extricated himself from the mess of paint cans, chemical cleaners, and maintenance supplies he'd toppled into when the door had knocked him off his feet.

Addison glared at her followers. "What are you doing?"

"I won't mess with Fiona," the woman replied. "Not after last time. Sorry."

"That's it." Johnny stepped fully into the closet and gestured toward the hallway. "Y'all hang tight for a second out there with Charlie, understand? No one's goin' anywhere until we give the go-ahead."

With a low growl, Addison leaned toward Johnny and pointed behind her at Bronson. "You can't simply storm in here to stick your nose into everyone else's business. I had this handled."

"In a broom closet."

"You didn't have anything handled at all," Lisa added. She paused in the doorway only to avoid knocking Rex and Luther aside as the hounds trotted through first to sniff Bronson. "We had a plan—a solid plan with numerous backup options if our first attempts didn't go the way we expected. You're the only one who went off-script. Why? Because it was convenient?"

"I did what you told me to do," Addison retorted. "But we didn't have a backup option for what happened when my part went completely sideways."

"That option was to call us." She laughed bitterly. "And even if you were caught up in something that prevented you from doing that—which you weren't—not answering your phone for two days doesn't exactly instill much confidence."

Johnny sniffed and scratched his cheek. "You didn't start with that much to begin with but we made a deal. And you tossed it out the window."

Addison turned her rage onto the dwarf this time and her blue eyes blazed from the center of so much dark, thickly smeared makeup. "And you think that gives you the right to barge onto my base and interrupt what I was doing?"

"Damn straight it does."

"It's not technically your base," Lisa added.

"He was about to talk!"

The hounds sniffed Bronson's prone legs and his bound wrists and nudged their noses against the back of his head. "Doesn't smell like he was about to talk, Johnny."

"Yeah. This guy smells like he was about to puke."

Rex sniggered. "Kinda like you smell sometimes, Johnny."

"Yeah, on a good day."

"Bad day for him, though."

Johnny raised a finger between himself and the furious Azure and muttered, "What the hell are y'all goin' on about?"

"Can't you smell that?" Charlie asked.

"Dammit, Charlie—"

"This trussed-up shifter smells like a week-old frat party, 'coz."

The bounty hunter paused, pressed his lips together, and looked slowly at Bronson. The young shifter glared at him and it seemed like his hatred intensified by the second. "Is that the reason why your part of the plan went sideways?"

Addison sighed. "Yeah. Plus a few other things."

"Huh." He raised his eyebrows at Bronson, who tried to lurch away from the hounds who pawed at his legs and sniffed him all over. "Excuse us, son. Me and my team gotta have us a little chat to Azure."

"I won't go anywhere with you," the transformed leader muttered.

"You will if you ever wanna get this guy to talk." Johnny gestured toward the hallway and she stormed past him like he wasn't even there.

One of the transformed in black stepped forward and peered through the door. "Do you want us to take the prisoner somewhere else?"

Addison opened her mouth to reply but Johnny cut her off. "Naw. Let him stew a little longer."

"Ha. Stew." Luther trotted through the door. "Funny."

Rex snorted and followed his brother into the hall. "Gross."

"Once we're done with him," Johnny continued, "I reckon he'll wish he was back in this closet anyhow. You know, in the dark. There ain't no goin' back after this, son."

"What does that mean?" Bronson snarled.

With a smirk, Johnny flicked the lights off and pulled the door shut behind him.

"Hey! *Hey!*" No one answered the young shifter's shouts and after a brief scuffle inside the closet, he fell silent.

*Huh. It doesn't take long to get a message through his head when he's tied up and all on his own.*

Addison glared at him and flung her hands in the air before she let them slap against her thighs. "Say what you came to say so I can get back to the interrogation."

"First things first." The bounty hunter pointed at the closed door. "We're havin' the kinda talk that needs more than a door for privacy."

She rolled her eyes, sighed in aggravation, and turned toward her followers. "Stay here. If he tries anything, throw him around a little. No one else opens that door. Got it?"

The three shifters nodded and darted wary glances at Johnny and his team before Azure stalked down the hall.

"Where are we going now, Johnny?" Rex asked.

"Yeah, you mentioned something earlier about steaks, right?"

He snapped his fingers and stared ahead at the back of Addison's head. "The work ain't done yet, boys."

"Aw, come on. We almost went to the pound, Johnny."

"Yeah, the least you could do is show us a little love."

Lisa shook her head. "It looks like the hounds are the only two in this entire facility who aren't mad about something."

"Trust us, Lisa. We will be if we don't get treats."

"We've been so good."

"When this whole thing is over, boys," their master muttered as Addison finally stopped in another nondescript corridor before she barged into the private room beyond, "Y'all can have a whole damn cow."

"Say what?" Both hounds stopped in their tracks and stared at him, completely oblivious to Charlie who passed them in the hall.

Luther's panting quickened. His sides heaved as thick strings of slobber spilled out of his open mouth to puddle on the floor. "Bro. Bro. I think I'm gonna pass out."

Rex sniffed the corner of his brother's mouth and followed the rest of the team into the room. "More cow for me, then."

## CHAPTER ELEVEN

After they'd all sat at the large round table that filled most of the makeshift conference room, Johnny folded his arms and nodded at Addison. "You were supposed to follow Bronson and talk to him. Tell him you ain't dead."

She scowled at him. "I did."

"Then what the hell happened?"

"He was wasted—worse than I've ever seen him." She swallowed and shook her head. "I tried to talk to him but he thought I was a hallucination."

"Did you try to get to him before he walked into a bar?" Lisa asked.

The transformed leader glared condescendingly at her. "He wasn't at a bar."

"And?" Johnny twirled his hand to keep her talking.

"He was…" The young woman glanced at the ceiling and sighed heavily. "He was at the cemetery."

"Doing what?" Charlie chuckled. "Robbing graves?" Everyone turned to stare at him and he looked from one to the other and shrugged. "What?"

"He was there visiting me, okay?" Addison added. "My grave."

"Oh. Shit. My bad."

Johnny leaned toward his cousin. "How about you keep your mouth shut from here on out, huh?"

The shifter dwarf mimed zipping his lips and throwing the key away.

"Then what happened?"

Addison lowered her gaze to the table. "Nothing. He…he tried to run away from me but he went down right there before I could explain. I honestly don't know if he passed out from the booze or the fall."

"Probably both," Charlie muttered and immediately noticed his cousin glaring at him and added, "Right. Shutting up."

"He passed out drunk in front of your empty grave." The bounty hunter leaned forward, propped an elbow on the table, and fixed her with a stern look. "So you thought that was a hell of a time to turn on the plan and kidnap your fiancé?"

"It seemed like the best option at the time."

"To do what? Make a point?"

"Johnny." Lisa placed a hand on his thigh beneath the table. "Right now, we need to focus on what happens next instead of rubbing it in her face, okay? Addison knows she made a mistake—"

"I didn't make a mistake." The young woman laughed bitterly. "I did what I had to do. I showed Bronson I'm still alive and offered to explain everything, and he didn't want anything to do with me. I couldn't let him go and risk him telling everyone that he saw me and I'm back from the dead."

"Darlin'…" Johnny cleared his throat. "You ain't been thinkin' things far enough through."

"I did think it through."

"Come on. Folks ain't gonna believe the ravings of a rich-ass shifter heir too drunk to know the difference."

"Then what do you think I should have done, huh?" She

pounded a fist on the table. "Stayed there and nursed him back to lucidity in the cemetery?"

"You should have called us, Addison," Lisa said calmly, although her voice had taken on a much stricter and more threatening tone. "We could have helped you smooth things over or at least given Bronson a chance to sober up before you tried again."

"He thinks I'm a figment of his imagination. He doesn't want to believe me. That was completely obvious."

"And now we'll never know, will we?" The half-Light Elf raised her eyebrows. "Because you thought you could do this on your own."

"I can."

Johnny snorted. "Is that right? Well, I think Fiona would have a couple of things to say about that. Should we call her to sit in on this mess too?"

Addison closed her eyes and raised her chin to take three long, deep breaths. "Fine. If you guys have any brilliant suggestions other than what I was already working on with my team, I'd love to hear them. Because Bronson's seen me like this—as Azure. He knows about my army and he knows we're coming for Kaiser."

"Dammit." The bounty hunter shoved himself back in his chair and growled in frustration. "You told him your goddamn plans to start a war against his uncle? It sounds like you've been hittin' the bottle a little too hard yourself."

"I didn't tell him our plans." The shifter woman sneered at him from across the table. "I was about to get information which won't happen now that he's seen you here. He won't take any of this seriously."

Lisa shook her head and fought to hold her anger under control. "None of this would have happened if you'd taken this seriously from the beginning."

"Are you for real?" Addison stood abruptly. "You guys aren't even a part of this. None of you are trying to stop an insanely powerful magical from murdering you and everyone like you simply because he feels like it."

"Um…" Charlie slowly raised his hand. "I kind of am, though."

"We don't have to be the ones getting hurt to care about what happens here," Lisa said calmly. "But we are the ones with experience who can help you if you'd simply stick to the plan—"

"What experience, Lisa? You used to work for the FBI and your partner's a bounty hunter who only helps people when someone pays him."

The Light Elf's mouth fell open. "That is so ridiculously far from the truth and you know it."

"Oh, yeah? Do you think he'd march out of here and finally let me handle my responsibilities if I paid him—"

"All right, that's enough." Johnny stood quickly from his chair and the hounds leapt away when the metal legs screeched loudly across the floor. "Y'all are makin' this way more complicated than it oughtta be."

Both women stared at him as he turned toward the door. Charlie sank a little lower in his chair.

"Where are you going?" Lisa asked.

"I think I know how to fix this whole damn mess."

Addison scoffed and folded her arms. "And how exactly do you think you'll do that?"

"The same way we fixed it the first time. With you." He opened the door and stormed into the hallway.

The two women shared a confused look and bolted across the room at the same time to follow him.

"Hold on a second," Addison whispered harshly and tried to not draw attention. "Do you mean the way you fixed it with me?"

"You have an advantage we ain't tried on him yet, darlin'. It's time to level the playing field."

"I have no idea what you're talking about."

Lisa sighed and forced herself to match her partner's rapid

pace as they turned down the corridors. "Honestly, Johnny, I have to agree with her on this one."

"If it gets y'all to quit gripin' at each other, even better."

"Yeah, that was me saying you should tell us the new plan."

The bounty hunter stopped at the next intersection of hallways and gestured in the general direction of the supply closet where Bronson was held. "You've seen both sides of him," he told Addison. "Now, he needs to see both sides of you. I think it's the guilt of havin' a double life without you knowin' that's keepin' him from believing you ain't merely his broken heart talkin' to him in a cemetery."

All the color drained from Addison's face.

"Do y'all have any rooms in this place with a two-way mirror?"

"We..." With a frown, she raised a weak hand to wave in a general direction. "Yeah, we have a few."

"Good. Choose one. Go in there as yourself and not a transformed warlord and wait for us there."

"Johnny, I can't do what you're suggesting."

"Sure you can. It's as easy as walkin' into the damn room and doin' it."

The transformed woman stepped back and shook her head. "No. It's not. It'll ruin everything."

*So the leader of the transformed army wants to have her cake and eat it too, huh? It sounds familiar.*

"Do it." He leaned toward her and narrowed his eyes. "I'm tellin' the magic-trick guards you have watching Bronson that you cleared the next part of the plan. And it's gonna turn out the way I say it is or I'll call Fiona and Connor Slate."

"Who?"

Johnny glanced at Lisa in disbelief and shook his head. "The goddamn director of the Coalition, girl. Christ, you and Bronson both need a hell of a better education than you've been gettin' so far." He spun to head to the supply closet. "Y'all are perfect for each other, that's for damn sure."

Addison bit her bottom lip and clenched her fists at her sides. "I can't do this."

"Yes, you can," Lisa said gently. "And you will because as crazy as it sounds, Johnny's right. Level the playing field. That's when the fighting stops and civilized conversation is possible."

"I…" The leader of the transformed resistance army took a deep breath and blinked away the angry tears that shimmered in her eyes. "Give me twenty minutes."

"You'd better make it ten. I'm very sure Johnny's done being patient and when that happens… Well, the civilized conversation gets replaced by explosives."

"Of course it does." With a snarl, Addison spun and stalked away across her base to get ready for the next part of the plan.

Lisa closed her eyes and drew a deep breath.

*Please let us get through the rest of this without explosives. Please.*

# CHAPTER TWELVE

Bronson strained to hear something through the closet door that might help him but the transformed stationed outside didn't say a word.

He couldn't believe the stupid, nosey, uncouth dwarf had weaseled into his personal affairs again.

*I guess I shouldn't consider Tyro a personal subject but come on. That woman with the face paint's completely psycho and he's helping her.*

Footsteps approached down the hallway outside and he held his breath to listen closely.

Three different phones buzzed, followed by Johnny's voice. "Do you know where that is?"

"Yeah."

"Then get it done." The dwarf snorted. "Azure's orders."

The heavy footsteps faded again and the door to the supply closet burst open.

The young shifter clenched his eyes shut against the blinding brightness after being left for so long in the dark. One giant shifter in all black darkened the doorway before he rummaged in an open cardboard box on one of the overfilled shelves.

"What did she tell you to do?" he muttered, stared at him, and hoped to catch his gaze.

"Stop talking." The man pulled a thick black bag out of the box and turned toward the prisoner.

Bronson tried to pull away while still lying on his side and snarled. "You know what? Forget what she told you. You'd better tell me you're letting me go now."

"Oh, yeah? Do you think we should simply forget about how many of us you've hunted and murdered for sport over the last two months? Nice try."

"Do you still think that's who I am?"

"Come on, Roger. Bag him already," Azure's female accomplice said from the hallway. "This guy doesn't know when to quit talking."

"You're tellin' me."

"Wait, bag me—" He snarled when the thick black bag was dragged over his head. Instinctively, he tried to struggle out of it but the transformed man rolled him onto his back and pinned him down with a knee on his chest. Lying there with his wrists bound beneath him under all that extra weight made him suck in a hissed breath.

"One more word and you'll make the trip dangling unconscious over my shoulder instead of walking on your two legs. Trust me, I'll have much more fun that way."

Bronson sighed and went completely limp as the guy fastened the bottom of the bag around his neck. It was way too tight to be comfortable but at least it didn't constrict his windpipe. After he'd spent who knew how long on his side, a lance of sharp, fiery pain coursed through his shoulder and hip when his captor finally hauled him to his feet and shoved him forward roughly.

"Is this—" He grunted when another pair of hands grasped his shoulders and jerked him forward again. "Come on. Is this necessary?"

Someone buried a fist in his gut and he doubled over with a grunt.

"That was a warning."

"Yep," he wheezed.

He was shoved, pulled, tugged, and jostled in all directions as the three transformed man-handled him over the tile floors. He only knew it was all three of them because the black bag didn't dampen his hearing. Still, he couldn't see a thing and he didn't hear any other movement around them as his captors escorted him down numerous branching hallways. When he stumbled under the dizziness of his massive hangover and staggered head-first into a corner before they turned, the transformed sighed with frustration and tugged him in the right direction.

Finally, a door opened slowly and he was jerked to an abrupt halt by the fingers digging into his elbow.

In a last-ditch effort to gain his freedom, Bronson tried to shift again. The familiar tingle raced across his skin but he remained in his human form with his wrists painfully bound behind him and a black bag over his head.

*I could take every single one of them if they hadn't...what did they do to me?*

He was pulled forward again roughly and this time, there was only the echo of his shoes and one other pair.

*No. What I want to know is who the hell this woman is. Psycho transformed acting like some kinda war criminal. So this is her POW camp then, huh? Fine.*

A chair screeched across the floor and he was shoved roughly forward and jerked to the side. The same gruff hands forced him down by his shoulders and he landed painfully on a hard metal seat. With a quick tug, the black bag was whipped off his head.

The young shifter jerked his head away from the man who balled the bag up into a tight wad. "What is this?"

"Your last chance, asshole. If it were up to me, you'd be dead."

The large man marched out of the room and slammed the door behind him.

He was alone again, still bound by the wrists but at least he had a chair.

*And I can see.*

They'd left him in a much larger room this time with the bright lights turned on. In front of him was a long, narrow metal table and an empty chair almost three feet from him on the other side.

The whole room was empty.

Bronson glanced at the large mirror on the righthand wall and snorted.

*So the dwarf and his FBI woman thought they could squeeze more out of me through a legit interrogation, huh? Right. If sticking me in an electric cage in a nightclub and then a leaking broom closet didn't work, this won't.*

He spent the next few minutes waiting for something to happen before he tried to wiggle to gain a little more room for his wrists between the cuffs binding him. They were clamped too tightly to make any kind of escape even remotely possible.

*This is the torture? That stupid dwarf's losing his touch.*

A moment later, the door opened and Johnny Walker strode into the new interrogation room with a long, thin metal rod clamped between his fingers. "Have you had enough time to consider your bad choices, son?"

"Screw you." He snarled at the dwarf. "When I get out of here, I'll destroy you."

"Is that a fact?" The bounty hunter stopped beside the chair and scrutinized him with a smirk. "Is Tyro gonna hunt me and kill me too?"

"I have more connections than you think."

"Sure. But there's no way in hell you can use 'em from in here. And in case it slipped your mind while you were drinkin' away what little common sense you have left, I think it'll help to remind you that I have contacts too."

"You don't scare me, asshole."

"Uh-huh. But your old man does, doesn't he? One word from Jasper and maybe a few strokes of the pen on some legal documents, and you lose everythin'."

Bronson clenched his teeth so fiercely that the massive hangover migraine intensified and brought a few dark spots to swim in the corners of his vision.

"Yeah, that's what I thought." Johnny shook the thin metal rod at him. "He's one of my contacts too, son. In case I ain't made that clear yet."

When the dwarf stepped toward him, he hissed and jerked away. "Don't touch me."

The bounty hunter ignored him completely and stepped behind the chair. A hand clamped around one of his forearms to hold him still while he picked the locks on the cuffs. They popped open with sharp clicks and made his wrists tingle with the surge of blood. The set of cuffs landed on the table in front of him before Johnny thrust his face mere inches away from the young shifter's.

He hissed a sharp breath.

Someone else chose that moment to walk through the door. As he rolled his shoulders back and rubbed his raw, aching wrists, he ignored the dwarf to watch their newest arrival instead.

When Azure came into view, she carried a metal tray with medical gauze, an unlabeled brown bottle, and cotton balls. She didn't look at him as she rounded the table and sat in the chair across from him. The tray clinked onto the table, and he thought he saw the glint of a scalpel under the cotton balls. She unscrewed the lid of the brown bottle slowly and didn't once look up from her task.

The end of the lockpick Johnny wagged in his face brought the shifter's attention back to the dwarf. "You listen to me real good, son. This right here? This is your last goddamn chance. You can make threats and keep hatin' me all you want, but I'm the reason you're gettin' a last chance in the first place. This is what you need. How you handle the hard truth ain't up to anyone but you."

Bronson studied the bounty hunter's gaze and his upper lip curled in a furious sneer. "I thought you didn't take sides."

"I ain't." Johnny nodded toward Azure. "You're as guilty as she is. Y'all have more than enough to atone for when all this is over. Any funny business, Bronson, and I swear on my paradise in the swamp, you ain't gettin' another chance to right your wrongs. That's a promise."

Johnny glanced at Azure again, stepped away from Bronson, and moved to the door.

"Don't make promises you can't keep, dwarf," he called over his shoulder. "If anything happens to me, you're finished."

"If anythin' happens to you, you're the only one to blame." The bounty hunter slipped into the silent hallway and pulled the door shut after him.

*What the hell is that supposed to mean?*

The young shifter gritted his teeth and stared at the insane transformed woman seated across the table from him. She still didn't look at him but busied herself with the collection of tools on her tray and soaked the cotton balls in whatever was in the brown bottle.

*Do they think this will scare me enough to talk? They're all insane.*

After several minutes of complete silence—and the distinct feeling that someone was on the other side of the two-way mirror, watching the whole thing—Bronson leaned forward with his hands in his lap and ignored the sting of his raw, aching wrists. "I'm not telling you anything. Not about Kaiser, not about Tyro, nothing. Do whatever you want but I thought you should know that first."

Azure's eyebrows twitched briefly and she shrugged and still refused to look at him. "That's not why we're here. Not now, anyway."

With a frown, he watched her calmly pour clear liquid from the brown bottle into a small glass bowl on the tray. She was serious. He didn't know how he knew, but her previous bravado when she'd threatened him with torture and bodily harm in the supply closet had disappeared.

*Now she simply looks sad. Right. I must be insane if I'm worried about the feelings of the transformed scum who kidnapped me and locked me in a closet.*

He cleared his throat. "Then what do you want?"

"Only one answer." When she'd finished screwing the lid on the brown bottle, Azure's gaze flicked up to meet his with severe intensity. "To one question."

"You expect me to believe that after everything you've done?"

She held his gaze without any reaction whatsoever and lowered her hands slowly into her lap. "Why do you hate us so much?"

Bronson scoffed. "That usually happens when you're kidnapped, locked in a closet, and interrogated by a group of criminals with…whatever kind of trick you tried to pull in there."

Azure shook her head slowly. "The transformed. All of us. Why do you hate us so much that you'd go out of your way to hunt us and murder us?"

The directness of the single question that had fueled his entire world for the last two months made him freeze. His heart thudded in his chest and the heat of his rage returned instantly when he recalled the night on the pier—the night he was supposed to propose to the love of his life but watched her fall into the bay instead, her body peppered with bullet holes.

He swallowed thickly and leaned back in his chair. "I don't have to explain myself to you."

"No. You don't." The woman's gaze was calm, steady, and fiery behind all that ridiculously thick makeup. Maybe it was the sharp tug of her severely pulled-back hair that made her look so dangerous. "But I wanted to give you the chance before I hurt you."

"I don't think that falls under the definition of 'leveling the playing field,'" Bronson retorted. "If you'd wanted to hurt me, you would have done it already."

"What I want doesn't have anything to do with this right now." She frowned and studied his face. "Are you sure you don't want to answer my question?"

"Screw you." He sneered at her and shook his head. "All this? Your secret hideout, the magical light show in the closet, you playing war and saying you've built yourself an army of transformed? I see right through it and it'll never be enough to stop what's coming for all of you. Believe me. If the transformed don't smarten up very soon and take the offers they are given, you'll all be dead."

With a heavy sigh and a glance at the two-way mirror, Azure grabbed a thin white cloth from beneath the pile of cotton balls and dipped it as much as she could into the glass bowl on the tray. "If you say so."

"Do you think I'm messing around?"

"I know you're not. That's the problem, Bronson. Neither am I."

When she lifted the soaked rag from the bowl, he flinched away from her in the chair and prepared to shift.

*The dwarf's been spewing nothing but empty threats. If she wants to fight me here, fine. That won't stop my uncle's wrath or mine.*

But Azure didn't stand from her chair, lunge toward him, or show any indication that she meant to attack. Her face remained a stony mask, even when she stretched the soaked rag and lifted it to her face.

Bronson snorted.

*Fine. I guess we're both insane. What is she trying to do? Torture herself to get at me?*

The liquid from the bottle, however, seemed to be as harmless as the cotton balls. She pressed it against her face and wiped her cheeks and temples slowly. Thick smears of black makeup came off and tinted the rag with dark smudges he could see from where he sat.

*Oh, so this is her version of taking a jacket off to get down to a fight, is it? Wiping off a mask of vigilante makeup won't do a thing to change my mind.*

When she removed the cloth from her face, she held it out in front of her with one hand to block his view before she used two of the cotton balls to wipe her eyelids.

The young shifter glanced at the closed door, then the two-way mirror.

*Maybe this is a test. They think I'm too scared or too stupid to get myself out of this. If she plans to attack me, she should do it already.*

The freedom of his unbound wrists and the short distance from his metal chair to the door were too much to ignore. He had to take his chance.

With a low growl, he shoved the table away from him. Azure must have caught it because something banged against the table and the tray and its contents clattered to the floor. He had already leapt across the room, his hand outstretched for the door handle and his pulse racing.

*Idiots.*

The door was locked.

# CHAPTER THIRTEEN

Bronson snarled and tried again. He cranked the door handle furiously before the clink of something breaking off in the mechanism made him stop.

"Bronson," Azure said calmly.

He stayed where he was, breathing heavily, and glowered at the door. Again, he'd let false hope and rage take over completely.

*And now I look like an idiot.*

"You aren't going anywhere until we've had this conversation," she added.

"What conversation?" With a snarl, he jerked his hand away from the handle and turned slowly toward her. "I want justice. You want a war. It sounds like the perfect—"

All the breath was sucked out of his lungs when he settled his angry gaze on the psychopath who called herself a leader. Now that she'd removed the ghastly black makeup from her face and had released the severe bun to let her light-brown hair fall around her shoulders, she looked completely different.

"No." His heel kicked against the closed door when he stepped back and made him jolt to a stop before he pressed himself against the wall.

Addison Taylor sat on the other side of the table, her hair pressed into a kink from the bun and her face slightly streaked around the edges with the remains of the face paint she hadn't removed completely. But the eyes that stared at him were unmistakable—the eyes he'd recognized in the closet and turned away from at the cemetery.

*I am insane.*

"I tried to tell you before," she said.

"No. You're dead."

She lowered her head. "Which is why I can't exactly run around showing my face. I know, a black mask isn't exactly all that original but—"

"Stop. Please..." The young shifter's mouth had gone dry and it was too hard to swallow, let alone say anything at all.

"You're not crazy, Bronson." Addison stood slowly from her chair and spread her arms. "And I'm not dead."

"You can't... You..." A pulsing wave of dizziness overwhelmed him and his knees buckled before he slid slowly down the wall and thumped to the floor. He couldn't look away. He couldn't stand being in the same room with her now but he couldn't get his legs to move the way he wanted them to either.

"I know it'll take some time to get used to." She stepped toward him and the closer she got, the more he felt like he couldn't breathe. "But this had to happen. One way or another."

"You..." His mouth worked futilely as he stared at his dead girlfriend in horror. "You're not real. You can't be—"

"I am." When she stopped in front of him, every part of his body felt numb. Then, she lowered herself to her knees and held a hand out.

With a sudden inability to move at all, he could only stare at her outstretched hand.

*Her hand—it looks the same. This has to be a joke. They have some kind of illusionist on their team. Like Kaiser has Agnes.*

That thought brought all the pieces whirling and crashing

into place in his mind. First was Agnes' magic, which had made them all think she was a rare and mysterious blood witch who happened to be unconscionably strong at the same time—shifter-strong. And Azure with her three transformed cronies had crowded around him in the dark closet and summoned the same powerful, deadly red magic that raced across their hands and arms.

Addison...alive.

"It's all a lie." Even his whisper trembled and he was vaguely aware that he was shaking now. Tears blurred his vision as he stared at her outstretched hand. "Everything I did. Everything he told me—"

His throat closed reflexively, and he wished he could stop breathing there and then so he didn't have to feel all of this. It was worse than watching her die.

Addison sat on her heels, took his hand from where it rested limply on the floor at his side, and held it between both of hers. "I'm here, though. This is real."

The simple act of taking his hand and telling him what he already knew but didn't want to believe shattered the rest of his resolve. A strangled groan escaped him and the tears were too much to hold back.

*She knows everything about me, about Mom. about Tyro—Jesus Christ, what have I done?*

The young shifter hung his head and didn't try to hold his sobs back. He didn't have the strength to continue the way he'd been going since the night that had changed everything. Stupidly, he didn't even have the strength to move his fingers pressed gently between the hands of the woman for whom he'd been ready to burn the world because he hadn't been strong enough to save her.

"I'm so—" A rasped breath finally filled his lungs between his choked sobs. "I'm so sorry."

"I know." She patted his hand, released it gently, and turned to sit beside him with her back pressed against the wall.

Not as close as she used to sit beside him before everything had changed. But it was so much closer than he'd thought he would ever be to her again.

"I'm sorry too," Addison muttered and stared blankly at the floor in front of them. "But I think it's too late for 'sorry' to mean anything."

Bronson clenched his eyes shut and bowed his head. Tears still streamed down his cheeks as he fought to catch his breath.

"We have so much to talk about."

"I...can't." Finally, he managed to close his fingers into weak, useless fists and shook his head. "I can't do this."

"You can." She turned her head to look at him but he couldn't bring himself to meet her gaze. "You simply don't want to. Neither do I. Like I said, what we want no longer has anything to do with this."

He drew in a long, jagged breath and it felt like he used every last ounce of his strength simply to nod a fraction of an inch.

"We tried to stay out of it." She inhaled slowly and ran her palms down the tops of her thighs over her pitch-black jeans. "But this whole situation has become so much bigger than either of us."

"Please..." What was he pleading for? For his resurrected girl-friend to stop talking? To keep going? To say everything he'd wanted to hear while knowing he never would?

To forgive him?

Addison didn't press him to explain but continued as if he hadn't said a word. "You know, in a weird way, maybe this was all supposed to happen the way it has."

"Don't say that," he whispered.

"So we could finish this."

When he finally gathered the courage to look at her, he was

glad to see a frown darkening her features above those glistening blue eyes. Seeing her gentle, loving smile might have killed him.

"I tried to finish it," he croaked. "Look what happened."

"Maybe that's the point. Thirty years of everyone trying to do it their way. We could keep going like that and see how far it takes us." She drew a deep breath and exhaled slowly. Her lower lip trembled. "Or we can do something different. We can show everyone—all shifters—that killing each other won't give one side or the other what they want. I think we all want the same thing, honestly."

A bitter laugh burst from his lips. "I don't think all shifters would agree with you on that."

"That's because it hasn't been done yet."

Bronson swallowed thickly, his senses overwhelmed with the scent of her that he'd tried so hard to forget, and the sour twist of shame filled his mouth. "And you think we're the ones who are supposed to do that. You and me."

"I do."

He looked at her and another wave of hot tears stung his eyes and blurred her face. If they spilled over again, he didn't care. "How are we supposed to do that, Addison?"

"We're already doing it. Sitting. Talking. But we still have so much to talk about."

"Talking doesn't do anything. That's how I—" He gritted his teeth. "That's how I lost you."

For a moment, they sat next to each other against the wall and both stared at the floor that reflected the bright overhead lights.

*This is too much. She wants way too much from me and I can't.*

"I won't force you into anything," Addison muttered. "That's how this whole mess started in the first place. So if you want to walk out of here right now, no one will stop you. That's a promise. But if Tyro doesn't give up his crusade, things will get worse before they get better. Much worse. For everyone."

Hearing that stupid name from her lips—Addison's this time

and not Azure's—made his gut twist painfully. He'd taken his rage out on transformed shifters for so long, thinking that would make things right and that the ones who'd pulled Addison away simply for being with him had to pay for thinking they could get away with it.

He'd killed shifters like her, knowing what life was like for the transformed. Knowing what she'd been through and what her parents had been through.

Because he and Addison were the same. Their mothers had both been turned thirty years earlier against their will, but Helice Harford had the means and the opportunity to hide her tragedy and convince the rest of the world she was natural-born.

"No." He raised a trembling hand to his mouth and grasped his jaw hard as he tried to recover whatever courage he had left.

"I understand." She pushed to her feet and nodded. "A promise is a promise." She knocked twice on the door and the heavy click of the lock turning echoed through the room. "I guess we'll see each other on the—"

"Addison." Bronson brushed his fingers against hers and she looked at him with absolutely no emotion at all behind her eyes.

That was the most terrifying part, he realized.

*That's not Addison. That's Azure. And she's not a psychopath leading a ragtag army. She knows exactly what she's doing.*

He placed his hand against the door to steady himself and stood, and the woman he'd wanted to spend the rest of his life with—the woman who was now a stranger—stepped calmly away from him.

"I'm staying." With a grimace, he shrugged. "Let's talk."

---

"Well, I'll be damned." Johnny chuckled and tugged his beard. "The little shit still has a conscience after all."

In the small, narrow room on the other side of the two-way

mirror, Charlie groaned. "Come on. He's been kidnapped twice, almost blown up, attacked by dogs, and punched in the face by you."

The bounty hunter snorted.

"And all it took was locking him in a room with his dead girl-friend who built an army against him."

"And his uncle," Lisa added, her arms folded as she studied the shifter couple in the next room slowly take their seats across from each other at the table.

"Well, shit." The shifter dwarf sighed. "Why didn't we start with this, huh? Seriously, no one in a million years would expect Tyro and Azure to sit together and hash out their differences over a—"

"I did. Thirty minutes ago." Without turning away from the window into the interrogation room, Johnny extended an open palm toward his cousin. "Nice try, though."

"With what?"

"I won, you lost. Pay up."

His cousin rolled his eyes and rummaged in his pocket before he withdrew his black leather wallet with its thick silver chain.

Lisa frowned at the dwarves as Charlie slapped two hundred-dollar bills into Johnny's hand. "Is that what I think it is?"

"If you're thinkin' it's two hundred bucks, darlin', then yeah." The bounty hunter pocketed the bills and folded his arms again.

"I call it theft," the biker dwarf muttered.

"You guys made a bet on whether Addison and Bronson would come to an understanding?"

"More than one."

Johnny smirked. "And I won 'em all."

"Wow." She looked from one to the other and laughed bitterly. "You two are unbelievable. Hundreds if not thousands of shifter lives are on the line and you turned it into a bet."

Johnny met his partner's gaze and raised his eyebrows. "They're makin' it work. Those two didn't have a chance in hell of comin' together the way they were goin' at it before. And by the looks of it, I'd say it's goin' fairly well."

"Seriously, Johnny."

"I am bein' serious, darlin'. It was Charlie's idea."

His cousin leaned away from him. "That's how it's gonna be, huh?"

"Besides." He tugged on his beard again and looked through the window at the two young second-generation transformed shifters who'd finally decided to stop fighting anything and everything that got in their way. "I imagine that when they're finished, those hundreds or thousands of shifter lives will be in a hell of a lot better hands than they have been."

"Not if Langley Appleman continues to run his Kaiser operation. We still have to deal with him."

"Uh-huh. But now we finally have a way to do that."

The small room fell silent as the team watched the heart-breaking reunion. Lisa glanced at Johnny's pocket and shook her head. "You're right. But all this was worth way more than two hundred bucks."

Charlie groaned again. "Don't tell him that. Who's side are you on, anyway?"

She slipped her arm through Johnny's and nodded at Addison Taylor and Bronson Harford. "Theirs. That's the point."

# CHAPTER FOURTEEN

Johnny and his team waited another two hours for the young shifters to finish the mother of all heart-to-heart chats. Charlie stepped out of the viewing room behind the two-way mirror first for a bathroom break, but he never returned. It took the bounty hunter a little over halfway through the observed conversation before he realized his cousin had been missing for at least forty-five minutes.

"I think I oughtta make sure Charlie ain't breakin' somethin' in this place 'cause I ain't payin' for anythin' else he screws up."

"You meant literally, right?" Lisa muttered, most of her attention still on the young shifter couple.

"Uh-huh. With cash." He sighed. "I might as well see what I can scrounge up for food in a dump like this. Do you want me to bring you somethin'?"

"Sure." She nodded. "Whatever you can find. I'm not fussy."

"If the hounds ain't found it and eaten it all on their own by now." He started to walk to the door and paused. "Are you doin' all right, darlin'?"

"What?" She glanced at him, then shrugged before she turned

toward the window again. "Yeah, I'm fine, Johnny. But I think someone should stay here and keep an eye on things."

"I'm sure this facility has security cameras in corners even I can't find."

"Maybe." She tapped two fingers against her lips and tilted her head. "But security footage doesn't react to real-time situations and the door's still unlocked."

"Huh. Good point. I'll make sure those... You know, what the hell are we callin' 'em now?"

"Who?"

"Addison's shifters. They damn sure ain't operatives."

"Soldiers, maybe?"

"There's nothin' military about this except what's for show."

"I don't know, Johnny. She rallied a group of rebel transformed with questionable intentions under a good cause. I don't think it matters what we call them, but I'm trying to listen. So can you—"

He snapped his fingers and pointed at her. "That's it. Rebels. We'll go with that."

"Great. Hey, if you find anything with caffeine, can you—" The door to the viewing room clicked shut, and Lisa turned to the door before she laughed wryly. "Fair enough. I said I was trying to listen."

Her stomach rumbled after the long day of fighting into a repurposed government facility, being threatened with guns, and threatening in return with a few phone calls. It was also challenging to hang on the edge of their seats while Addison revealed herself as alive, well, and the leader of Azure's army.

*I would never have guessed we'd be here almost three weeks after taking this case. It didn't even seem like a real case back then. None of this has been normal but here we are.*

Now that she was alone—without Charlie to complain about the noise or Johnny saying he couldn't have cared less about the details of such a private exchange—Lisa reached for the control console on the intercom and turned up the volume of the conversation in the interrogation room.

"He won't stand down simply because you bring an army to his front door," Bronson said. "If anything, it'll make him push that much harder."

"Maybe." Addison folded her arms on the table and leaned forward. "But he has no idea that we can push back. Or how hard."

"You don't understand. Langley's—" He licked his lips. "He's not the kind of guy to rethink his priorities because someone finds enough courage to confront him. He doesn't stop and he won't stop. And he has way more leverage than you give him credit for."

"So tell me about his leverage."

He took a deep breath. "He's persuasive. More than most people I know and I've met as many politicians and philanthropists and CEOs as he has."

She smirked. "You don't usually hear all three of those in the same sentence."

"Right." He responded with a small smile. "But that's what I'm saying. Langley has connections. Maybe even more than Dad, and most of them aren't the kind to shy away from getting their hands dirty—legally or physically."

"Okay. So your asshole uncle has buddies who might back him up—"

"They will, Addison. Because he'll ask and no one refuses Langley Appleman when he calls to collect on IOUs."

Her smile flickered. "We have connections too."

"What, you mean the hick bounty hunter and his sidekicks? Please."

Lisa's mouth popped open in indignation. "Sidekick my ass."

Addison laughed, and the sound startled both Bronson and the former FBI agent behind a wall of glass. "Yeah, Johnny's a little...rough."

"And nosey."

"Seriously nosey, right? He thinks he can run around telling everyone else what to do when he has no idea what he's talking about."

Holding back her laughter, Lisa folded her arms.

*I think I'm gonna keep this one to myself for now.*

Bronson's low chuckle was as unexpected but it died quickly, his smile replaced by wide-eyed realization. "I told him I'd kill him."

"Seriously?"

"Uh…I think so, yeah." The young man glanced at the mirror and swallowed. "I might have to clear that up."

"I'm sure he knows you didn't mean it."

"No, I meant it. At the time."

"You're allowed to change your mind." Addison chuckled before her smile faded too. "Wow. I just realized I can't remember the last time I laughed."

He stared at her for a long moment before he nodded. "Yeah it feels…weird."

She cleared her throat and glanced almost wistfully at him. "We can talk about that when this is finished—if you want. Trust me, I'm looking forward to being able to sit down with someone and have a real conversation about anything that isn't…well, this. But that's not why we're here."

"Right. No, I know."

"Good." The woman studied her ex-fiancé from across the table while he scrutinized the thin scratches on the table's metal surface.

Lisa bit her lip.

*They're only kids but they have to sit here and hash out battle plans together because they were forced into someone else's fight. Addison was right. It shouldn't be their responsibility, but they might be the only ones who can fix this before it's past the point of no return.*

The young woman tucked her hair behind her ear and looked like she was about to throw in the towel right then and there.

*Come on, Addison. You said you could do this. Keep going.*

"So."

"So." Bronson looked at her with a slightly wary frown.

"Leverage."

"Beyond Langley's connections?" He sighed. "Come on. If you've watched him as closely as you think you have, you already have a clear picture of—"

"Anything you can tell me right now will be incredibly helpful, Bronson. No matter what it is—even if I might already know —there's always a different angle."

He wrinkled his nose and leaned away from her. "You have been through…so much. I've never heard you talk like this."

"Yeah." She folded her arms. "That tends to happen when you die and wake up on a middle-aged couple's couch in the Midwest."

His mouth dropped open before he could find the right words. "I know what you went through—"

"No, Bronson. You don't know." There was no anger or venom in Addison's voice, merely a calculated detachment so she could get to the truth the way she had to as Azure. "You can't know. It didn't happen to you."

"Hey, I'm sorry. I'm only saying… I mean…"

"I don't blame you if that's what you're worried about."

He clenched his eyes shut and lowered his head.

"Not for what happened that night at the docks and not for being unable to know what I went through. None of it is your fault. But I'm not…" She straightened in her chair and raised her chin. "I'm not the same person. Trying to pretend I am will only make all this harder than it has to be."

"That I do understand," he muttered.

"I know."

They stared at each other for a moment longer and Lisa's stomach growled.

*Johnny had better hurry with something to eat. It can't be that hard to find food in a place like this.*

Bronson drew a sharp breath. "I don't know what else I can tell you, Addison. Honestly. Langley's already untouchable when he acts like he's a part of normal society. As Kaiser? He's...I honestly don't think he has any weaknesses."

"That's a load of crap." She tilted her head and looked at hom sternly. "Everyone has a weakness somewhere."

"What, you think it's me?"

"Is it?"

"No. No, not even a little. I'm simply a thorn in his side." The young shifter shook his head vigorously. "My uncle's tried to pull me into his circle for my entire life. My mom did what she could to stop it and it worked for a while until—"

Until Addison was killed. That truth didn't need to be said out loud for either of them to know what he meant.

"So you don't think he'll listen to you," she prompted.

"He never does. He gave me the resources I needed when I wanted them and aside from that, all I ever got was a slap on the wrist. Any time I wanted to sit and talk, it was like he wanted me to get out of the way so he could call in his favorite little—"

Bronson froze and his eyes widened as he stared at the blank wall behind her.

"What?" She tilted her head to try to meet his gaze. "His what, Bronson?"

"Agnes," he whispered.

Lisa turned the volume up in the viewing room and leaned closer to the glass. "Now we're getting somewhere."

"Agnes." Addison glanced at the two-way mirror and covered her mistake quickly but Bronson didn't notice. "I don't know—"

"His shifter hunter." Bronson flicked his gaze to meet hers

again and uttered a choking sound. "The blood witch. At least that's what we all assumed she was. But she's not, is she?"

The girl shifted in her chair. "I wouldn't know."

"Yes, you do. You do. She was there that night on the docks. You saw her. And even if you haven't seen her since then, it's impossible to forget what she can do." He lowered his gaze to her arms folded on the table and pointed at her. "It's what you can do. Isn't it? The red lights—magic. How…"

"I don't know how it's possible but it happened." The young woman darted another look at the mirror. "I don't think I have to tell you what it means, though, do I?"

He choked out an angry laugh and his eyes bulged as he thumped his palms on the table. "That bastard."

Lisa rubbed her hands together and listened intently, her growing hunger forgotten as the real point of this entire mini-operation finally came into play.

*She's good. No one else knows him well enough to pinpoint his thought process like this. He has no idea she's been feeding him the answers and now, he's about to come up with our next steps all on his own.*

"No wonder none of us could work out what she is," Bronson muttered. "Jesus, I merely thought she was some kind of freak—some messed-up chick who wanted to play with fire and ended up working for my uncle."

"She's not a freak," Addison said flatly.

"What? Oh. No, of course. That's not what I meant."

"Then what are you trying to say, Bronson?"

His eyes widened when he met her gaze again. "That's it. Agnes. That's how we get to him."

"You mean take her out of the equation."

"Take her—" The young man looked horrified when he realized what she meant and saw no trace of distaste or hesitation after her suggestion. "No. I don't mean—we can't do that."

"Why?" Addison folded her arms and leaned back in her chair again. "It's not like you have a problem with killing."

"Don't. Addison, that's not... It's different."

"How? How is it different?"

"Agnes is...she helped me."

The woman sneered. "It seems like even more of a reason to get her out of the way."

"You can't sit here and tell me I need to take her out of the equation and expect me to jump to attention and do it."

"Why not? If Agnes is leverage, we—"

"Because that's not the point!" Bronson pounded a fist on the table but she didn't so much as flinch. "You said there was a better way. One that doesn't involve hunting magicals and killing them because it's part of war or whatever the hell this is. I thought you were serious."

"Don't I look serious now?"

"You look..." Bronson hissed and leaned toward her. "You look like my uncle. I'm done being manipulated."

He shoved away from the table and launched the metal chair across the room behind him before he turned toward the door.

"So, what?" Addison called after him. "You're gonna run away to come up with another half-baked plan on your own and use your uncle's resources to get it done?"

"I don't need anything from him." He snarled, whirled to face her, and pointed a finger at her. "And I don't need anything from you."

"Then it sounds like you're out of options."

"Ha. Does it?" He grasped the door handle and glared at her. "You know what, you're right. I have no idea what you've been through. But that goes both ways, Addison. You have no idea what it was like to watch you—" He swallowed thickly and grimaced. "Forget it. Good luck with your war."

She stood and raised her voice enough to make it echo around the room. "Where are you going?"

"To find someone who doesn't give a shit about what I am. I'm done being used. And I'm done…doing horrible things I wish I hadn't because someone else told me it was for the greater good. You're exactly like Langley. Honestly, I have no idea which of you is gonna come out of this alive but I hope you two tear each other apart. Without me."

Lisa laughed in surprise and pumped a fist tightly at her side. "Yes! Here we go."

He jerked the door open so hard that it slammed against the interior wall and left a new divot in the plaster. He was halfway through the doorway when he stopped with a snarl. "Do you not have anything better to do than stand in my way?"

"Not when it's this much fun, pal." Johnny clapped a hand on the shifter's shoulder and Bronson immediately stepped aside with a snarl. "And trust me, I ain't had this much fun tryin' to figure a fella out in years."

"What?"

"Oh, sure." Charlie entered the room right behind his cousin. "You're only having fun because you keep taking my money."

"It ain't my fault you can't smarten up and quit takin' the bait. Hell, I seen catfish more discernin' in what they bite than you, 'coz."

The hounds trotted through the door after them. Luther sniggered. "Charlie the catfish. I like the sound of that."

"Bro, you're not any better than he is."

"I don't bet with money, Rex."

"Good thing, 'cause you always lose."

"What the hell is going on right now?" Bronson turned toward Addison with wide, furious eyes. "You said I could leave whenever I wanted."

"You can." She looked at the dwarves who stepped into the room and shrugged. "But ten seconds ago, it sounded like you wanted to stay."

"You didn't hear anything I said, did you?" He growled and turned toward the door. "I should have kept my mouth—"

"Where do you think you're going?" The giant shifter who'd strapped the black bag over Bronson's head loomed in the doorway and his massive chest blocked any form of escape.

"Get out of my—"

"Y'all quit standin' there and let everyone else have a turn, huh?" Johnny waved them forward into the room. "Hurry the hell up. We ain't got all day."

"Oh, yeah?" Charlie sniggered at his cousin as another half-dozen rebels of Azure's army trailed into the room. Each of them scrutinized Bronson from head to toe. "Do you have big plans for the rest of the afternoon, 'coz?"

"Uh-huh. Takin' whatever cash you have left on ya, to start."

Bronson gazed around the room in disbelief bordering on fury again. "You're all completely insane."

He turned to the door again, but the giant transformed man slammed it shut with a meaty hand. "You wanna stay for this, Tyro."

"Don't call me that."

"Whatever your name is, you'd better not screw this up."

The Harford heir stepped back and grimaced in frustration and confusion as the big man leaned against the door and folded his arms. "Will someone tell me what the hell is going on here?"

"Where's Lisa?" Johnny asked and completely ignored the question as the rebels took their places around the room. "Lisa! Are you still in there?"

A sharp click activated the overhead speakers. "Did you bring me anything to eat?"

He snorted and Charlie lifted his arm toward the two-way mirror to show her the plastic bag dangling from his fingers. "Get excited, Lisa. This is probably the worst meal of processed snack food you'll ever have."

The speakers crackled again. "Don't start without me."

Charlie frowned at his cousin. "Is she talking about the food or the meeting?"

"Both. Don't test her." Johnny pointed at Bronson. "Take a seat, son."

"Not until someone either lets me out like I was promised or explains to me what this is."

"Like I said. Take a seat. You can skip on outta here as soon as we lay out another plan."

# CHAPTER FIFTEEN

Bronson had refused to take the only other available chair in the interrogation room filled with seven other transformed shifters, two dwarves, two coonhounds, and a Light Elf. Once Lisa had joined them, she gladly accepted the open chair since no one else was using it and snatched the bag of snacks from Charlie's hand without a word.

Everyone else was focused on getting down to business.

"All right. Let's talk about Agnes." Johnny hooked his thumbs through his belt loops and squinted at all the faces around the room. "It sounds like that's our best way in."

"If we can even get to her," the giant man grumbled.

The bounty hunter pointed at him. "Who are you?"

"Roger."

"Well, Roger. That's what he's for." He nodded at Bronson, who widened his eyes when all heads turned to face him.

"I'm not getting involved." He shook his head and darted Addison a livid glare. "I already said that."

"You're the one who knows how to find Agnes," she replied. "You also said she helped you, which means she's probably still willing to help you. As long as she doesn't have a reason to suspect you've been here with us for the last twenty-four hours."

"Twenty-four?"

She shrugged. "Give or take."

"She ain't got one of those trackin' devices shoved into your pockets or anythin', right?"

Bronson gaped at the bounty hunter. "What?"

"Does anyone know? Aw, come on. Y'all can kidnap the son of one of the wealthiest shifter families in the country, but none of y'all thought to check his damn pockets?"

"Don't get your panties in a twist, dwarf." Dee folded her arms and smirked at him. "He's clean."

"Ha. Where did you come from? You know what, I don't care. Bronson, how do you normally get in touch with Agnes? You know, to tell her y'all are meetin' up to go after someone or meet up again after y'all break out of the kinky nightclub. That kinda thing."

Bronson narrowed his eyes at the bounty hunter but didn't say a word.

"It's important, man," Charlie muttered. "You know, lives on the line and everything. You understand, right?"

"I am not helping you with this," Bronson seethed. "I will not call Agnes or set a trap for her. I won't trick her into meeting me somewhere so you lunatics can attack her. No."

"Hell, we ain't said a thing about doin' any of that. She's Kaiser's weak link. All you gotta do is—"

"I won't kill her!" Bronson snarled and his eyes flashed silver.

The room fell completely silent as everyone stared at him. His fists clenched and his lips curled in fury again.

"Whoa. Okay…" Charlie turned slowly toward Addison and exaggerated a grimace. "I thought you guys, like, settled your differences or whatever."

She pressed her lips together and tried to choke down a laugh. "I didn't exactly have the time to explain."

"Explain what?" The Harford heir gestured impatiently. "That this whole thing was simply another lie?"

"You have to be kidding me," Lisa shouted as she tossed a half-opened candy bar onto the table between her and Addison.

Johnny cleared his throat. "I didn't think you felt so strongly about it, darlin'."

She pulled a package of pretzels from the plastic bag and shook it at him. "Did you even look at the expiration date?"

"They're pretzels," Charlie said. "July seventeenth wasn't that long ago."

"Yes, Charlie. That would be true if it was July seventeenth of this year."

"Oh…"

The six rebel transformed looked at one another in confusion and wondered silently if this was some other part of Johnny and Lisa's plan to bring Bronson Harford onto their side or merely a regular day.

The young shifter closed his eyes, stepped back, and shook his head. "I'm never getting out of here. And I have to deal with this for the rest of my life."

Lisa dropped the bag of expired snacks onto the floor, stood from her chair, and ignored everyone else as she moved closer to him. "Since no one else seems capable of explaining the situation to you through to the end—or of finding anything edible in this entire building…" She looked at both Walker cousins in exasperation. "I guess I'm the only one who realizes we won't get anywhere by standing around yelling at each other."

Johnny snorted. "He's the only one yellin'."

She ignored him and closed her eyes for a brief moment to collect herself.

*I'm in a room with over a dozen hotheaded transformed shifters and my dwarf partner who might as well be one too. This is not my idea of a good time, but we're working with what we have.*

"No one wants you to kill anyone," she told the angry,

confused young shifter. "I'm very sure that goes without saying but we're now all on the same page."

He gritted his teeth and stared unblinkingly into her eyes. "But someone's going after Agnes."

"Yes. You. Because you're the only one of us she knows and trusts. We want her alive because if she's as important to your uncle as you think she is, Agnes will be the one to rip the rug out from under him."

"What rug?"

Dee snorted and darted Bronson a cruelly joking grin. "That his favorite little blood witch isn't a witch."

Johnny grunted. "I think Kaiser will have a hell of a time reconcilin' his perfect little crusade knowin' he's been puttin' all his eggs in one transformed basket without even recognizin' it. Maybe it's enough to break him or maybe not. At the very least, we start unravelin' the threads."

Bronson shook his head. "You want me to take Agnes to my uncle and spill her secret right there for her? He'll kill her and I don't think he'll go much easier on me either."

"Let Agnes decide," Addison said as she stood from her chair. "It's her secret to tell, after all. All you have to do, Bronson, is meet her. Tell her you know and we'll see what she does."

"Right." He laughed bitterly and turned in a quick circle before he fixed everyone in the room with a crazed, disbelieving grin. "It seems none of you thought this through."

"It's a good thing you're on our side then, ain't it?"

"I'm not on anyone's—" The Harford heir growled and pinched the bridge of his nose. "Look, you don't send the guy who's been...on his own crusade to go threaten the muscle whose hands are as dirty as his. Agnes knows exactly what I've done. And the only thing she'll think about when I tell her I know she's a transformed is how to slit my throat and get rid of my body."

"It has to be done," Johnny muttered. "If anyone else tries to reach out to her, we'll blow this whole thing wide open or lose even more lives than we oughtta." He frowned and hooked his thumbs through his belt loops again. "Which is one, by the way."

"No, you don't get it," Bronson shouted. "She'll kill me!"

Everyone in the room stood perfectly still and silent. The six rebels glanced knowingly at each other. Addison's lower jaw jutted in frustration. Johnny raised an eyebrow and Charlie's mouth fell open.

"Yeah." The young shifter nodded and his gaze darted from one staring face to the next. "That's right. She will. I can't take her on my own. Hell, even the dwarf knows that."

Still, no one else had a response to his outburst.

The hounds sniffed under the table and moved to the far end of the room near the door.

"Dangit. No snacks down here either, bro."

"Hey, Rex. I think that's the bag." Luther trotted toward the abandoned snacks to investigate, whipped his head up, and looked around the room. "Yeesh. It's quiet in here, huh? Big-bad Tyro said he's gonna get killed and it's like no one believes him."

"Thank you," Bronson muttered and immediately felt like an idiot for talking to the hounds.

Rex zigzagged across the floor toward him, then stopped to look him in the eye. "It's 'cause no one cares, shifter."

"Oh, yeah." Luther sniggered and thrust his nose into the bag. "'Cause he's been killing extra stinky shifters the whole time. Ha. That guy needs a new plan if he thinks anyone's gonna feel sorry for him."

With a barely perceptible twitch of a smile at the corner of her mouth, Dee looked at the hounds before she swung her gaze lazily to meet Bronson's. "Even the chatty dogs can pick up on that much."

Roger growled through a leering grin. "It sucks to be one of us, doesn't it?"

The other rebels sniggered and nudged each other, shook their heads, and fixed Bronson with hateful stares.

Addison cleared her throat and drew everyone's attention. She nodded at Bronson. "You'll set up a meeting with Agnes and tell her what she needs to hear and we'll go from there."

"I—" He turned to Johnny and Lisa but received the same response from them.

If he wanted to survive—especially in the middle of a transformed base surrounded by the faction of shifters he'd hunted and killed one by one—he needed to sit down, shut up, and do as he was told.

When he finally realized this, he pressed his fist to his mouth and couldn't look at anyone. "Yeah. Okay. I'll call her."

Addison nodded. "Have her meet you tomorrow. She can choose the location as long as it's not Kaiser's farm or somewhere very public where more people can get hurt. We'll take care of the rest."

"Fine." No one else said or did anything and Bronson shoved his hands into his pockets.

"Now would be great, Bronson," Addison added. "Thanks."

Charlie whistled quietly, headed toward the Harford heir, and clapped a hand on his shoulder. "I'll keep you company. It's hard to have a decent phone conversation with everyone packed into a room this small, right?"

Rex sat and scratched behind his ear with a rear paw. "Sounds quiet in here to me."

"Yeah, we could make a phone call in this room." Luther removed his head from the plastic bag of snacks and a four-year-old candy bar's silver cellophane wrapper glinted between his jaws. "You know, if we had thumbs."

"Or phones."

Charlie opened the door and quickly ushered a thoroughly berated and shamed Bronson into the hall. The second the door closed again, Johnny snapped his fingers. "Drop it, Luther."

"Seriously? Lisa's not gonna eat it—"

"Now."

With a low whine, the hound's tail drooped between his legs and the candy bar toppled on the floor.

Roger shook his head. "Can someone tell me why we don't simply shoot him now and dump him somewhere in the desert?"

"Hey." Luther stared at the massive rebel shifter. "It's only a treat, shifter. Relax."

"Not you, dummy," Rex clarified.

"Oh, okay. We're cool then."

Addison frowned at the hounds and when she looked at Johnny, the bounty hunter shrugged. "We need him, Roger."

"Yeah, about as badly as he needed us dead," one of the other rebels added. "We shouldn't make deals with him. If the others found out we're letting Tyro—"

"No one will find out about this." She pointed at each of her rebels. "No one. If Bronson can—"

"You mean Tyro," Dee said haughtily and earned a warning stare from her leader in response.

"If he pulls this off with Agnes, we'll get what we need. If it goes south, it won't matter because no one else will know. Got it?"

The other shifters grumbled their assent, and Johnny grunted. "Way to draw it out of him, by the way. What did you have to say to get him to turn around?"

Addison raised her eyebrows. "Exactly what I needed to say."

"Sure. Right. It must have been one helluva yarn, though, huh?"

Lisa shook her head. "She didn't have to lie to him, Johnny. I think Bronson already knew what was happening. He merely spent the last fifteen years trying to bury his mom's secret—"

"Ugh. Come on." Dee rolled her eyes. "No one wants to hear poor little rich boy's sob story."

"What?"

Addison clapped and nodded curtly. "I think we're done here for now. Right?"

"Yeah…" Lisa eyed the scowling rebels all around her and tilted her head. "I feel like I'm missing something."

"Only the cues, lady." Roger gestured toward the door.

"I need some privacy with my team," Addison added. "And we'll fill you in on the plan when we have something solid."

"Well, I'm sure we could help with—"

"I think we oughtta head out, darlin'." Johnny placed a hand on her lower back and guided her gently toward the door. "There might be a few rooms in this place I ain't searched yet for somethin' edible."

"Johnny—"

"Y'all know where to find us when you're done with your secret meetin'." He opened the door and practically shoved her into the hall as the hounds scrambled to catch up with their master.

As soon as he closed the door, she whirled on him. "What was that about?"

"You didn't feel it?"

"Feel what?"

"Woo!" Luther shook himself vigorously, his usually sleek coat now ruffled and sticking out in places. "Now that's what I call a good tingle. Hey, Johnny. Let's go back in there and do it again."

"Bro, you're insane." Rex shook his head and panted heavily. "I can't even smell myself right now."

Johnny hovered his palm above Lisa's shoulder and her dark hair fell over it. The top layer rose five inches to meet his hand and popped with static electricity.

"Whoa-ho-ho! Hey, Rex. Check it out. Lisa's floating."

She stared at her electrified hair and frowned. "Is that from…"

"Transformed shifters with magic they ain't fully learned how to use. Uh-huh." He removed his hand but his partner's hair still hovered erratically above her shoulder. "I ain't exactly sure what happens when one of them gets mad enough to let loose but I assumed it's best to not stick around to find out."

Lisa tried to smooth her hair into something resembling neatness. "That adds a whole new level of 'don't screw this up,' doesn't it?"

"Yep. Addison thinks her magic-wielding rebels are enough to eliminate Agnes all on their own if Bronson can't convince her she's throwin' bombs for the wrong side."

"But Agnes has enough control over her magic to make Kaiser's entire organization think she's a witch."

Luther giggled nervously. "Sounds like we're screwed."

The two partners glared at him and he immediately lowered his head to lick enthusiastically between his legs.

"They might not be enough," she added.

"We still have a few things goin' for us, darlin'. But we gotta convince Azure she ain't ready to move until we are."

"Right." Lisa's stomach growled ferociously and both the hounds whipped their heads up to stare at her. "Please tell me one of the rooms you haven't checked for food is the kitchen."

Johnny scratched his head and turned down the hallway. "Yeah, we're gonna have to find it first. These rebels ain't exactly forthcomin' with directions through their maze."

"We're on it, Johnny." The hounds trotted dutifully past their two-legs and sniffed diligently.

"Yeah, if there's food here, we'll find it."

"And then you'll have to share."

# CHAPTER SIXTEEN

When Bronson finished making the call to Agnes, he slipped his phone into his pocket and wiped the thin layer of beading sweat from his forehead. "This won't work."

Standing beside him in the empty hallway, Charlie wrinkled his nose. "I'm very sure no one ever got something done by deciding it was pointless before they even started."

The shifter snorted. "That's a weird thing to hear coming from a guy like you."

"I don't know how that was supposed to be a compliment, but thanks."

Somewhere down another branching corridor in the maze of Azure's compound, hurried footsteps echoed and faded again in the opposite direction. Bronson puffed his cheeks and blew out a long, slow breath. "You know, you kinda seem like the only shifter here who doesn't want to strangle me."

The biker dwarf grimaced and shook his head as he stepped away from him. "Trust me, I do."

"Oh."

"Seriously, you gotta know you won't get away with...you know, killing transfor—"

"I know that." Bronson growled. "And I know it doesn't mean anything to anyone here, but I never —"

"What?" The dwarf raised an eyebrow. "Regretted it? Knew what you were doing? Thought about how shitty it is to go after innocent magicals who can't protect themselves because they had no one to show them how?"

"Yeah, never mind."

"Nice try. No one's brushing this under the rug, Bronson. Just so you know." Charlie hiked the waistline of his pants up and sniffed. "It's a good thing we arrived when we did, though. You'd probably be dead without us."

"I'm probably dead anyway."

"Aw, come on." Charlie rolled his eyes and hissed a sigh. "You screwed up. Big time. Do you know how lucky you are that I got Johnny to take this case in the first place?"

The young shifter's eyes widened. "You?"

"Yeah. It didn't cost me a dime either until we started making bets today on— You know what?" Charlie pointed at him. "That doesn't matter. What I'm telling you right now is you owe Johnny and Lisa a hell of a lot for putting up with your dumb ass and hauling you out of the hole you dug yourself like…like…" He laughed. "Damn. I think I get it now."

"Get what?"

"Family stuff. Don't worry about it." When Rex and Luther appeared around the corner at the end of the hall, followed closely by Johnny and Lisa, he slung his arm around Bronson's shoulders again and held him a little tighter than necessary. "The point is, man, you have a ton of work to do. Serious work. And you're gonna hate every second of it."

"Please remove your arm," the shifter said flatly through gritted teeth.

"Manners. That's a good start." He thumped him on the back instead. "Now, how about an apology?"

"What?"

"Come on, Harford. You know what you did."

Bronson glanced at the ceiling and muttered, "I'm...sorry I kidnapped you."

"And?"

"What else do you want me to say?" The young man stepped away from the dwarf and forced himself to lower his voice as he darted a glance at the two partners approaching with the hounds. "I'm a terrible person. I should be killed and left to rot. I don't deserve a second chance. Is that better?"

"Well, damn." Charlie backed away with his hands raised. "I was talking about my bike, man, but okay. You have serious issues."

"I realize this was probably meant to be a private conversation," Lisa said and her eyebrows flicked in and out of a frown. "But everything echoes in here, so... Do we need to go over the plan one more time? Make sure you don't get cold feet or anything?"

Bronson grimaced and looked away. "No."

"Did you talk to Agnes?" Johnny asked.

"Yeah. She sounded normal so I don't think she knows about any of this."

"Uh-huh." He studied the Harford heir carefully and ran his tongue along the edge of his upper teeth. "You ain't done yet, son. You know that?"

The young shifter fixed him with a bitterly insincere smile. "Maybe you guys should tell me a few more times to let it fully sink in."

Lisa squinted at him. "What's going on?"

"What?"

"Okay, I understand all this has been a lot to take in and you haven't exactly had a good day. I don't think any of us would call it a good day. But you look like you have something else you need to say."

The bounty hunter snorted and rolled his eyes. "Ain't everythin' gotta be talked to death, darlin'. What else would the guy need to say that ain't already been said, huh?"

"I don't know, Johnny. That's why I'm asking him."

Bronson fought to raise his gaze from the hallway floor before he finally looked at her. Still, he struggled to find the words.

"Well, spit it out already, son." Johnny pointed down the hall. "My hounds ain't stoppin' and they're likely to eat everythin' left in this whole damn buildin' first if you don't say what you gotta—"

"Why?" Bronson cleared his throat and couldn't decide what to do with his hands until he finally folded his arms. "Why did all of you walk into that room after Addison tried to tell me we needed to get rid of Agnes?"

The partners shared a knowing glance.

Charlie stared at them.

"Simple." Johnny shrugged. "You were fixin' to leave, and we weren't fixin' to let you."

"No." He pointed at them and shook his head. "Something changed right before that. I know you were watching us through the mirror. That was obvious. But why then? She was trying to get me to join...her army or whatever—which is weird to say out loud. You didn't step into that room to stop me from leaving. You came in to start making a different plan that had nothing to do with killing anyone. Even...Agnes."

Lisa gave the confused shifter a small, sympathetic smile and nodded. "We had to make sure you were ready, Bronson."

"For what? To help everyone who would rather shoot me in the head than let me help?"

Johnny sighed. "You have some serious self-esteem issues to work on after this."

"Oh, you think?"

The half-Light Elf caught Johnny's arm gently to stop him

making another rebuttal. "When you realized Agnes isn't what you thought she was, you were angry."

"Of course I was." Bronson scowled and rubbed his chin. "She lied to me."

"Huh." Johnny cocked his head. "That's one hell of a grudge for a vengeful murderer to hold onto against his murdering friend."

"I didn't—" The young shifter shut his eyes, took a deep breath, and clenched his fists again. "What's your point?"

"My point," Lisa said and lowered her head toward him, "is that you were angry enough to want to hurt someone. Exactly like you've been angry at the transformed you wanted to blame for Addison. It would have been very easy to give in to that again and go after Agnes now that you know Addison is alive and what she's trying to do. What we're all trying to do."

"Yeah. And the more you keep talking about it, the more it sounds like a good idea."

Johnny tsked and shook his head. "You have a lotta spit and vinegar in you, son. But we walked into that room 'cause you changed your damn mind. If Tyro's done killin' transformed, it means we knocked some goddamn sense into you. That was all we needed to hear."

"You guys…" Bronson raised a hand to his forehead and muttered, "You guys honestly think I—"

"Johnny! Hey, Johnny!" The hounds raced around another corner and skittered across the tile floors.

"We found it, Johnny!"

"The motherlode!"

"Paradise!"

"Hound heaven, Johnny!"

The bounty hunter hurried down the hall. "All right. Where is it?"

"Right by the kitchen, Johnny."

"Yeah, you can't miss it."

"By the what?" Johnny frowned at them. "I'm talkin' about the kitchen."

"Yeah, but wait until you see the giant trashcan."

"All you can eat, Johnny."

He bit his bottom lip and his mustache bristled. "I swear. One of these days, y'all are gonna get yourselves into more than you can handle."

"You mean like a landfill?"

Luther cackled and trotted down the hall, followed by everyone else. "Bro, imagine that. Trash for miles."

"Trash for days."

"Trash coming out your ears."

Charlie pulled his phone from his pocket to check the cell reception. "Hey, guys. What if we, like, order a pizza or something?"

"Dammit, Charlie. This ain't a party."

"Well, it could be. With pizza. Am I right?"

Bronson wrinkled his nose. "In the middle of the desert?"

"Hey, just because you feel like a giant screwup doesn't mean the rest of us can't enjoy ourselves. Oh, hey. But Johnny's paying. He took all my cash."

# CHAPTER SEVENTEEN

Two days later, Johnny, Lisa, and the hounds sat in the rental SUV across the street from the Mission Dolores Public Park in San Francisco. She peered through the binoculars they'd purchased at the sporting goods store on the way out of Nevada and drew a deep breath. "Any minute now."

"It ain't like we won't know when she's here, darlin'." Her partner leaned back in the driver's seat, his arms folded as he scanned the park. "A tiny girl with red hair wearing a black trench coat in August. She should be easy to see."

A thick rustling came through the earpieces they'd been given at Addison's Coalition-approved compound before Charlie's spoke over the comms. "You haven't had her sneak up behind you, 'coz. Believe me, she's like a ghost."

The dwarf scowled through the windshield. "This ain't a private line, Charlie."

"Well, nothing's happened yet." His reply was followed by a muffled thump. "Man, how do those guys see when they run around in these things?"

"Wait." Luther chuffed in the back seat. "Johnny, is he inside that thing in your ear?"

Rex pressed his nose against the window. "And how'd you get him in there in the first place?"

The bounty hunter ignored them and muttered into the comms, "You damn well better make it so you can see, Charlie. And get into position."

"I already have it covered, 'coz. I'm staring at the back of your car."

Johnny turned in his seat to scan the street behind them. "Jesus Christ."

One block down from their rental, a purple-and-blue polka-dotted creature the size of an average-height dwarf stood at the corner. It spread its arms and turned in a slow circle. "What do you think, 'coz?"

"I think you need a reeducation about what it means to blend in, Charlie. What the hell is that? A dinosaur costume?"

The giant cartoonish head lowered comically for a long look at its body. "I was thinking more like...fantasy yeti, you know? Where did you get dinosaur?"

"And you ain't stopped to think how goddamn weird it is to see a purple dinosaur standin' on the street corner doin' nothin'?"

"Hey, it's the best I could do, okay? That blood witch— whoops. Strike that. Agnes knows what I look like, Johnny. It's kinda hard to hide the mohawk and the guy at the shop threw in some of those long clown balloons and a pump for free. I'm merely a regular guy in California trying to make people happy with a—"

"Will you two shut up?" one of Azure's rebels snapped into the comms. "We can all hear you."

Johnny scowled through his window at the park bench where Bronson waited for Agnes to meet him. He tapped the unit in his ear to mute it and said flatly, "If we make it outta this mess in one piece, I'm gonna kill him."

Lisa rubbed her forehead. "So he's not stakeout material. Noted."

"We should have left him at the hotel."

"He might still be helpful. I'm not sure how a giant costume is supposed to fit into it but—"

"There she is," Dee said over the comms. "Southwest corner of the park."

"Wait," Charlie whispered. "I think I see her near the statue—"

"That is the southwest corner. Who gave that idiot an earpiece?"

"Everyone shut up." Addison's terse command was the final word in that useless conversation.

The bounty hunter tapped his earpiece again to unmute himself.

*This is what we're workin' with. A group of transformed shifters playin' at special ops because Fiona and the Coalition thought it would be fun to give 'em some toys. We should have told everyone else to stay behind.*

Lisa raised the binoculars to her eyes again and whispered, "That's her."

Bronson had refused to go into this meeting wearing any kind of wire or communication device whatsoever, and no one had tried to argue with him on that point. Now that everyone knew Agnes the blood witch was Agnes the well-concealed transformed shifter, they also knew she'd be able to hear everything Azure's team might have said to him over the comms.

*She ain't dumb, that's for sure. Merely hard to kill.*

"Okay, stand by," Addison muttered. "And remember, no one moves until either Bronson gives the signal or the shit hits the fan."

Johnny snorted.

*Now she's speakin' my language.*

Bronson sat perfectly still on the park bench, his arm draped over the metal armrest as Agnes marched down the path toward him. The hem of her trench coat fluttered around the ankles of her black combat boots.

*Wherever they are right now, they had better not screw this up. We won't get a second chance at this.*

She stared at him the whole time, her face perfectly blank like it always was. When she reached the park bench, she didn't look around or scan the area before she turned with a thick swing of her coat and dropped onto the metal seat beside him. "You look like shit."

He darted her a sidelong glance and scowled. "Thanks."

She crossed one leg over the other and slung her arm over the back of the bench, her fingertips poised near his shoulder. "Is there a reason we couldn't have this little chat over the phone?"

"Obviously." He tried to maintain his usually stoic demeanor around her but it was harder than he'd expected, knowing he was about to drop a massive bomb on his uncle's pet attack witch.

*Shifter. She's like you, Bronson. Don't screw this up.*

"Listen," he started, "I got new information a few days ago—"

"Something's bugged me for the last couple of days." Agnes shifted on the bench to face him without moving her arm. "Maybe you can help me clear it up."

Bronson drew a deep breath and nodded. "What?"

"Why did they let you go?"

His stomach flipped uncomfortably and a cold wave of doom washed over his skin and raced through his veins.

*She's been watching me. Dammit. If I don't play this right, it will turn bad before I even have a chance to tell her anything.*

He tried to make his shrug look as apathetic and careless as possible. "They think they know everything, Agnes. But they didn't have proof so here I am."

"Don't tell me a group of wannabe secret agents or whatever

the fuck they think they are let you go simply because you said please."

His growl sounded suitably irritated. "I've fooled them all for the last two months, Agnes. Nothing's changed."

She shook her head and stared across the park. "I should have been there with you. If I had, they'd all be dead and we wouldn't have this giant mess to clean up before Kaiser finds out about it."

"He won't." The young shifter pressed his lips together and forced himself to not move. If he did, he was sure she'd see him shaking.

*Do it now. Catch her off guard, and maybe she won't put the pieces together.*

"Because you won't tell him."

Agnes snorted. "Trust me, he has much bigger problems than you playing innocent victim here."

"I know. You're one of them."

The redhead stiffened and turned her head slowly to scrutinize him warily. "They drugged you, didn't they?"

"That's the new information I wanted to talk to you about, Agnes." He met her gaze and his palms grew instantly clammy. "It's about you."

"Right. More rumors about Tyro and his partner in crime, huh? What are they saying now? We can grow wings and breathe fire?"

"They're saying you're one of them."

She leaned away from him, her lips parted in as much surprise as she was capable of displaying. "Say that again."

Bronson clenched his jaw and studied her face.

*That's either rage, complete disbelief, or murder in her eyes. I guess we'll find out.*

"You're one of the transformed, aren't you?"

With a terrifying sneer, she leaned toward him and hissed in fury. "You need to get your head checked, Bronson, because those morons calling themselves shifters can't do what I can do. And you're listening to the wrong rumors."

"They aren't rumors."

"Oh, yeah? Since you're so big on proof, where's your—"

"Your magic." He glanced at her hand that grasped the opposite armrest of the bench tightly. "I've seen it."

"Yeah. Every time I use it to do your dirty work for you." Agnes' eyelids fluttered before she snarled warningly. "Unless you want that snippet of new information to go public—about how Tyro doesn't have the balls to do the deed himself?—I suggest you drop whatever you're trying to pull right now and get back to what matters."

"This does matter, Agnes." Bronson glanced around the park before he leaned slightly toward her and lowered his voice. "Because the transformed who took me can do the same thing."

"Bullshit."

"That's how they tried to get me to talk." He laughed wryly. "They had no idea I'd already seen your magic in action and it didn't go the way they wanted. But it's the same."

"Right. Because you're suddenly an expert on different kinds of magic when you're trying to not be made by the enemy."

"I could smell it."

"That doesn't mean shit."

With a smile that was more a grimace, he leaned away from her and gazed across the park again. She probably interpreted it as his frustration with her denial, but it was because he couldn't believe how hard it was to convince her they were still on the same side despite what he was telling her.

*We can still be on the same side even if it's not my uncle's side. She has to know that.*

"Are you telling me a shifter's ability to pin magic by scent doesn't hold any weight?"

Agnes shifted on the bench again, this time away from him. Her eyes widened with fearful realization. "You're lying."

"I'm not, truly. I don't know how you managed to keep it a secret for so long, especially from Kaiser, but it's not a secret anymore."

"Is that why you're here?" She snarled and stabbed a finger toward his face. "He sent you to try to shake me, didn't he?"

"No, that's not—"

"You're a real piece of work. It's not my fault you can't get ahold of yourself. Or that I have to come running after you to save your ass from every stupid, juvenile mistake."

"Agnes, you need to listen to me."

"Tell Kaiser he can interrogate me himself. I have nothing to hide."

"Until he finds out about you like I did—"

"Piss off." She started to stand but he caught her wrist and stopped her from rising all the way.

Agnes froze over the bench and glared at his hand. "Don't touch me."

*She could toss me and this bench halfway down the path but she hasn't. This caught her attention.*

"I'll let go as soon as you sit and hear what I have to say."

"I'm not listening to a crazy-ass shifter telling me I'm one of them."

"You still work for my uncle and he still doesn't know a thing. Sit." Bronson tightened his grasp around her arm. "Unless you think he'll listen to you and give you another chance once he finds out about this."

She jerked her wrist out of his grasp with a snarl and dropped onto the bench. "What do you want, Bronson?"

"The truth." He slid away from her to put more space between them. "And there hasn't been nearly enough of that going around as either of us deserves."

Agnes raised her eyebrows and the sharp, bitter laugh that burst out of her made him frown.

*Does she know something I don't? Jesus, if I went into this without all the information, I'm as good as dead.*

"I've been at your side, feeding you the transformed you wanted so badly for your little revenge scheme without saying a word about any of it to your uncle. And you want to talk to me about the truth we deserve? You're the one who called this meeting, Bronson. You just threatened to feed Kaiser a bunch of bullshit lies you know would get rid of me forever." She studied him for a long moment and her upper lip curled in disgust. "Don't start talking to me now like we're still in this together. Say what you have to say, then you and I are done."

Bronson nodded slowly.

*At least she calmed down enough to listen. I can't say what this next part will do but she has to hear it. I have to say it.*

He held her gaze and drew a deep breath. "You don't have to keep hiding, Agnes. Not with me. You can trust me—"

"Ha! Do you hear yourself right now? Make up your mind, asshole."

"Listen, I know it's hard to admit that someone else found out what you thought you'd buried forever—"

"Please. After what you pulled with this transformed-magic crap, why the hell would I trust you?"

"Because we're the same," he shouted. A few pedestrians along the walking path cast wary glances at them but he ignored them and lowered his voice. "And I've kept my secrets locked up for way too long. You deserve to know."

"That you're insane?"

"That I'm one of them too, Agnes."

She stared at him with such intense disbelief that he thought she hadn't heard him. After a moment, she opened her mouth, paused, and snarled. "You what?"

"My mother. She was turned with the rest of them. Before she died, she made me promise to keep her secret for her. For us. And—"

"She should have taken it with her to the grave."

"Agnes, this is real."

Her fingers, still clamped around the metal armrest of the bench, flared with crackling red light. "Why are you telling me this?"

Bronson looked around the park but no one seemed to notice the petite woman in all black throwing sparks on a park bench. "Because this has to stop. All of it—Kaiser's offers, the skirmishes, and carrying his insane crusade to the transformed. We have to stop it all before things get so much worse but I can't do that unless you let me help you—"

"I don't need anything from you!" Agnes lurched to her feet with a hiss. "I should have left you locked in that cage."

"Wait. Let me show you—"

The transformed witch snarled and tossed a bolt of red light at the center of his chest. It struck him with a muffled crack and a debilitating wave of heat and electric magical energy coursed through his limbs. His body went completely rigid and he slumped against the back of the bench, completely unable to move as the agony of her attack raced through him.

She leaned toward him, her lips pulled back in fury. "If you want to be one of them so badly, you can die with them too."

Without another word, she spun and stalked across the grass toward the street on the other side of the park. A group of kids playing soccer shouted happily and raced after the ball that rolled into the shifter witch's path. She stamped on it and burst it with a sharp snap to leave a ripped and deflated rubber casing in her wake. The kids skidded to a stop and stared after her in horror.

Bronson panted on the bench, immobilized by the attack and unable to look away from her figure as it grew smaller in the distance.

*Why the hell hasn't anyone stepped in to take care of this? She'll go directly to Kaiser, and if she tells him about anything I said... Dammit, how long does it take to get out of a car and follow her?*

# CHAPTER EIGHTEEN

"What's she doing?"

"She looks pissed. I think rich boy blew it."

"They're still talking. No one moves yet."

Lisa and Johnny listened to the constant updates from Addison's team stationed around the park. She looked through the binocular again and shook her head. "This doesn't look good at all."

"We wait for the signal," Addison repeated. "That's the plan."

She gritted her teeth.

*Oh, sure. Now she's all about the plan.*

Another long, tense minute passed. The conversation between Bronson and Agnes heated quickly. Finally, the woman in the trench coat leapt from the bench and snarled something.

"Shit. Look at her hand."

"He couldn't stop her even if he wanted to—whoa!"

The red light that crackled around Agnes' hand launched toward Bronson's chest and the shifter slumped on the bench.

"And...he's down."

"Did we honestly think he could keep it together out there on his own?"

Lisa jerked on the handle of her car door. "I knew we should have spent more time coaching him on what to say. We need to get to her before she does any more damage."

"Everyone stay where you are!" Addison shouted through the comms.

Johnny opened his door swiftly. "Think what you want, but that's what I call shit hittin' the fan."

"If you two start running right now and she sees you," the transformed leader snapped, "we have nothing left to work with."

He gestured toward the opposite side of the park. "She went around the corner and Bronson might be dead on a bench for all we know." He whistled and held his door open for the hounds to scramble over the seat before he slammed the door shut. "Let's go."

"Ethan, do you have eyes on her?" Addison asked.

"Yeah, in the parking lot behind the coffee shop right here. She has a car."

"Then stay on her. We'll catch up with you in—are you serious?"

Muffled sniggers came over the comms and the bounty hunter stopped in his tracks when the bulky, hairy blue-and-purple polka-dotted monster that had swallowed his cousin loped clumsily across the grass toward Bronson.

Roger chuckled. "There's something seriously wrong with that dwarf."

"I only see the abominable snowman."

Johnny ripped his earpiece off and clenched it in his fist. "Dammit, Charlie."

The shifter dwarf reached the park bench before anyone else and drew stares from pedestrians and families enjoying the sunny day. He struggled to remove the giant head of his costume before he dropped it onto the grass and knelt at the young shifter's feet.

The hounds laughed uproariously and raced toward the bench, barking madly.

"Hey, check it out. It's the boogeyman."

"It's a sick bear."

"Hey, Rex. It's your mom."

"Bro, we have the same mom."

Lisa sighed in exasperation. "I'll be seriously surprised if this doesn't end up in the local paper."

"Oh, sure. Hairy beast stoppin' to help the Harford heir passed out in the park. It makes for real good copy."

"We should go help him."

"He got himself into that damn costume, darlin'. He can get himself out of it."

"I'm talking about Bronson." She paused and raised a finger to her ear. "Yeah, yeah, I hear you. No. That's not a good idea. Listen to me, if we—" With an aggravated grunt, she muted her headset and stormed across the grass. "Johnny, we need to hurry."

He looked at the earpiece in his hand. "Why? Are the reporters on the way?"

"No. Agnes left in her car and Addison won't listen to me. She left with everyone else to tail her."

"There is no way in hell those rebels know how to tail someone on the road without bein' seen."

"Yeah. I can't believe I'm saying this but when we get Bronson to the car, you need to do whatever you can to make sure the others don't engage Agnes before we catch up to them."

Johnny snorted. "Are you givin' me permission to drive like Charlie?"

"Don't push it."

---

With Bronson unconscious in the back seat of the SUV and the hounds panting over him, Johnny raced up Highway 80. He and

Lisa had kept their comms muted but listened to the conversations between Addison and her team as they followed Agnes' car. She tried to call the transformed leader several times to talk some sense into the woman but of course, her calls went unanswered.

"This is bad." She gazed out the window and scanned the dry, browning valley that stretched on either side of them.

The bounty hunter tapped his earpiece. "Azure. Do you hear me right now?"

"Johnny, if they haven't answered us for the last ten minutes, they won't answer now."

"Well, there's always a chance."

"Look. There's Charlie." Lisa pointed as they came over the top of the hill and the shifter dwarf's orange Harley disappeared down a righthand turn behind a high stone wall.

"Where the hell is he goin'?"

"I don't know. He's supposed to be following the rebels."

"Dammit. If that's private property, we'll land ourselves in a whole different kinda mess. I ain't fixin' to clean up after young, headstrong shifters and their hot tempers."

"Addison wants something with her," she added. "Agnes isn't going to Langley's pot farm or his house in the mountains. Those are both in the complete opposite direction."

"I assume she thinks a transformed-hunter who ain't runnin' to her boss will be easier to deal with alone than with an army and a hell of a lot of guns."

Lisa shook her head. "That's not helping. Here. Take the turn here."

"I can see the wall, darlin'."

"Well, I can't see Charlie, and that admittedly makes me very nervous."

Johnny took the righthand turn with a sharp jerk of the wheel. The hounds yelped and slid against each other in the back. The turn and the switch from relatively smooth asphalt to a bumpy gravel road jostled Bronson enough to bring him back to consciousness. As Lisa thumped her hand against the passenger-side door to steady herself, the shifter in the back seat groaned.

"Whoa. Hold on. Where—ah! What the hell is—" He kicked at the giant monster-costume head Charlie had unceremoniously dumped into the SUV before getting on his Harley.

The hounds burst out laughing. "Hey, now it's a party."

"Hey, guy. Hey. Throw it here!"

"Keep it away from Luther, huh? We can play Hound In the Middle."

The monster head toppled into the back seat and Bronson braced himself against another bump in the road. "Why am I in your car?"

"Why?" Johnny glanced at him in the rearview mirror. "Did you want us to leave you on the park bench instead?"

"What? No. I mean where—oh, shit. Oh, no. No, no, no." The shifter kicked at the seats to push himself into a seated position and stared through the windows. "Please tell me we're not outside Colfax right now."

"We're followin' my cousin. I ain't got time to see exactly where this is on a map."

"And Charlie's following Addison and her team," Lisa explained.

"Why the hell are they out here?"

The Light Elf turned in her seat to look at him. "Well, Addison decided to follow Agnes—against our suggestion."

Rex snorted and shook his head. "Whew. That's making me dizzy."

"So we're bringing up the rear to make sure they don't get themselves in even more trouble," she added.

Johnny grunted. "Or dead."

"Yeah, okay…" Bronson leaned forward and grasped the backs of both front seats. "See, that's the problem. None of us wanna be out here right now. Even Agnes knows that."

"It certainly doesn't look like it." The bounty hunter gestured at the road that stretched beneath the cover of thick overhanging trees. "Everyone's headed this way—"

"Yeah, but Agnes is the only one who knows where to turn off before she gets herself killed. Stop here. Now."

"Bronson, I ain't pullin' over 'cause you reckon—"

A high-pitched whine filled the air outside the rental SUV, loud enough to make all three magicals in the car cringe and try to cover their ears.

"What is that?" Lisa shouted.

"I told you to stop the car!"

At that moment, a massive shadow streaked over the SUV, followed by the thud and deafening roar of an explosion. The blast launched the vehicle down the road and it veered alarmingly from side to side across the dirt while Johnny tried to correct the movement with quick jerks of the steering wheel. A shower of dirt, thick dust, and pebbles plinked on the vehicle's hood and roof, and he finally managed to straighten the car before he braked sharply. Another rumble of tires skidding on gravel followed until they finally stopped.

He spun in the driver's seat and stared at the massive crater in the road where they'd come frighteningly close to being pulverized. "Was that a goddamn missile?"

Bronson fought to catch his breath. "Probably."

"Who the hell is launchin' missiles in the middle of the Sierra Nevada Mountains?"

"The guys we seriously don't wanna piss off and probably already did. We should—"

"Wait." Lisa raised a hand to silence them both. "Where's Charlie?"

"Aw, hell."

The cloud of dust and debris still hadn't cleared but a dark silhouette stumbled down the road toward them. When the shifter dwarf finally came close enough to see him clearly, he was covered in dirt, bloody on one side of his face, and wiggled his pinky in his ear to clear the ringing.

"Dammit, Charlie." Johnny pushed the door open and hopped out.

"Wait, wait. Johnny!" Bronson tried to grab him but was too slow. "You truly don't want to—"

"Oh, my God." Lisa unbuckled quickly and got out too.

With a frustrated snarl, the young shifter followed them and flailed to avoid a fall when his legs didn't quite work the way he wanted after he stepped out of the car. The hounds almost knocked him over again when they leapt from his open door and raced after their master.

"Whoa." Charlie shook his head vigorously, which made him stumble sideways dangerously. "Did you guys see that? It came out of nowhere and blew the road up."

"What's wrong with him, Johnny?" Luther asked and crept toward the biker dwarf to sniff his dust-covered knees.

"Yeah, why's he yelling?"

"We can hear you, Charlie."

"Hush." The bounty hunter snapped his fingers and caught his cousin by the shoulders. "Hey. Look at me. Right here. In my eyes."

"What?"

"Charlie." He snapped his fingers in his cousin's face and pointed at his eyes. "Look at me."

"I can't hear you, 'coz."

"Hey, Rex." Luther cocked his head. "Are those his brains smeared over the side of his face?"

"Well, if they're not his brains, they're someone else's, right?"

"We need to get out of here!" Bronson shouted as he staggered toward the group in the center of the quickly dissipating dust cloud. "That was only a warning."

"That's a hell of a warnin' for the folks who end up dead after one of those."

"Yeah, which is why we need to go. There's a shitload more where that came from."

Lisa examined the cut on Charlie's temple. "It doesn't look too bad and I don't think he has a concussion."

"Huh?" the shifter dwarf shouted.

She leaned away from him and gave him two thumbs-up. "Johnny, as weird as it is to use the phrase 'civilian missile,' I'm very sure that's what we're dealing with. We were very lucky but we need to find Addison and her team."

"Uh-huh. And hope they were as lucky. Hey." The bounty hunter snapped in his cousin's face again. "Did you see Addison's team before you were hit? Or their other cars?"

"I still can't hear you." Charlie shook his head. "Hey, can a magical be deaf if they only hear ringing? 'Cause that's what this feels like."

"Charlie—"

"You know, the only reason I didn't get blown into a million pieces by that giant bomb was because I saw the first explosion at the end of the wall." Charlie's eyes widened. "Shit! The others cars!"

"Johnny, make him stop yelling," Luther whined.

"To me, boys." Johnny jogged down the road and the hounds raced after him.

Lisa and Charlie were close behind and Bronson turned in a slow dizzy circle to regard the SUV that still idled in the middle of the gravel road. A massive dent in the top of the frame around the windshield had barely missed splintering the glass, and the hood was covered in tiny, dusty bumps from a hailstorm of gravel. "They're insane. Why doesn't anyone listen to—"

Another high-pitched whine filled the air, followed by the hounds' mad barking and Charlie shouting, "Another one!"

Bronson searched the sky and saw the glint of metal a second before the road exploded behind Johnny and his team and shielded them from view. When the blast debris settled enough for him to see the crater in the road, his unlikely new friends were gone.

"Oh, come on." With a snarl, he forced himself into a wobbly run and hoped he wasn't too late.

*I still will be if I can't get anyone to listen to me.*

## CHAPTER NINETEEN

With his ears still ringing, Johnny could barely make out the shouts, snarls, and coughs coming from ahead. Another dust cloud from the explosion obscured half the stone wall on their right and a good portion of the trees hanging over it. A splintered branch groaned overhead, and he skipped forward to place a hand on the small of Lisa's back and nudge her forward.

"Johnny, what—"

The branch snapped and fell with a crunch and the rustle of violently fluttering leaves.

She spun and stared at it before she glanced at the other overhanging branches. "I think Bronson was right."

"We ain't leavin' until we see what happened to the others. And I have half a mind to march up to whoever owns this place and give 'em a piece of my mind. Blowin' up folks in cars drivin' down a damn road."

"I assume this is private property."

"I ain't seen a sign for it. Did you?"

"No."

"Hey! There they are." Charlie pointed up the road to where

one of the rebel SUVs had rolled onto its side and the other had spun a hundred and eighty degrees on the gravel.

The partners raced toward the group of shifters who struggled to collect themselves again. Dee had hit her chin in one of the explosions and now sported a long cut and smeared blood down the side of her neck. The others were covered in dust and dirt and looked shaken but were otherwise unharmed.

"Is everyone okay?" Lisa asked.

Addison looked up from where she'd doubled over with her hands propped on her thighs to catch her breath. "I think so."

"Good." Johnny pointed at her. "'Cause I'm very sure we told y'all not to follow Agnes. Is all this enough to convince y'all, or do you think you need a little more?"

"We almost had her," she snapped through gritted teeth. "She raced out here and pulled over at the end of the wall. Then the—were those bombs?"

"Missiles, most likely." The bounty hunter tugged his beard and searched the sky. "And we're gettin' outta here before the next fun surprise. The chances are it ain't gonna miss."

"Azure." A tall rebel man with shaggy blond hair pointed into the trees beyond the end of the high stone wall. The ground dipped into a ditch before it continued down a steep incline. "She went down there."

"Agnes?"

He nodded.

"Track her scent. Look to see if she's injured and if you find her, subdue her however you can and wait for us to catch up."

Lisa stepped toward the leader of the transformed with wide eyes. "Addison—"

"That's not my name. Not out here."

"Fine. We need to get out of here."

"No, we need to make sure Agnes won't be able to run to her boss to tell him what she heard and saw today."

Roger hissed and pointed at Bronson, who struggled to bring

up the rear of their shell-shocked group. "What did you say to her?"

"We can talk about that later. Right now, we need to get out of here."

"You blew this whole thing before we even had a chance to—"

"Now!" He cut her off sharply. "Forget about Agnes."

"We don't take orders from you." Roger nodded at the blond shifter standing at the top of the steep drop into the woods. "Go find her."

The other rebel nodded and started to step sideways down the incline. The sharp crack of rifle fire split the air a second before the bullet glanced off the closest tree trunk in a spray of splintered wood and sawdust.

Everyone ducked and the shifter who'd almost been shot in the head froze and stared at the bullet hole in the wood.

A second later, the rumble of a Jeep rose over the fading echo of the gunshot and the shooter came into view in the field beyond the end of the high stone wall. He was hard to miss where he stood at the back of the rapidly approaching vehicle with the rifle still raised in both hands and aimed at the intruding party.

Two more Jeeps followed close behind and their high speed churned clumps of dirt, dry grass, and dust in plumes behind them.

"Great. Now they know we're still here," Bronson muttered.

"They don't look like military," Lisa added.

"Hey." Charlie squinted and leaned forward. "Does anyone else get a weird feeling that we're on safari out here? As in we're the animals?"

The vehicles closed rapidly on the haggard transformed and the bounty hunters.

"Can we all please agree to not make any sudden movements right now?" Bronson raised both arms high above his head. "Or do anything stupid."

"Who are they, Bronson?" Azure asked.

"Fanatics. Extremists. Take your pick."

"What kinda fanatics?" Johnny asked.

"The kind who support Kaiser's message and have no issue getting their hands dirty when they have the opportunity."

"Wonderful," Lisa whispered. "The whole point of the last few days was to avoid more fighting."

Azure looked at her rebels and smirked. "How much do you wanna bet these fanatics still don't expect transformed to fight back?"

Dee snorted and cocked her head. Roger grinned like a lunatic and nodded at the blond shifter who stood at the tree line. "It seems to me like they could use a little educating."

"No." Lisa pointed at Addison. "No. We stand down."

"That's not what Azure's Army does, Lisa." She settled her gaze on the approaching Jeeps and her eyes flashed with silver light before they took on a deep-red hue. "We could use the practice anyway."

"Whoa." Charlie stepped away from the rebel leader and looked at her with wide eyes. "It's still totally weird to see that."

"Y'all ain't fit to practice a damn thing if y'all can't see this is a bad idea." Johnny snorted impatiently.

"You're free to go whenever you want, dwarf." Addison didn't look at him. "We're not going—" Another rifle shot cracked a second before the ground at her feet erupted in a spray of dirt and shredded brown grass. She looked at what could only have been another warning shot and sneered.

The hounds barked at the approaching Jeeps, their tails sticking straight out behind them as they bared their teeth. "Those guys don't look happy to see us, Johnny."

"Yeah, they're worse than you when two-legs show up at the swamp."

"First, they launch missiles at the road and now, they're shootin' rifles in a damn parade." The bounty hunter moved a hand to his belt and retrieved an exploding disk. "That's unnecessary flexin'."

"Johnny, we can't engage these shifters," Lisa warned. "We're trespassing. That's on us."

"It ain't if they don't post signs."

"You don't post signs."

"I don't shoot strangers on my road either, darlin'."

The closest vehicle skidded to a stop fifty feet from Azure and her rebels. The driver slid out as the other two vehicles veered slightly to flank the first. All three shifters standing through the roofless frames of the vehicles held their rifles trained on the group of trespassers while two more shifters emerged from each vehicle.

The man leading them was only five-foot-five, although his hulking shoulders and massive biceps bulging from beneath the sleeves of his plain white undershirt made him look much bigger. A toothpick dangled from the corner of his mouth as he walked toward the group and he tongued it to the other side before he stopped fifteen feet away.

"Most people get the hint after the first explosion."

"We don't want any trouble," Lisa said.

Johnny looked at her in disbelief. Charlie nodded and raised both hands. Addison and her rebels sneered and held their ground while they focused on the half-dozen shifters who took their places behind their leader, as well as the three still in the vehicles with fully loaded rifles.

The shifter snorted. "Even if I couldn't smell the stink of your lies, elf, that's not gonna fly out here."

"It ain't a lie." Johnny nodded toward the parked vehicles. "With the way y'all have those Jeeps loaded, I reckon y'all are itchin' to start somethin' anyhow."

The natural-born shifters growled in response and Azure's rebels snarled.

"You know what else stinks?" A shirtless man with a shaved

head made a show of sniffing the air before he stabbed a finger at Addison. "Transformed. Your kind doesn't belong here."

"We have as much right to be anywhere as you do," she retorted.

The leader laughed. "On our land? I don't think so. You came looking for trouble and here it is. If you were smart, you would have gone to the man who hands out free passes to mutts like you. We're not as understanding."

"As Kaiser?" Dee scoffed. "Neither are we—"

"I wasn't talking to you." He drew a massive, heavy pistol from the holster at his belt and his gang did the same.

The shifters on both sides snarled and growled. Lisa shifted her hand instantly to her shoulder holster to draw her pistol, and she clasped it with both hands as Johnny raised his exploding disk with his thumb hovered over the red button on the top.

"Everyone needs to think about this," the half-Light Elf shouted. "This isn't why we're here and none of us want a blood bath."

"Says the Light Elf with a gun," one of the natural-born said. "You made a big mistake getting mixed up with this scum."

"Whoa, whoa. Hold on." Bronson stepped forward with his hands still raised in surrender. "We were following the witch with red hair and a black trench coat. She left her car back there on the—"

"Who the hell are—" The leader's eyes widened as he studied him intently. "No fucking way."

"Listen, this isn't about—"

"I know you." The giant barrel of the natural-born's pistol trailed up and down Bronson's body and the young shifter grimaced and turned his head away in discomfort. "Does your boss know you're mixing with these lowlifes?"

"Watch it, asshole," Roger snarled.

"Come on, guys." Charlie chuckled nervously. "There's a lotta name-calling going on. Do we have to—"

The thick, intimidating click as the leader thumbed the hammer of his giant handgun made everyone freeze. "This is turning into a very good day for us. Bad for you—and your last."

Addison stepped forward with a loud snarl and summoned her transformed magic. Red light flared behind her eyes and crackled into two violently sparking blood-red orbs in her raised hands. Her magic flared up her arms and hissed like snakes, and each of her six rebels who'd unlocked the same unexplained abilities followed suit.

The gang of natural-borns growled and stepped back but they recovered quickly and kept their weapons trained on the intruders. Their leader snarled and swung the barrel of his gun toward Lisa again. "Cut it out."

"I'm not—"

"I swear on both planets, elf, whatever trick you're trying to pull with a shitty illusion like that isn't gonna work. Either you kill the whole thing or I put a bullet between your eyes before I gun these mutts down for showing their faces out here."

"You ain't listenin', pal." Johnny stepped slightly in front of his partner to draw the furious shifter's attention. "She ain't doin' a thing. If y'all can't handle a few transformed evenin' the odds against your outdated artillery, y'all might wanna turn around and hop in your—"

The shifter squeezed a shot off, although it was clearly meant as a warning. Even then, the bullet whizzed so closely past the bounty hunter's head that he felt the rush of air flutter his hair and tickle his beard.

Bronson dropped into a crouch at the sound. Charlie spun to stare at the second tree caught in unfriendly fire. The hounds erupted in angry howls between intermittent snarls.

"You almost shot him, you moron!"

"Moron! He's gonna blow you to smithereens now."

"Let us at him, Johnny. We'll show him—"

A rebel woman whose name Johnny hadn't caught yet

launched a crackling orb of red magic at the natural-born in front of her. He seized immediately and his rigid finger clenched around the trigger of his firearm against his will, and the bullet went wide into the woods on the incline.

The first man to be attacked by transformed magic uttered a series of choking sounds before he crumpled. His comrades stared at him in horror, their standoff momentarily forgotten.

"Do you still think it's not real?" the rebel woman demanded.

The shifter leader roared in outrage and swung his pistol toward her.

This immediately triggered the kind of skirmish between natural-borns and transformed that Johnny and his team had tried to avoid and the situation descended into complete chaos. The deafening crack of gunfire echoed across the valley, joined by the heavy sizzle and snap of transformed magic launched in return. Somehow, in those ten seconds of anarchy, only one of Azure's rebels took a bullet in the knee and fell with a snarl.

The hounds leapt toward the shifter leader to do exactly what they'd promised. Luther jumped up and clamped his jaws around the man's wrist to jerk the gun down before Rex launched himself at the guy's chest and knocked him onto his back.

Lisa unleashed no more than three fireballs and aimed them carefully to not obliterate the natural-borns but to distract them from making a deadly shot.

Johnny thumbed the button of one explosive disk while he jerked another off his belt. The first one hit the hood of the closest Jeep and startled the shifter posted there with his automatic rifle before the first explosion hurled him between the other two vehicles. The second disk landed in front of the second and the gunman there threw himself over the side in the opposite direction before the disk detonated in a spray of dirt and grass. The second Jeep's front tires bounced under the impact.

Oblivious to the bounty hunter's collection of throwable weaponry, the shifters spun to find the source of the new attack.

"Behind the Jeeps!"

"Get him down!"

They opened fire on the grass around their vehicles while their teammates with rifles scrambled frantically out of the way.

Johnny lunged at the closest natural-born's back and swung his fist into the guy's kidney. The shifter fell with a cry and he delivered a blow on the side of his head for good measure before he turned to the next guy with a gun.

"Now you know what we can do!" Addison screamed as she gestured at her team. "This is only the beginning."

The hairs on the back of Lisa's neck tingled and stood on end. She turned to where the rebel leader glowed with a dangerously intense red light. Surges of red energy crackled around her head, streaked down her shoulders, and grew at the center of her chest between her outstretched arms.

The electricity in the air thickened by the second and a low roar vibrated not from her throat but from the insanely powerful magic she concentrated between her hands.

Even her rebels paused in the fight to stare at her in a mixture of adoration and terror.

Lisa was rendered speechless.

*She doesn't know how to control that. She thinks she does but even her team looks ready to run for cover.*

"Someone stop her!" Johnny shouted as he punched another natural-born in the gut hard enough that the man lost his hold on his pistol, which sailed over the grass.

Azure's eyes blazed with red light that drowned any trace of their natural blue. Her chest heaved in short, sharp breaths, and her open mouth twisted into a vengeful grin until she looked completely insane.

"Addison!" Lisa darted toward her "Stop!"

"No one will stop us ever again," she shouted.

Bolts of red light burst from the massive orb of crackling magic that had grown to half her size between her hands. They struck the ground in all directions and threw up clumps of dirt and grass. One of them hit Dee in the shin and the rebel cried out as her legs buckled. Another crashed into the trees behind her. A third shot streaked toward the shifter leader, who had managed to get to his feet after the hounds had joined their master to attack the rest of the natural-borns. It glanced off his shoulder and spun him sideways with a roar of pain.

*She's turning herself into a bomb.*

Lisa caught Johnny's gaze and knew he was thinking the same thing.

"Addison, you have to—"

A sharp crack from the woods behind the battle was followed by three flashes of blue light.

The bounty hunter turned to search the tree line and pulled another disk from his belt.

*Someone else came to join the party and get blown to pieces with the rest of us. Good for them.*

Tree branches rustled violently, the thick bushes growing at the top of the incline exploded to the side, and leaves and twigs flurried against the surrounding trees. Three more shifters stepped through the wreckage, all of them armed with small gadgets strapped to their field vests and two of them carried weapons that looked like a hell of an upgrade from Johnny's laser-bomb cannons.

The redheaded woman who led the small team snarled and charged forward through the bushes directly toward Addison Taylor's ticking magical time bomb.

It was Fiona.

Johnny's hand went slack around his knife.

*What the hell?*

# CHAPTER TWENTY

The three Coalition delegates moved fast. In moments, the two shifters on Fiona's small surprise team leveled their strange-looking hand cannons at both Azure's rebels and the group of snarling natural-borns who tried to aim their weapons at the newcomers.

"Who the hell are you?" The shifter leader growled, the sound both belligerent and confused.

Both Coalition shifters activated their heavy-duty weapons and a burst of shimmering energy exploded from the wide barrels. A high-pitched whine sounded a warning and the pulse from the cannons spread in the blink of an eye to wash over every single shifter in both factions who'd been intent on killing each other. The powerful force of the shockwave knocked them off their feet and catapulted them away from the delegates with the giant guns.

The moment the shifters had fired their weapons, Fiona raced up behind the transformed leader and drew what looked like a close-range taser from her belt. She pressed the device to the girl's back and a wave of blue-and-silver light bloomed around Addison's body and immediately snuffed out her transformed magic. She sagged a split second after everyone else who had been overcome by the energy cannons sprawled where they'd landed.

With a snarl, Fiona jammed the modified taser onto her belt and blew a few straggling locks of red curls out of her face.

Lisa extinguished her fireballs and stared at the dozen shifters spread across the ground. With wide eyes, Johnny turned slowly to stare at the Coalition delegate, who now tugged two black earplugs out of her ears and slid them into one of the smaller pockets of her vest.

"You gotta be shittin' me."

The woman met his gaze and raised her eyebrows. "What did he say?"

"Who?"

"The guy with the toothpick hanging out of his mouth." Fiona leaned forward to study the shifter, who lay completely unconscious on the ground with the others. "Or at least it was in his mouth."

"He asked who you are," Lisa muttered flatly and struggled to pull her attention away from the instantly neutralized battle.

"Oh." The redhead nodded at the other delegates as they removed their earplugs. "Yeah. We're the ones who saved his life."

"Before you took 'em all out with those…" Johnny pointed at the energy cannon as the other delegates strapped the weapons over their shoulders. "Lemme take a look at one of those."

"That's not gonna happen, dwarf." Fiona pulled her loose hair away from her head to retie a ponytail of wild, barely containable curls before she settled into a crouch to check Addison's pulse with two fingers. "I promise you, those are Coalition property. One hundred percent. Patented and everything. Kind of."

"Holy crap!" Luther darted between the fallen bodies of the shifters. "Johnny, they're all dead."

Rex sniffed at Charlie's mohawk. "They killed your cousin, Johnny."

"What?" The bounty hunter whirled to where Charlie sprawled on the grass like everyone else, his fingers inches from the shifter leader's giant discarded pistol.

"Wrong." Fiona retrieved another device from a separate pocket on her field vest and peeled the strip off the adhesive backing. "No one's dead. Thanks to us—again." With a sigh, she slid her hand under the back collar of Addison's shirt and pressed the square adhesive patch to the base of the woman's neck.

Her team members repeated the same process with Bronson and the six other rebels. They moved quickly and slapped the patches on shifter skin with far less care than Fiona had used on Addison.

"Seriously, I gotta take a look at one of these." Johnny reached for one of the cannons strapped to the closest delegate's back but the man slapped his hand away and stood from his crouch before he moved on to the next unconscious shifter.

"That's what you're the most concerned about right now?" Lisa frowned at him. "A fun new toy?"

"I know you saw what it can do, darlin'."

"It's an EBP transmitter, not a toy." Fiona stood and dusted her hands off. "But I see how someone like you might get confused, Johnny."

Lisa frowned and scanned the bodies again. "EBP?"

"Yeah. Electro-biometric pulse."

"To take down everyone but us?"

The redhead snorted. "Calibrated for shifters of all—" She glanced at Charlie and shook her head. "Shapes and sizes, hence the earplugs. Come on, man. Get with the program already."

"You're pullin' my leg," Johnny muttered and circled the other delegate in an attempt to get another up-close look at the transmitter cannon.

Fiona raised an eyebrow and snorted. "You know, I expected complete cluelessness from your partner, Johnny. Not from you."

"I'm not clueless," Lisa muttered.

"Oh yes, you are." She glanced at her fellow operatives, snapped her fingers, and pointed at the unconscious rebels. "Both of you. Completely clueless and completely useless. Otherwise, you wouldn't have facilitated another skirmish out here in the middle of nowhere...this doesn't look like Nevada. Kyle, what state is this?"

Her fellow operative finished dragging Bronson by the arms across the ground toward the tree line and dropped the unconscious shifter's body carelessly with a thump. "California."

"Huh. It's not as dry out here as I expected."

"We didn't facilitate a skirmish," Lisa corrected. "We were trying to— What are they doing?"

Kyle and the other delegate collected the last two rebels and dragged them quickly to the group of unconscious bodies at the edge of the sharp drop into the forested valley.

"Like I said." Fiona shrugged. "Cleaning up."

"What about the rest of 'em?" Johnny nodded at the gang of natural-borns who lay motionlessly in the grass.

She sighed with exaggerated patience. "They'll wake up. Eventually."

Lisa's mouth dropped open. "Fiona."

"Fine. I'm ninety-five percent sure they'll wake up. And when they do, they won't remember anything from the last..." The woman glanced at her watch. "I don't know. Twenty minutes, give or take."

"You're real precise with your gear," Johnny muttered. "Did you make those EBPs yourself?"

"Are you kidding? Come on. I don't waste my time with tinkering."

"Or with knowing exactly how your weapon will affect these magicals." Lisa gestured at the shifter gang. "You said those weapons were patented."

"I said mostly. And these morons aren't my problem." Fiona pointed at Addison, who lay in a heap at her feet. "She is."

"Because you have no idea how to handle her when she gets out of control." The half-Light Elf folded her arms. "That's what happened, isn't it?"

With a snort, the woman crouched, grasped the unconscious girl under the arms, and dragged her toward the rest of her team. "See what I mean? Completely clueless."

"Hey. You can't simply show up in the trees to knock everyone out and start calling me clueless."

"Darlin'." Johnny sidled closer to his partner and scowled at the Coalition shifters. "Now is probably not the best time to start grillin' her."

"Now is the perfect time." Lisa stormed toward Fiona and her team. "You've known all along how dangerous transformed magic is. You knew Addison and her followers needed more training, at the very least, and you still gave her the go-ahead to wage war against—"

"You know what?" The redhead dropped the girl's limp body and straightened. "You try rounding up all the most stubborn, hotheaded, furious young shifters intent on making history before you tell me how to do my job."

"I don't even know what your job is!"

The Coalition delegate rolled her eyes and glanced at her watch again. "Well, I can tell you it's not standing around out here arguing semantics with a Light Elf. We have thirty seconds. So if you don't wanna be stranded with the nutjobs driving artillery Jeeps, close your mouth and grab someone."

"What?"

"An arm or a leg. Whatever's closest."

"Twenty seconds," Kyle muttered as he crouched beside Bronson and placed a hand on the shifter's shoulder.

"Your call." Fiona crouched to rest a hand on Addison's forearm and widened her eyes. "Johnny."

"What?"

"You might wanna get your dogs too."

"What is going on?" Lisa shouted.

Johnny scowled at Fiona, who shrugged and looked at her watch. "Ten seconds."

*They showed up from the trees. In a ditch with no vehicle and no airdrop—aw, shit.*

"To me, boys!" He uttered a piercing whistle. "Now!"

Rex and Luther stopped sniffing around the tree line and whipped their heads up toward their master. "What's up, Johnny?"

"More shifters?"

"We can handle those guys no problem."

"Five," Fiona declared.

Johnny grasped Lisa's wrist and tugged her toward the pile of unconscious transformed surrounded by Fiona and her team. "I said now!"

"Okay, okay. Jeez."

"Everyone keeps yelling today. What's up with that?"

"Four."

The hounds raced toward their master, their tongues lolling.

"Three."

"Dammit, Fiona. You couldn't warn us?"

"Two."

With a growl, Johnny shoved Lisa onto one of the rebel's backs, lunged at the hounds, and wrapped his arms around them to haul them closer.

"Whoa, whoa, hey."

"We can walk, Johnny."

"One."

He tossed them toward the pile of bodies. They yelped and flailed while he dove to catch hold of Kyle's black boot at the edge of the rough circle. The second his fingers clamped around rubber, he was jolted through a spinning world.

A blue light overwhelmed everything and the sudden intensity of the painful ringing in his ears made him cry out. At least he thought he did but couldn't be sure because he could no longer feel Kyle's boot in his hand or see anything but the blue light. He couldn't even feel his body until he realized he'd suffocate if he didn't start to breathe again real soon.

*I'm gonna kill her for this. If I make it.*

# CHAPTER TWENTY-ONE

The bounty hunter's senses rushed back all at once and he fell face-first onto the cold linoleum floor beneath him.

"Holy shit!" Luther leapt off the bodies of unconscious transformed rebels, staggered sideways, and shook himself vigorously. "You threw us, Johnny. You picked us up and threw us."

"Totally undignified, Johnny. Not cool." Rex snorted and circled the pile of bodies toward his master. "Oh, hey. Talk about stripping dignity away …"

"Bro, what's wrong with him?"

Johnny managed to use his shaking arms to push onto his hands and knees before he vomited.

"Oh, whoa." Luther backed away from his master, sniffed the air, and padded slowly forward again. "Want us to clean that up for you, Johnny?"

"Dogs." Fiona snorted and shook her head as she stood. "I don't see the appeal."

"Hey." Lisa crawled toward her partner and placed a hand on his back. "Are you—"

"Fine." Johnny jerked away from her and tried to wipe his

mouth. One hand wasn't enough to support himself so he immediately slapped his hand onto the floor and heaved again.

"Okay, okay." Fiona took a thin, almost translucent phone from her pocket and lifted it to her ear. "Yeah, we need a cleanup in…" She turned before she nodded at the sign on the door. "4C. Yeah, a dwarf through a teleport web. I know that but we couldn't leave him there. He's the one who jumped on. Send a bucket and mop."

"Where are we?" Lisa stood and looked around the room with one door and no windows.

The other woman grimaced at the mess in front of Johnny, who finally sat and grunted before he wiped his mouth. "That's classified."

"You bring us here and say here is classified." She pointed at the unconscious shifters. "You teleported us off that property, didn't you?"

"Yep. Look, if I had any other choice…well, I didn't. So this is as good as it gets."

"You should have said somethin' before the countdown." The bounty hunter rose on wobbly legs and held a hand flat against the wall to steady himself.

"Oh, come on. You worked it out all on your own. Just in time, too."

A quick knock on the door announced a man in a gray jumpsuit who entered the room pushing a mop and bucket. He scanned the rather large group of unconscious transformed and glanced at Fiona before he pushed the wheeled bucket forward. "This many bodies should have overloaded it."

She scoffed. "Well, it didn't."

"A transport web." Lisa smoothed her hair over her head and frowned. "What is that?"

"Let's move somewhere a little…uh, easier on the nostrils, huh?" The redheaded woman gestured toward the door. "Then I'll answer your questions. It's not like I have anything better to do while we wait for Sleeping Beauty and the Seven Dwarves to wake up."

"Only one of them is a dwarf. And that's not even the right—"

"I'll take care of it." Johnny motioned for the shifter on clean-up duty to step away from the mop and bucket.

"It's his job, Johnny," Fiona protested.

"It's my mess and I need a minute to cool off so I don't strangle you for puttin' me through that."

"Fine. Let him clean up his vomit." The Coalition delegate nodded at her operatives and headed to the door. "Give me a call when you're done."

"Go on, darlin'." Johnny wrung the mop out and slopped it onto the floor. "I'll catch up."

"I think I'll stay with you." Lisa watched Fiona and the other two delegates—plus the relieved janitor—walk swiftly out of the room. "Honestly, I don't think I should be with her either right now. Without you."

"Why?" He stopped mopping to look at her. "Are you feelin' sick too?"

"No, that went away quickly, I'm relieved to say."

He shrugged and continued his task, scowling the whole time.

"I haven't seen you react to anything quite like that before, though."

"Teleportin' ain't meant for dwarves."

"It's not meant for anyone. It involves massive amounts of power and magic, sure, but—"

"Dwarves are affected the most. I ain't used that way of travel since I was young enough to think it was a good idea."

"Fiona and her friends didn't seem all that bothered by it."

He snorted and stuck the mop in the bucket again. "Did you ever stop to think about how that redhead gets to and from a place so fast? It ain't with the tech she slapped on all these transformed either."

Lisa shook her head quickly and glanced at the open door into the hallway. "Fiona can teleport on her own?"

"Yep."

"With magic."

"It ain't that big of a shocker, darlin'. Hell, Amanda's fixin' to start trainin' with her magic."

"I simply…" She shook her head. "Didn't realize shifter magic went that far."

"Sure. Now, it goes as far as an untrained rebel leader on the verge of blowin' herself up in her first real fight. It looks like Addison still sees natural shifters as the enemy."

"And Fiona arrived at the perfect moment to shut the whole thing down." Lisa folded her arms. "I thought she said the Coalition doesn't take sides."

"I assume that ain't changed."

"Maybe not when she stepped in to train a group of transformed on how to use magic most of us don't understand the first thing about. But she stepped in to stop a fight. That changes things."

The bounty hunter finished cleaning the last of his lunch off the floor and placed the mop in the bucket. "Do you think we'd be better off if she hadn't stepped in when she did?"

"Of course not, Johnny. I don't even want to think about what would have happened if Addison kept going with that…uh… Did it look like a magical bomb to you?"

"It probably was. And Fiona was right. We'd most likely be dead." He sniffed and studied the still-unconscious shifters in a heap on the floor. "We oughtta have us a nice long chat about how the Coalition's a part of this whole shifter war now. And if I don't get my hands on one of those EBP guns those fellas carried, Fiona sure as hell had better hand 'em to someone who could use the backup."

Together, they turned and moved to the open door. "You mean Azure and her army, don't you?"

"It's a hell of a way to stop a fight before it even starts."

"Johnny, I don't think those would pass any kind of field test. She didn't sound all that confident about how they work."

"Which is why I wanna take a look."

"Or we could stick to the original plan and undermine both factions' ability to fight each other at all. The idea is without weapons. You know, the whole diplomatic approach we've aimed for from the beginning."

He grunted and snapped his fingers. "Boys. Let's go."

Luther sniffed the newly cleaned floor and whined. "Aw, come on, Johnny. You got rid of a perfectly good snack."

"Bro." Rex trotted past him. "Give up already."

The smaller hound licked the floor anyway before he scurried to catch up with his master.

"Are we leaving them in there?" Lisa asked with a final glance inside.

"I ain't fixin' to drag eight bodies out into the hall. Are you?"

"I…guess not." She turned to study the hallway that stretched in both directions. "Do you have any idea where we are?"

"Coalition HQ would be my best guess. Lucky us. The first dwarf and Light Elf to make it through the doors."

"And hounds, Johnny," Rex added.

"Yeah, don't forget about us. The first hounds to walk around on this floor."

"Hey, I was the first one to lick it."

*Every damn door here looks the same.*

Johnny stopped turning and started walking.

Lisa jogged after him. "Do you know where you're going?"

"Nope. But we have a pissed-off transformed out there callin' herself a witch and she does know how to use her magic. It might be she ran to Langley to spill the beans on our failed plan, or she simply tried to give us the slip. It doesn't matter much now 'cause those shifters in Jeeps took one look at Bronson Harford and knew exactly who he was."

She stopped short and drew a deep breath. "That's not good."

"Nope. And if all that ain't enough to get Fiona to talk, I have enough other ways to knock some sense into her." The bounty hunter balled his fists, turned abruptly down the next corridor, and strode noisily through the headquarters of the Coalition of Shifters.

Lisa stared at the place where he'd disappeared and sighed with exasperation before she hurried to catch up with him. "Again, I'm very sure physically fighting anyone is the reason we're still in this mess."

"Sometimes, darlin', it's the only way to get ourselves out of a mess like this too." He turned to face her as she opened her mouth to remind him of the fallacies in that line of thinking. "Trust me. I ain't fixin' to join a war either. If we can get these shifters to fall in line and play by a new set of rules, that's priority number one."

"I'm…very glad to hear you say that."

"Yeah, well, we gotta get that far first." He nodded toward the other end of the hall and they continued to walk. "I can't believe we took this case for free."

She snorted a laugh and searched the doorways for any sign of Fiona. "It's a good thing we're not doing this for the money, then."

"Sure. Fiona can pay us with one of them electro guns."

---

That night, Langley Appleman sat behind the desk in his home study and glared at the far wall. He wanted to throw his phone across the room but he kept it pressed against his ear as the man on the other side finished his story.

"There was nothing we could do—"

"With all the resources at your disposal?" Langley snarled. "I find that hard to believe, Thompson."

"I've never seen anything like this. Trust me, it's not something I ever want to see again. I thought I was dying when I came to."

"Well, it's a good thing you're still here to tell me what I could have gone without hearing tonight."

"What do you want us to do?"

"Whatever you want, Thompson. It's your property."

"That's not what I meant. I'm talking about the boy."

He pressed his lips together firmly and straightened in his reclining executive chair. "You let me take care of him. He's family, after all."

"Right. If…if they come back—"

"Then you give them everything you've got. It's self-defense at this point, isn't it? They were trespassing. If they're stupid enough to try it again, I'd say they deserve it."

The line was quiet for longer than Thompson usually allowed. Finally, the other shifter cleared his throat. "Right. Self-defense. Do you want us to call if we see or hear anything else?"

"Not really." Langley ended the call and dropped the phone on his desk. None of this was part of his plan.

*I let it all go on for way too long. I tried to be fair and tried to give everyone the opportunity to make the right choice. And now, my nephew's turning against me.*

With a heavy sigh, he settled his hands slowly in his lap and considered his next steps.

*Bronson can be reasoned with. He has no idea what he wants. But these transformed abominations are starting to fight back. That's the bigger problem.*

He snatched his phone again and pulled up Agnes' number. The line rang through to the robotic voice of her voicemail message that told him the number he'd called was unavailable to answer at this time.

Frustrated, he tried three more times and on the last attempt, the phone went directly to voicemail without a single ring.

"I didn't give you that phone so you could ignore me." He snarled his displeasure.

Langley finally admitted to himself that he should have at least given his nephew a little more of his undivided attention over the last few days. The string of drunken texts and incomprehensible voicemails Bronson had left him had turned him completely against the idea.

The Harford heir was no longer a child. True, his uncle hadn't been around much when he was young but that didn't mean he needed to step in and pick up the slack.

*He's a grown man. And if he was out at that ranch this morning, it means someone else stepped in. Why would he align himself with them? And why now after everything he's done?*

With a scowl, he turned slightly in his chair and looked at the portrait of his son hanging on the wall beside the fireplace in his study. He hadn't seen Peter in the ten years since that picture had been taken.

*There's nothing more important than family. Isn't that right?*

When the realization sank in completely, he leapt to his feet.

"That bastard." He snarled and slammed a hand on the desk. "Tucked away in his own little world this whole time and now he decides to step up and play his hand?"

*I should have gone to him the moment Helice died and told him to stay out of this.*

Langley picked his phone up, slipped it into the pocket of his slacks, and stormed across his study before he turned the lights off.

*If you want something done right, you have to do it yourself. Tyro might be out of the game, thankfully, but Kaiser sure as hell isn't.*

# CHAPTER TWENTY-TWO

After two hours of being examined by medics, tested, observed, and asked more questions than they could answer, Charlie, Bronson, Addison, and her rebel team were finally released from the makeshift medical unit. The only thing they were told was that Fiona Damascus and her friends were waiting for them.

"Friends?" Charlie rubbed his pounding temple as he staggered down the hall with the other transformed. "I didn't realize the woman had any friends."

Addison rolled her shoulders back and stretched her neck from side to side. "I wonder why."

"How did she know where we were, huh?" Dee asked and limped on her bandaged leg. "Because if she put some kinda tracker in us—"

"She probably did." The rebel leader looked at the other woman's leg and bit her lip. "Listen, guys. About what happened back there—"

"We don't need to talk about it," Roger said quickly. "It could have been any one of us."

"And it could have been worse," Kyle added.

"But it's not the way to lead anyone into anything." Addison studied her hands as they followed the silent Coalition shifter down the halls toward their imminent meeting with Fiona Damascus. "I thought having magic would solve our problems but I think I made them worse."

"Like I said." Roger cleared his throat. "We don't need to talk about it."

"You didn't do anything wrong," Bronson added and placed a gentle hand on her shoulder. "You couldn't help it. It's okay."

She stopped and stared at his hand. "I know you're trying to make me feel better. But coming from someone who spent the last two months not being able to help himself, it doesn't have the desired effect."

He swallowed and removed his hand immediately before Addison and the rest of her team continued down the hall.

Charlie uttered a low whistle. "Tough break."

"She still blames me."

"Bronson, we all still blame you. You're Tyro—or you were. Please tell me you're done with all that, right?"

The young shifter grimaced and pushed himself forward down the hall. "I wouldn't be here if I wasn't."

"Well, good." Charlie shrugged. "I wish I could say she'll come around but you seriously screwed up. You killed more than a few—"

"I didn't." Bronson snarled in his face and the shifter dwarf backed away with his hands raised.

"Okay, okay. Sure. You keep telling me that, but it's kinda hard to take it seriously when you won't tell anyone else. Like the people who still think you did."

"It wouldn't matter. No one wants to believe I'm not the one who's been killing transformed. Even if they did, it wouldn't change the fact that I was still a part of it."

The dwarf nodded, then winced when the migraine flared. "Maybe. Maybe not. Still, there's a very big difference between killing someone and…you know, not killing them."

"You know what, dwarf? I'm done talking about this."

"Hey." Charlie raised a hand. "You keep calling me dwarf. That's not all I am, okay? Can't a guy have a little pride in both parts of his thrown-together self?"

Bronson glanced at him in exasperation.

"Yeah. That's right. I am proud. I'm all dwarf and all transformed shifter at the same time. I can't do shit about it, so what's the point of getting all bent out of shape, right?" He thumped the young man on the back. "You might wanna try looking at it that way, bud. Now that all the secrets are out, embrace it. You're one of us—"

"No." It came out more sharply than he'd intended and he cleared his throat. "No, I'm not. I can't do...all that—the magic. And I can't walk around in broad daylight saying I was born a transformed shifter. I have a life."

"Yeah." Charlie snorted and nodded at Addison and her rebels who stood around a heavy steel door being opened by their wordless guide. "So do they. And so did I before I ended up in the wrong place at the wrong time and all my magical parts were turned inside out and made into something else."

The young shifter wrinkled his nose. "I didn't mean it like that."

"Sure you did. You think you're so different from the rest of us. Hell, it makes sense. That's what you were told to believe, especially when your mom made you promise to not tell anyone. I get it. You're seriously screwed up."

"Charlie—"

"Exactly like the rest of us." The dwarf thumped his back again and chuckled. "Trust me, Bronson. When you find somewhere you don't have to be seriously screwed up all by yourself, it's a hell of a lot easier to deal with. You should try it sometime."

Bronson gritted his teeth and didn't say anything else as they joined the rest of Azure's rebels inside the room. Their guide pulled the door shut with a loud bang and Fiona stood from her chair behind the long desk that stretched across the far end of the room.

"Huh." Charlie scratched the side of his head. "You know, this looks like a courtroom in Nebraska I had to go to once. It was a total misunderstanding, of course, but it looks bad on paper if you don't show for—"

"No one cares about your legal troubles," the redhead said and shook her head. "You're in my house now so sit down, keep your mouth shut, and listen."

Seated two seats down from her behind the long table, Johnny looked at her and narrowed his eyes. "You don't live here, right?"

"Please. I wouldn't tell you either way. Now." She clapped briskly and scanned the faces of the newly awakened transformed that she was responsible for. They all sat gingerly in the rows of chairs across the room, grimaced, and sucked in sharp breaths. She smirked. "It's good to see everyone up and at 'em again. Honestly, I thought you'd be out for another three hours, but this is progress. We're gathering data."

"You knocked us out with cannons," Dee muttered.

"Wrong. My associates and I saved your lives and we knocked you out with electro-biometric pulse transmitters that pack one hell of a punch. That stopped the fight and got you out of that giant pile of dogshit you dove into head-first when you decided to engage those natural-borns with way too many weapons for civilians and a serious issue with you."

"Hey, wait a minute." On the floor at Johnny's feet, Luther raised his head from his front paws. "Why does it have to be dogshit?"

"Johnny." Fiona pointed at the bounty hunter. "Put a muzzle on your pet."

Beside his brother, Rex uttered a short, low growl. "Johnny, she knows that won't shut him up, right?"

The bounty hunter snapped his fingers and shook his head.

"So here's the deal," the woman continued. "We need—" Charlie's hand raised sharply and she burst out laughing. "What do you think this is? First grade?"

"I still don't know how you got us all here," Charlie said and ignored her jab. "Wherever this is."

"Oh. Yeah. We used a teleport web. It works well on shifters and we know for sure from this experience it works semi-well on Light Elves, dwarves, and pets. Now—"

"Teleport?" Dee leaned forward, her eyes wide. "We teleported?"

"No, you were teleported. There's a big difference."

"Wait, do I have a black eye from that or the knock-out cannon?" Kyle pointed at his swollen eye lined in purple.

The rest of the rebels started asking questions all at once and talked over each other until it was clear that no one was ready to listen to anyone else.

Fiona rolled her eyes, exhaled a massive sigh, and stretched her neck from side to side. A series of pops rippled down her spine before she glanced at Johnny. "What? No whistle?"

"It's your meetin'."

"Fine." She cleared her throat, pounded both fists on the center of the table, and bellowed, "I said sit and shut up!"

The table splintered beneath her fists with a loud crack, and the rebels fell perfectly silent.

"Jesus Christ, I thought I left middle school assemblies behind me for good years ago."

Lisa leaned toward Johnny and whispered, "What kind of middle school did she go to?"

"You'd have to ask her, darlin'."

"Nope. I'm good."

The Coalition delegate smoothed her frizzy red hair away from her face with both hands and scanned the faces of the transformed shifters seated in the small lecture hall turned training room. "I'll only say this once and to save time, I'll give you curious little shifters a rundown of everything the grownups have talked about while you were gone for naptime."

Addison frowned and shook her head.

Johnny rubbed his mouth.

*I hope to hell she ain't fixin' to talk to Amanda like that. Then again, the kid would probably dish it right back.*

"And no," she continued, "there won't be a Q and A afterward because we don't have time. We found you in California because the Coalition watches everything. We know where most shifters are most of the time, and because you answer directly to me, you'd better believe we have eyes on you even when yours are closed.

"The EBPs knocked you out because that's what they were made for—to control shifters who start getting a little too big for their hairy britches. Yes, the idiots with their private missiles got the same treatment. No, we didn't stick around to see how they felt afterward because someone tried to make a statement with shifter magic in a big way. That statement would have spelled 'magical bomb' in blood and guts all over that valley."

She pointed at Addison. "Don't do that again. And if you tell me you don't know how to stop it, you and I are gonna have a talk about self-control. Again."

Lisa grimaced and covered her mouth with a hand before she muttered, "I can't imagine that this will go over well with them."

"Fiona's runnin' the show, darlin'. It's best to not question it."

"Yeah, I get that impression."

"No, you won't get access to teleportation technology because I don't trust you. No, you can't have the EBPs because I don't trust you. And no"—she pointed at Kyle—"you didn't get a black eye from any of our gear because that happened when you were unconscious. Johnny threw a dog on you."

"What?"

The bounty hunter scowled at her and Luther snorted. "So not cool, Johnny."

"Yeah, there's more." Fiona put her hands on her hips. "I don't want to get any more involved in this buffoonery than I already am. The Coalition doesn't want to get involved. You all came up with some touching plans to turn this Agnes so she would come to the good side to help you do…whatever you're trying to do. Mainly not get killed. But it backfired. She's gone. Escaped. No one will go after her.

"And not only that, I received an email half an hour ago saying a giant group of transformed outside Las Vegas is waiting for Azure to give them a timeline on when her army will be ready to attack Kaiser. Jesus, I can't believe I had to say all that."

"Who emailed you?" Addison asked.

"Someone who was trying to give *me* information, kid, not you. I have my contacts and you have hundreds of pissed-off, geared-up transformed storming the proverbial gates because you told them you knew where Kaiser's running his base of operations."

"I do."

"Great!" Fiona flung her hands in the air. "But it doesn't matter because you blew it out there when you went all death-and-destruction on someone else's private property."

"We can't tell hundreds of transformed we're calling the whole thing off," Dee said. "They're counting on us."

"Not to blow them up, they aren't." The redhead rolled her eyes. "I knew you weren't ready. I didn't think you'd have such a hard time handling your magic with a few measly guns pointed in your faces, but hey. Sometimes, I'm simply overly optimistic."

Roger scowled at her. "You don't have any idea what it's like."

"Oh, don't I?"

"Great." Johnny raised his eyebrows and leaned away from the angry woman. "Here we go."

"Yeah, you're a natural-born," one of the rebels added. "Regular shifters don't have magic."

"Ha." Fiona waved a hand toward them and looked at Johnny. "Do you hear this?"

"I'm stayin' out of it."

"This is why two different kinds of magicals who can both turn into wolves are running around trying to kill each other. Everyone thinks they know what everyone else is and isn't capable of." She gestured expansively. "Are you gonna try to kill me too? Because I'm a regular shifter?"

The rebel shrugged. "I'm just saying."

With a snarl, the Coalition delegate slammed her hands on the table again although this time, she wasn't trying to make a point by breaking the wood. Her eyes flashed silver and a massive wolf of ghostly white light surged from her chest before it darted across the room. The projection of her magic tossed its head back and uttered a chilling howl. A scant second before it washed over the first row of rebels, it dissipated in a few thin whisps of smoke.

No one said a word.

"Shifters," Fiona said slowly, "have magic. Anyone who tries to tell you otherwise is a complete idiot. Most of the world, magical or human, has no idea what we're capable of. And I am telling you right now that you're not ready to show anyone else what you can do because I'm very sure you'll kill yourselves first."

"Fiona, we have to stop Kaiser," Addison said. "We have to. I've spent the last few weeks standing in front of so many transformed shifters and promising them we would stop him."

"We will," Bronson muttered.

The rebels glared at him.

"Well, he's mostly right." The redhead shrugged. "Someone's gonna stop him. But it won't be Azure or an army of transformed or even the psycho's prodigy who had a sudden change of heart and wants to try to redeem himself."

Charlie leaned forward behind the young shifter and muttered in his ear, "She's talking about you."

"Yeah, thanks."

"If you won't let us do it," Roger said, "who will?"

Fiona folded her arms and stepped aside to look at Johnny and Lisa. "Who indeed?"

"Huh?" The bounty hunter looked from the rebels staring at him to the Coalition delegate staring at him and snorted. "No."

"Come on." The redhead grinned. "Johnny Walker. Best bounty hunter on this planet, right? Okay, fine. Top three."

Lisa stared at her partner but kept her mouth shut.

"Listen." Johnny pointed at Fiona. "I already got pulled in way too deep. And Lisa and I did what we set out to do, anyhow."

"Which was what?" Addison asked.

"Mostly, it was findin' Tyro and stoppin' him from goin' after any more transformed simply for fun. Figurin' out why he had such a grudge on everyone and stoppin' him. We did that. Bronson had a good dose of reality. I ain't sayin' it's all smoothed over and squared away, but I'm fixin' to call this one closed and move on."

Everyone stared at him. Lisa drew a sharp breath, frowned, and tilted her head.

"You're giving up," Fiona accused. "Just like that."

"No, I'm handin' this over to the Coalition. If I'd known you were trainin' transformed who can zap a guy unconscious with a bolt of red light, I'd have stepped outta your way and let you handle it."

"The Coalition doesn't get involved in wars, Johnny." She narrowed her eyes. "And it doesn't go after individuals for making bad choices."

"Johnny." Lisa fixed him with a firm look. "If we can find concrete evidence that Langley's calling all the shots, we can bring him in."

"We already showed up at his weed farm and his house, darlin'. The man's as clean as a whistle on paper. He gets everyone else to do his dirty work for him. We have nothin' to go on."

"I'm very sure we have enough right here in this room to set something up. We could force him into giving us something to go on."

"Wait, wait, wait." Fiona chuckled and pointed at her ear. "Did I hear you say weed farm?"

"Uh-huh." Johnny scowled at her. "One of Kaiser's operations."

Charlie laughed. "Yeah, and he bought fifty pounds of it."

The bounty hunter gritted his teeth and glared scathingly at his cousin. "That was a play to get him to talk."

"And a hefty chunk of change," the Coalition delegate added through her grin.

"I ain't fixin' to collect on it if that's what you're worried about."

"It's still a bummer," the shifter dwarf muttered.

"Payment." Lisa widened her eyes and a slow smile grew on her lips. She leaned toward Johnny and whispered in his ear.

His frown deepened for a moment before he clicked his tongue and nodded. "Fine. We'll do it."

"Good."

"I'm gonna need a few things."

"Anything you want, Johnny."

He grinned at Fiona and nodded. "Call it official if we shake on it, yeah?"

"Fine." She shook his hand and he tightened his grasp before she could pull away again.

"Anythin' I want. You have a whole room of witnesses who heard you say it."

Her smile faded. "No."

"I heard it," Charlie interjected.

"No, Johnny. That's classified technology and—"

"That I'm gonna need to take a look at before Lisa and I clean up this little problem so everyone can get back to livin' their lives in peace without killin' each other."

"What about me?" Charlie asked.

"That's a given."

Fiona tugged her hand out of his grasp and looked like she was ready to punch him in the face. "Fine. But you give it back when this is over."

"Sure. All I need is one look inside."

"That's what you said the last time." She leaned toward him and growled her frustration. "It took us two months to put that prototype back together again."

"It took me two days to build a better one."

"Get out of here." She pointed at the door. "I'm done making deals about things I know are gonna come back to bite me in the ass."

# CHAPTER TWENTY-THREE

It took them the rest of the day to come up with a plan that satisfied both Johnny and Addison's rebels. When they finished deliberating, Dee was the one tasked with reaching out to all of Azure's transformed followers who were waiting for her signal to rally. Now, they'd be told that new information had come to light and Azure's army was trying another tactic.

"Feel free to tell 'em to stand by," Johnny muttered as Addison and Dee drafted the final email. In front of him on the table was a set of tools he'd specifically asked for and one of the Coalition's new and still-unapproved EBP transmitters. He'd taken it apart hours earlier and was already halfway through putting it back together again.

*The Coalition ain't gonna notice a few minor upgrades. I'm sure they don't even know exactly how this works, which only makes improvements that much easier.*

"It's a weird way to send orders to wannabe soldiers, sure," he continued and pressed the small tip of a miniature welding gun against the inside of the cannon's wide barrel. "But it's the only way we have right now."

Addison folded her arms and looked over Dee's shoulder as

the other woman typed the email. "I can't believe we're backing down like this."

"It ain't backin' down. It's bein' smart."

Fiona shook her head. "I gotta say, though. The most impressive part of all of this is how you managed to build up such a huge following before I even got it in my head to reach out to you. Well, that and the fact that you're bulletproof."

"I'm not bulletproof." The rebel leader glanced at Bronson seated in the corner of yet another room they'd been moved to—this time specifically to use the Coalition computers and Wi-Fi to send an email. He slouched in his chair, his arms folded, and stared blankly at the tabletop. It looked like he was more involved in his own world than in anything the rest of them were saying. "And you make it sound like I went viral on social media or something."

"Ha. That's the last thing we need. Transformed shifters with unknown magic sparking rebelliousness and courage all over the Internet." The redheaded woman pointed at the rebels. "Don't get any ideas."

"How many shifters would consider themselves in your army?" Lisa asked.

"I don't know. A lot."

"And you were fixin' to bring *a lot* to Kaiser's farm so you could...what?" Johnny looked up from his work. "Kill him a lotta times?"

"Sometimes, a show of force is all it takes," Addison said flatly. "And I don't know what we were gonna do when we got there. Maybe it would have turned into an actual fight. Maybe it would have merely been... Mostly, I wanted to show him and any of the others who hate us for being what we are that we won't put up with it anymore. That we will fight back if we have to."

"Well, now you can." Lisa smiled at the young woman and nodded. "But with a much smaller group and some help from magicals who know how to handle this kind of thing."

The bounty hunter snorted as he returned his attention to the half-assembled device on the table. "We ain't been through anythin' even a little like this, darlin'."

"Fine. This is on a much larger scale, admittedly."

"And with more damn pseudonyms."

Fiona smirked and headed to the door. "How much more alone time do you need with that weapon?"

Johnny shrugged. "About another hour."

"Great. You have thirty minutes before we send you to your hotel. In California. Don't screw this up, Johnny."

"I never do."

She raised an eyebrow at Lisa, who shrugged in reply, then spun and left the exhausted team to complete the rest of their preparations.

Dee finished typing, clicked send on the mass email to be distributed to Azure's rebellion subscribers, and leaned back in her chair with a heavy sigh. "I say we simply go out there and burn the whole place to the ground."

"That also defeats the purpose," Lisa warned.

"We'd get rid of all the assholes hanging out there first."

"That's not any better."

"I meant, like, lure them out." Dee rolled her eyes. "But instead, we'll…what? Plant bugs? Spy on Kaiser and his gang of murderers? How is any of that gonna help?"

"That's the plan," Johnny muttered as he picked up a tiny screwdriver and squinted at the weapon in his hands. "But it ain't the whole plan."

The rebels all turned to look at him.

"What's the rest of it?" Addison asked.

"That's for me to know and you to quit askin' about."

Roger paced the room. "So we spent all this time going over a plan with Fiona and now you want to change it?"

"I'm addin' to it. Fiona ain't the type to care about the details, in case y'all haven't picked up on that by now. But the rest of y'all stick to what we went over. That's enough to keep y'all busy. Bronson."

The young shifter still stared at the table, completely oblivious to the conversation let alone his name being called.

"Hey." Kevin picked a pen up and threw it across the room.

With a jolt, Bronson flinched from the projectile that flipped past his face and looked at everyone with wide eyes. "What?"

"Take this." Johnny tossed him a small black square the size of a fingernail.

"What is it?"

"All-in-one recon."

Charlie chuckled and shook his head in amazement. "You can't get it microscopic, huh?"

"If you think you can build somethin' better with Coalition scraps, Charlie, have at it."

"This is…" The young shifter turned the tiny device in his hands. "It looks like a magnet."

"Some of it is." Johnny pointed at him. "The rest will pick up audio and visual. Send it back to us. We'll be watchin' and listenin' when you go to have a chat to your uncle."

"Wait, what?" Bronson straightened in his chair and looked at all the faces gazing at him. "I can't—"

"Oh, come on." Dee wrinkled her nose. "You gave yourself a stupid fake name so you could play rich-boy philanthropist by day and murder us by night."

"Dee." Addison shook her head.

"I didn't—" Bronson closed his fist around Johnny's newest spy cam and clenched his jaw.

"You didn't what?" Roger growled. "Think the rest of us would still want to make you pay for what you've done?"

"Okay, guys. That's enough." Addison swept her gaze across her closest rebel soldiers, who already knew enough about their leader's old life to understand the dynamics. "Bronson's helping us. That's good enough for now—"

"Bullshit." Dee stood from her chair and scowled at the other woman. "You wouldn't shut up about all the things you were going to do to Tyro once you got your hands on him. And now that you know he's your boyfriend, you're trying to protect him instead."

"He's not my boyfriend."

Bronson closed his eyes and frowned but said nothing.

"Three days was all it took to make you go soft," the rebel woman whispered. "And now we don't even get to fight."

She brushed past her in a huff and walked to the door.

The other rebels followed quickly with disappointed glances at the woman they called Azure and growls at Bronson as they passed him to leave the room.

Addison pressed her lips together and watched them go, her nostrils flaring.

Charlie sighed. "See? That right there, Bronson. That would have been the time to tell everyone the truth."

"What truth?" Lisa turned her gaze on the young shifter as well and he bowed his head.

"It doesn't matter."

"Well now, if you have more secrets hidden up your sleeves, son, this is the time to share with the rest of the class."

"I'm good."

"He keeps saying he didn't kill anyone," Charlie said with an edge of irritation in his tone. "Except it seems I'm the only one he feels like telling."

"Why's that?"

"No clue, 'coz. Maybe I simply have one of those faces."

"Yeah, that's it."

"Bronson." Addison stepped toward him and her frown darkened. "Is there something you want to say?"

"No." He stood and gazed at the device Johnny had given him. "It doesn't change anything."

"So why would you tell Charlie you didn't kill anyone and not the rest of us?"

"Well, no one seems to take him seriously."

"Wait, what?" The shifter dwarf gestured in protest. "Come on, man. You already kidnapped me. Now you gotta add insults to the list?"

"I'll be at the…teleporting station—or whatever the hell these shifters call it." Bronson left the room quickly and the others fell into a tense silence broken only by the sound of Johnny's tinkering and the hounds' light panting.

Addison pointed at Charlie. "Did he tell you anything else about this?"

"Uh…do we look like best friends?"

She paced in front of the computer table. "Okay, I now honestly feel like I'm missing something here."

"I think that's standard for all of us right now." Lisa placed a hand on the young woman's shoulder and guided her toward the door. "When we finish this, we'll sit down with Bronson and decide where to go from there— including what to do about his version of events."

"Which we still haven't heard yet."

"Yep. We'll get there when it's time. Johnny?"

"Yeah, I'll meet y'all out there in a sec. I'm finishin' a few last things."

"Okay. Well, Fiona said thirty minutes so that most likely means fifteen."

The bounty hunter smirked and lowered his head to focus on his work. "She ain't sendin' y'all back without me, darlin'. I'll be there in a sec."

"Okay."

Once the two women had left the room, only Johnny, Charlie, and the hounds remained.

The biker dwarf popped his lips and smacked his palm repeatedly onto the side of his other fist. "So…"

"Uh-huh."

"What's the last part of that shifter-stunner…thing?"

"If you wanna hang around, Charlie, quit askin' questions."

"Can I help—"

"No."

"All right, all right." He raised both hands and chuckled. "One of these days, I'm gonna get you to show me how you do what you do, 'coz."

"Instead of simply takin' my things without puttin' in any of the work?" Johnny reattached the back panel of the weapon and refastened the screws. "That'll be the day."

"I know, right?" His cousin hissed a laugh and turned in a slow circle around the room. "Forget teaching me, Johnny. It's cool. I got everything I need—my buddies, a place to crash in all fifty states, my bike—no!"

Johnny jolted at his shout and threw the screwdriver at the table. "Dammit, Charlie."

"My bike." The other dwarf spun with his hands upturned in front of him like claws. "No one thought to get my bike?"

"I wasn't exactly worried about grabbin' a hunk of metal half a mile down the road when we were almost blown up. Or when we were teleported."

"Aw, come on, Johnny. We can't leave it there."

"How much you wanna bet that it's been put out of its misery already?"

"I…" Charlie shook his head. "No. I don't wanna bet anything."

"Smart choice." With a sniff, the bounty hunter picked the screwdriver again up. "Maybe now you can get yourself a real vehicle."

"Do you know how long I've had that Harley?"

"Too long." After a few minutes, the bounty hunter straightened the tools neatly on the table, stood, and lifted the EBP transmitter against his shoulder. "Worry about that later. Right now, we have a shifter pot farmer to catch in the act."

"That's what you're going with?" His cousin laughed bitterly. "Call him screwed 'cause he is now, isn't he?"

"When we're done with him? You bet." Johnny whistled sharply. "Boys. Time to get movin'. The day ain't over yet."

"Yeah, Johnny. We're coming."

"Hey, are we getting out of this place the same way we came in?"

"I hope not," he grumbled.

"Probably," Charlie stated cheerfully.

"Hey, Johnny. Are you gonna puke again?"

"Listen, bro. As long as he doesn't throw us onto a pile of bodies again, I'm good."

"Yeah, that sucked, Johnny."

The shifter dwarf sniggered as they left the room and hurried down the hall to catch up to the others. "Did you truly throw your dogs?"

"It wasn't one of my proudest moments, all right? Don't worry." He clapped a hand on his cousin's shoulder and jostled the other Walker dwarf. "I would have done the same to you."

"Oh. Yeah. Real nice, 'coz."

"Family, right?"

## CHAPTER TWENTY-FOUR

It was almost dark by the time Fiona and a few Coalition assistants set up a much larger and more gently prepared teleport for Johnny and his team to return to California. That didn't mean the journey was any easier on his stomach, but at least it was empty this time.

And the woman had gone above and beyond and provided them with a vehicle after they'd been forced to leave their rental on the private road belonging to a gang of psychotic, missile-wielding shifters in the Sierra Nevada Mountain Range.

"I ain't drivin' that."

Charlie sniggered and pressed a fist to his mouth.

"It's the only option we have right now," Lisa said and fought her laughter back. "Until we think of a way to get the rental back without getting blown up, this'll have to do."

"It's yellow."

"Canary-yellow," his cousin pointed out.

"Aw, hell." The bounty hunter glanced at the keys in his hand, grimaced, and stormed toward the car. "Every damn chance she gets, that redhead has to screw with me."

"Well, it's—" Lisa finally couldn't help herself and laughed before she forced a frown in an attempt to recover. "It's kind of easy when you know which buttons to push."

The hounds sniffed the rear tires of the Kia Rio as their master strode to the driver's door. "Hey, Johnny. What's this—"

He snapped his fingers and pointed at them. "Don't say a word."

"You know what?" Rex stared at him with pure canine adoration. "I bet we'd be far less willing to say anything about your new ride if you got us that steak you promised."

"I promised that when we're done with this whole situation. We ain't done."

The door slammed shut behind him, and Lisa and Charlie shared an amused glance before she slid into the passenger seat and he opened the back hatch. "Your carriage awaits, hounds."

"You mean our birdcage?" Luther leapt up into the back.

"Ha. 'Cause it's canary-yellow." Rex followed his brother. "That was kinda funny."

"Thanks, Rex."

"If we had feathers."

Charlie shook his head, shut the hatch, and turned. "Do you need a ride?"

Bronson stood in the empty parking lot with his hands in his pockets and shook his head. "Nah. The cemetery's only a couple of blocks away. I'll walk."

"Cemetery?"

"Where I left my car."

"Oh. That cemetery. Right." The shifter dwarf snorted and crossed his pointing fingers in front of himself. "When you thought your girlfriend was still dead. But she's not so it's kinda... I mean, I bet that's awkward."

Bronson widened his eyes. "Well, now I seriously wanna ride in bright yellow car with you."

"Good point."

Johnny rolled his window down and draped his forearm over the outside of the door. "We ain't got all night, Charlie."

"Yeah, yeah. Pot farms to bug and murdering shifters to catch red-handed. I get it, 'coz."

"Do you still know what you gotta do?" Johnny asked Bronson and twisted in his seat to look at the young shifter behind the car.

"Yeah."

The bounty hunter squinted at him, then flung his hand in the air. "Go ahead and repeat it to me, son. I learned my lesson thinkin' enough of y'all young folks can stick to the plan without makin' y'all say it first."

Bronson closed his eyes with a sigh. "Keep your tiny spy-square with me at all times. Head out to Langley's tomorrow after you guys bug the place tonight. If he's not at the farm, I'll try his house. Either way, I get him to talk or meet me in person. Get him talking about the rebels and Agnes. Then you guys handle the rest you still refuse to tell me."

"Good." Johnny pointed at him. "And if anythin' goes wrong?"

"Seriously?"

"Say it, Bronson. I didn't make Addison say it and that's what got you kidnapped and tied up in a broom closet."

The young shifter stared across the street. "I call you."

"And if you ain't sure exactly what to do next?"

"I call you."

"And if you talk yourself into a corner with your uncle, if he makes you, if you see anythin' wrong when you're with him…"

"I find a way to work the signal word in," Bronson replied flatly. "Listen, I memorize speeches to give in front of thousands of people waiting for me to convince them to donate to the foundation. I know how to—"

"And the word is?"

He gave the bounty hunter a deadpan stare.

"It'll be over if you give him what he wants," Charlie whispered.

"Margo. It's Margo, okay? Who is that anyway? I don't even know a Margo."

"It's not a who," Lisa called from the passenger seat.

"But it means you need us to storm in and stop your ass from gettin' squashed," Johnny added.

"By his uncle." Charlie shook his head. "Well, he's not technically your uncle—"

"I'm done now." Bronson raised both hands and turned away. "I'll let you know when I head out there tomorrow, okay?"

"We'll be watchin', son." Johnny adjusted the side mirror of the Kia Rio to center him in the reflection as he walked away. "And listenin', waitin' for a sign that somethin' still ain't right—"

"Give him a break, huh?" Lisa nudged her partner in the arm. "He's been through more in the last seventy-two hours than most people or magicals could ever handle. Honestly, I'm very sure that if I were in his shoes, I would have already booked myself a therapy session."

Johnny turned to scrutinize with a curious expression. "You go to therapy?"

"Well, not now. I said I would." She laughed. "But maybe I should start."

"Naw. There ain't nothin' a shrink can say that you don't already know, darlin'."

"Oh, that's sweet. It's probably not true, though."

Charlie got into the back seat and closed the door with a sigh. "I love therapy."

The two partners turned in their seats to look at him. "Say what, now?"

"Yeah." The shifter dwarf buckled his seatbelt and grinned at his cousin. "It's great. You walk in, you get to talk about yourself for a whole hour, and someone tells you what to do to fix all the holes in your brain. What's not to love?"

With a snort, Johnny turned to look through the windscreen and started the car. "See, I understand you lovin' a whole hour to talk to yourself and a so-called professional tellin' ya exactly what you wanna hear to make you feel like you're doin' somethin' productive."

"Johnny, licensed therapists are professionals," Lisa muttered.

He ignored her. "But then you start talkin' about fixin' all the holes in your brain, Charlie, and I gotta say it. I ain't sure this therapy of yours is workin'."

The shifter dwarf laughed and waved the comment off. "You should have seen me before therapy."

Johnny shifted into reverse and glanced at him in the rearview mirror. "I have. It wasn't pretty then and it ain't pretty now."

"Oh, come on. But I can at least laugh about it now."

"That makes one of us."

Lisa choked on her laughter as her partner pulled onto the side street to head north out of Sacramento.

"Hey, Johnny." Luther popped his head over the back seat and his tongue flopped out of his mouth. "Hey, you think I could get someone to shrink the holes in my brain? I think I might have worms."

"Bro. That's it!" Rex snorted. "You explained how the word dumbass was invented."

"Huh. It's about time someone appreciated me for my genius. Thanks, Rex."

Charlie threw his head back and roared with laughter. Luther skittered away from him and thudded against the car's rear hatch.

Johnny tightened his hands on the steering wheel and focused on the road.

*It's gonna be a hell of a long night.*

## CHAPTER TWENTY-FIVE

After leaving Johnny and his team in the parking lot, Bronson took his time walking the five blocks through Sacramento toward the cemetery. His visit to Addison's empty grave three days before was a complete blur, which was understandable on multiple levels.

He remembered being way too drunk to drive and furious at the entire world for trying to shove him into a box and force him to take a shape that didn't belong to him. And he recalled being terrified when he'd seen the ghost of his past standing there as he'd wept over her grave.

*I wasn't all that worried that I was losing my mind. That I can deal with. I was more terrified that she was real.*

Of course, knowing his fiancée hadn't been killed and had come back from the brink of death months later was completely different than realizing that the same fiancée was a rebel leader. She was a transformed shifter with transformed magic and a powerful force determined to face those responsible for killing her kind.

A knot of guilt and shame tugged at Bronson's chest as he entered the cemetery parking lot.

The fact was that he'd done unspeakable things. He'd kidnapped transformed, heavily interrogated them for information on those he'd specifically wanted for his revenge, and had practically tortured several others. Worst of all was that he hadn't stopped anyone around him from taking things too far—his thirst for vengeance and his uncle's plans refused to be denied.

*I don't have the blood on my hands. I'm merely bloody by association.*

The young shifter slid into his car, started the engine, and gave himself a moment of real solitude before he set off for Sausalito and the Harford estate again.

"Three days with a rebel army and that relentless bounty hunter." A bitter laugh escaped him.

*Who knew three days was all it took to start undoing the last few months?*

He backed out of the parking lot, careful to not accelerate away or draw any more attention to himself than he already had. They would simply see a regular guy driving a slightly dented Bentley away from a cemetery where he'd visited an empty grave.

While he drove the hour and a half back to San Francisco and his family's property across the bay, Bronson couldn't stop thinking about the last conversation he'd had with Addison.

They'd only had half an hour before Fiona had stormed in with her gadgets and snapped orders—plus a few flippant insults —to send him and Johnny's team back to California.

Half an hour wasn't nearly long enough after a whirlwind of three days spent questioning everything he had been raised to believe and everything he'd thought he knew once he'd turned against his better judgment. It hadn't been nearly long enough to tell Addison everything he'd wanted to say, especially after her quest to bring a mostly justified war to Kaiser had been cut off at the head—all because she wasn't ready and couldn't control herself or her magic.

But it had been enough to make one thing perfectly clear.

"You might not be the same person anymore," he had told her. "But nothing can change the fact that you'll always be the one who saved me."

She had responded to that with a weak, disbelieving laugh. "I kidnapped you and threw you in a supply closet hoping to turn you against your uncle."

"Well, yeah. That was weird." They'd shared a laugh and he hadn't been able to stop himself from growing immensely serious, knowing what might happen after he played his final part in this mess. With Johnny and Lisa's help, of course. "But none of that outweighs everything you've done for me. Before we... before we were caught up in this mess and after."

Addison had looked at him with a mixture of pity, regret, and hope in her eyes. It was the hope that had kept him talking.

"You were right. What you said in the cemetery."

She'd given him a small smile at that. "You remember that conversation. I'm impressed."

"You told me it sounded like I needed to start trying to forgive myself first. I didn't think that was possible. Honestly, I don't know exactly how to start or how long it'll take, but I know I can try." He'd raised his hand slowly to cup her cheek and wanted to tell her that it had been seeing her as Azure and then as Addison Taylor back from the dead in the span of five minutes that had finally convinced him he wasn't unredeemable. It had hurt to see it, yes. But he'd needed to see it.

He'd wanted to say many things, but she had pulled away from his touch and made it equally clear she didn't want to open that door then. Maybe she'd never want to reopen it.

"We all have work to do when this is all over," she'd said. "Including me. I have to forgive myself too, Bronson. For so many things. If you can do it, so can I. And...well, I guess we'll have to see how things go after that."

That had more or less been the end of their conversation and certainly the end of their time spent together trying to stop this war Langley had started. The war Langley wanted.

*First things first. I get him to talk. He pays for what he's done. Then I can start trying to find out how to keep moving forward after this—with or without Addison.*

At least the love of his life—the woman he was willing to kill for and to die for—was still alive.

---

The front gates of the Harford estate opened smoothly for Bronson when his Bentley rolled to a stop in front of the gate towers. None of his father's usual guards were out this late at night but the automatic security system had let him in.

He pulled his car around to the row of detached garages behind the main estate house and frowned at the fist-sized dent his anger had left in the driver's door.

*I guess forgiving myself might as well start with getting to know the family I do have. The family who's worth my time, even if they are only human.*

The estate grounds were silent and dark, lit only by the flood-lights interspersed every few yards around the perimeter of the main house. He pulled his phone out to check the time and found five missed texts and an astounding number of unanswered calls, all in a group text from his friends.

*Where have you been, man? We've been worried.*

*There's some weird talk out here in the valley. You should call us.*

*Seriously, Bronson. We know things are rough. It'll get better. Just call us back.*

*Okay, guys. It's been almost a week. We have to do something.*

*I know he told us to keep his dad out of it, but maybe we should go talk to him?*

Bronson checked the timestamps of the texts as he walked

across the grounds toward the back entrance of the estate, which he always preferred to use.

*How did I miss these on the drive home?*

He had two voicemails too. The first one was from Adam.

"Hey, man. It's Adam. Listen, I know you're trying to not be around anyone right now. Whatever's going on with you, I get it. You're having a rough time. But we got some calls from Steg out in the valley. He said to call him if we see you or hear from you, which is weird, man. Steg never asks about you. I think something came down from the top if you know what I mean. Probably shouldn't talk about it over the phone, so... Just call me back, huh? Me and the guys are worried about you. Or at the very least, let me know you're alive. We've heard some seriously weird stuff while you were MIA, so... I guess that's it."

Bronson swallowed and almost pulled the group text to his friends open to let them know he was home and alive and didn't have the time to talk about anything right now. Not yet.

But then he saw the voicemail from Jasper Harford's private home number. Usually, he ignored these. For some reason, tonight he couldn't.

"Hi, son. I realize you don't want to talk to me for whatever personal reasons you might have. I understand personal reasons and I'm trying to give you space. But there are some things I want to discuss with you that... Well, I suppose I'll say they're important. For both of us. I've been staying up late working on a few things I'd like to go over with you when you're home. Ten o'clock is my new bedtime. Stop by my office if you're in before then. I... I love you, Bronson."

With a sigh, he stopped in front of the rear entrance to the estate and stared at his phone. He must have received all these calls and texts somewhere during the drive with terrible reception. His dad's message was timestamped almost forty minutes earlier. It was now 9:45 pm.

*That might be the best-timed message he's ever left me.*

Tears shimmered briefly in his eyes when he thought about the kind of conversation he had to have with Jasper Harford. He quailed when he considered all the things he had to tell his father about who he was, what he'd done, and what he had to do now to try to set things right. Whatever Jasper wanted to go over with him could be folded into that.

*The bounty hunter and his weird team are handling things at Kaiser's. I gotta step up and handle things here. Fine.*

Bronson drew a deep breath, slipped his phone into his pocket again, and felt the small black square of the strange recording device the bounty hunter had made him.

*How does a guy like that make something like this and expect it to work without even testing it?*

That thought made him chuckle as he opened the rear door and stepped into the dimly lit hallway mostly used by the estate's staff.

*Trying to understand that dwarf is way harder than what I'm about to do. Keep it on me at all times, huh? Okay.*

As he moved through the back hallways of the main house, he pulled the device out and tried to find a decent place to put it that would catch at least some kind of visual to go with the audio. Unfortunately, it didn't have a clip or an adhesive back or anything he could use to pin it on his shirt.

The sound of a door closing somewhere on the first floor startled him out of his frowning investigation, and he cursed under his breath when Johnny's device fell from his fingers. "Where... Huh."

The small black square had attached itself neatly to the face of his wristwatch.

*Only kind of magnetic, huh? Okay, I'll roll with it. This had better work, Johnny.*

Bronson normally liked to use the central staircase from the front foyer to the second floor. He still had so many memories of climbing those stairs with his mother, playing on them, and laughing as she shouted at him and pretended to be mortified by the fact that Helice Harford's boy would dare to slide down the intricate banisters in the middle of the day where everyone could see. But in the interest of time and not wanting to miss his father's newly announced bedtime, he took the service elevator beside the kitchens instead.

It was a little odd that he hadn't heard or seen any of the round-the-clock staff he usually passed in the house, even this late at night. Of course, he had heard someone shut a door on the first floor.

*Maybe Dad told everyone to keep quiet and stay out of my way in case I showed up tonight. He's done it before.*

When the elevator doors opened on the third floor where the Harfords had their living quarters and Jasper's private study—the one in which he didn't take visitors—the halls were also completely silent. Another glance at his watch showed him six minutes until he knew his father would remove his gold-framed glasses to place them neatly in the center of his desk before he retired to his massive bedroom that rivaled most five-star suites.

The young shifter lowered his head and quickened his pace down the hall toward the study.

*How the hell am I supposed to do this? Okay. Be honest. Tell him you need to talk to him about something tonight. It has to happen tonight or I'll completely lose my nerve. And it's not only me anymore. It's all of us.*

He stopped outside the French doors into Jasper's private study and rolled his shoulders back.

*Looking confident makes you feel confident. Jesus, I can't believe I'm pep-talking myself for Dad.*

He raised his hand to knock gently. The small creak of the hinges startled him when the door swung inward a fraction of an inch and cast the warm glow from the ambient lighting inside across the soft carpeting of the dimly lit hallway.

*Weird. He doesn't leave doors open.*

"Dad?" He knocked again. "Are you in there?"

The sound of his father clearing his throat at the opposite end of the room brought a mixture of relief and mild, fleeting panic.

*Yeah, he's still there. Punctual as ever. Which means I can't put this off.*

Bronson pushed the door open slowly, which didn't creak at all now that it moved much faster beneath his hand. "I got your voicemail on my way in from the garage. There's something I want to—"

A low groan rose from across the room beside the crackling fireplace nestled between the full bookshelves but there was no one there. Only the two armchairs, the couch, and the coffee table between them on the rug.

His father wasn't behind the desk where he expected him to be. He wasn't anywhere at all.

"Dad?"

"How nice of you to join us."

He whirled to where his Uncle Langley stood where he'd expected Jasper Harford to be. "What are you doing here?"

The older shifter pressed a hand against the well-polished wood of the open door and shut it again gently. "I came for a little chat. It looks like you and I had the same idea."

The door clicked shut.

A thump came from the other side of the room near the fireplace, followed by another muffled groan.

*He's behind the couch. He has to be.*

"What did you—"

Langley's grin flashed in the low light before his fist swung into Bronson's face. The young Harford crumpled and his eyes rolled back in his head before he uttered a similar groan.

With his hands pressed together, the man studied his nephew with a tight-lipped smile and nodded. "This isn't usually the way I like to conduct business but I'd call these special circumstances.

And you're in luck, Bronson. I've completely cleared my schedule for this."

# CHAPTER TWENTY-SIX

Johnny and his team had stopped for a quick meal at a Mom-and-Pop burger joint off 49 on the way out of Sacramento. Mostly, it was to stop the hounds' incessant pleading for the steak their master had promised. He ordered them burgers instead.

The bounty hunter had forced himself to wolf his meal despite the lingering nausea from his second teleporting trip in less than twelve hours.

*That's one thing Fiona got right, at least. It wasn't nearly as bad as the first time, I'll give her that.*

Once they'd eaten, the team set off for Kaiser's unmapped farm in the middle of the Sierra Nevada Mountains with two happily sated coonhounds in the back. Lisa sat in the front and slurped the last of her root beer. Charlie sprawled in the back seat with one leg propped up and the other stretched beside him as he leaned against the rear door.

As Fiona's joke of a canary-yellow Kia Rio raced down the winding, hilly frontage road toward the farm they'd visited multiple times, Johnny glanced in the rearview mirror at his cousin. "All right. What's wrong?"

The shifter dwarf met his gaze briefly in the mirror. "Nothing."

"You ain't said two words since we ate."

Charlie snorted. "You've told me my whole life to shut up, 'coz. Now you're pissed that I'm quiet?"

Johnny could feel Lisa's gaze on him as he focused on the road.

*Yeah, yeah. I get it. He's right and there's still somethin' wrong.*

He cleared his throat. "I ain't pissed, Charlie. But if there's somethin' you gotta get off your chest, now's the time. We're goin' into this under the radar without announcin' ourselves to make sure we have eyes and ears on that farm when Bronson makes his move to talk his uncle into proof we can use against him. It's a simple thing tonight. Not havin' your head in the right space makes simple things way harder than they oughtta be."

"My head, huh?"

"I think Johnny's using the universal 'your' for this one," Lisa said gently.

"No, I'm talkin' directly to my cousin."

Charlie turned his head to face the front and raised an eyebrow at the rearview mirror. "So I'm the only one who messes up when my head's in the wrong space."

"All right, fine. I'm talkin' about everyone. The universal 'your.' Whatever." Johnny grunted, shook his head, and tried to focus on the hill rising in front of them beneath the Kia Rio's muted headlights. "So what's goin' on?"

"You wouldn't understand."

"Huh. Try me."

His cousin rolled his eyes and leaned back against the interior wall of the vehicle. The hounds popped their heads over the back seat and panted happily. Rex licked the taste of burger off his muzzle. Luther rested his chin on the back of the seat and stared at Charlie, his tail thumping against the side of the car. "You're sad about something, two-legs."

"Yeah, we can smell it. Johnny, how do you cheer up a guy who's sad about something he won't tell you?"

"We already had treats. What more do you need?"

A bitter laugh burst from Charlie's mouth as he looked at the hounds hovering over him. "My bike."

"Aw, that again?" Johnny adjusted his grip on the steering wheel. "You damn near lost your hearin'—even shifter hearin'—and bloodied your face gettin' thrown off the damn thing. Why you gotta keep obsessin' over a damn motorcycle, Charlie? It ain't a person."

With another scathing glare at the rearview mirror, his cousin shook his head. "See? I told you you wouldn't understand."

"He understands," Lisa said.

"I do?"

"You merely have to put it into a perspective that applies to him."

Charlie snorted. "Oh, you don't say."

"All right, y'all. This ain't open season on the dwarf."

"But I'm right." She patted her partner's thigh twice and raised her eyebrows when he glanced at her in confusion. "How would you feel if you were out one day in Sheila, minding your own business, and someone decided to try blowing you up or off the road?"

"That ain't gonna happen."

"And then you had to deal with the guys who did it, and the only option after that was to leave without her. No going back to check if she survived. And you had to keep pushing forward with a case before you could even think about going back to get her. You had to leave her out in the road for…I don't know. Alligators and snakes."

The bounty hunter snorted. "I've seen a lotta things, darlin'. Gators and snakes tryin' to get themselves a piece of what's mine ain't never been on the list."

"You know exactly what I'm saying."

He gritted his teeth and stared at the road racing beneath them. "Hell. I'd be drinkin' every damn bottle of whiskey I could find."

"Thank you. See?" Her smile widened as she nodded and shifted more comfortably in the passenger seat. "It merely takes a little perspective."

"That ain't perspective. That's plain torture—" Johnny froze, cast his partner a sidelong glance, and hissed a sigh. "Sure. I'd be as rough as the grown-ass dwarf slumpin' in the back seat like a moody teenager."

"You know, none of that sounds like you understand any of it," Charlie muttered.

"Well, I'll tell you one thing." The bounty hunter looked into the mirror again, but his cousin had returned his gaze to his open hands resting in his lap. "To you, that ugly-as-hell bike is your Sheila, yeah. I get it."

The shifter dwarf frowned. "We're not talking about an actual person, right? 'Cause your kid's name is Amanda and I didn't see or smell anyone else at your house."

"Ha." Luther sniffed the shifter dwarf's head and his tongue hung out of his mouth. "Everyone always asks about Sheila."

"Yeah, she's the best," Rex added. "Takes us out for long rides. Growls louder than a wolf."

"Louder than a hound."

"And no one touches her but Johnny. Right, Johnny?"

"That's right, boys." He forced himself to not look at Lisa.

*Why the hell am I talkin' about all this when we're five miles from a damn operation?*

"Huh." Charlie looked up at the sounds from the passenger seat. "It kinda sounds like you have a little competition, Lisa."

She laughed and cleared her throat. "Against a cherry-red Jeep Johnny rigged with artillery and secret compartments? There's no competition, Charlie. Sheila's one of a kind. So am I."

Johnny smirked.

*Yes, ma'am.*

"Oh. That's right." The shifter dwarf heaved a sigh and placed a hand half-heartedly on Luther's head. The hound's tail whacked the inside wall of the car with renewed vengeance. "I forgot you name your stuff."

"Only my favorites." They passed the last bent, weathered street sign Johnny recognized as the marker for slightly less than two miles to go until the unmarked road that would take them down the bumpy, perilous entrance to Kaiser's undocumented farm.

Rex shuffled in the back, licked his muzzle again, and whined. "You gotta do something, Johnny. It's killing me."

"Yeah, it's like he spent the last ten minutes digging for a bone only to find some other jerk dug it up first," Luther added. "No. Worse."

"Much worse, Johnny."

"Thanks for the concern, boys." Charlie heaved a sigh and closed his eyes. "I've lived through a lot of crappy stuff—rejection, heartache, loneliness, trying to fill the holes with drug after drug after drug. I'll survive somehow."

The bounty hunter rolled his eyes.

*Here he goes now. Layin' on the guilt and all his sob-story poor-me crap.*

"Listen here. You—"

Lisa cleared her throat and when he glanced at her, she fixed him with another of those wordless looks he could read better than if she'd written the meaning of it on her face with a permanent marker.

*Aw, hell. I still gotta be the bigger dwarf here? Fine.*

"Charlie."

"Johnny."

"Look at me."

The shifter dwarf swung his head slowly to the side to look at the rearview mirror. If Johnny wasn't about to do something he'd sworn he would never do again for this particular cousin, he might have laughed. How many times had Amanda looked at him exactly like that when she was in one of her moods?

*The kid has an excuse. She is a teenager.*

"All right." He sniffed and divided his focus between watching the road for the unmarked turnoff and meeting his cousin's morose gaze in the mirror. "Mostly, I ain't in the habit of makin' promises before I go into something like what we're doin' tonight. But I need you on your game, understand?"

"I'm on my game." Charlie shrugged. "We're still in the car."

"Yeah, I know where we are. But..." He drew a deep breath to steady himself and didn't dare look at Lisa again. However impossible it was, he could feel her smiling now and trying to hide it. "Listen. We do this right, we get this job done and get outta here in one piece so Bronson can get us what we need to put away the right guy and... Hell. I'll take you out to get a new damn bike myself."

The biker dwarf stared at the mirror, then shook his head. "I can get a ride to a dealership on my own, 'coz. But thanks."

Lisa cleared her throat again and tilted her head gently toward the back.

*Oh, come on. If I gotta go any farther out on this limb, it'll snap out from under me.*

"And I'll buy it for ya," he blurted quickly.

"You know what? Don't even worry about it." Charlie waved him off. "I'll work it out somehow and—wait, what?"

"You heard me."

"Did you say you'd buy me a new Harley?"

Johnny clicked his tongue. "You said you wanted a bike. I ain't payin' for the twin to that eyesore you already ran ragged across the country."

"Johnny." Charlie pushed away from the inside of the door to sit fully upright, his eyes wide and glistening. "Oh, man, Johnny. Do you honestly mean it?"

"Well, now I'm startin' to think I ain't."

"That's... Ha!" His cousin lurched forward and grabbed the back of his seat. "You'd do that for me? Truly? I mean...you don't have to."

"Do you have the money to cover it yourself?"

Lisa scoffed and frowned exasperatedly at him.

"Well... No, not really. I don't exactly have much cash flow right now, but—"

"I don't wanna hear about your cash flow." Johnny slowed the vehicle as they approached the massive boulder that marked the turnoff he wanted. "We'll call it payment."

"For what?"

"Hell, Charlie. I don't know. Services rendered."

The shifter dwarf laughed and grasped his cousin's shoulder this time to give him an enthusiastic shake. "As a consultant. Yes! I knew that was what I needed to get into. Thanks, 'coz. Seriously."

"Yeah, all right. Get your hand off me. I'm tryin' to drive."

With a thump on his cousin's shoulder and another breathless laugh, Charlie leaned back in his seat and grinned. "I can't believe it. The best choice I ever made was coming to visit you in the swamp, 'coz. The best choice."

*And I'm never hearin' the end of this.*

"Keep your head in the game for now," he muttered. "I need you sharp."

"As a fucking tack." The shifter dwarf slapped his thighs. "Let's do this. I'm pumped!"

Lisa lowered her head to hide another smile, but she couldn't quite stop a soft chuckle. "Let's do this."

"Uh-huh." He turned the wheel hand over hand before he guided the car along the poorly maintained road that was little more than tire tracks in the grass. The vehicle jostled and bounced as he navigated the uneven terrain.

*At least if I lose control of this one, it ain't nearly as bulky as the last car I almost flipped comin' down here. It ain't nearly enough to keep us from crashin' with it, either. It might be the only thing that gets me outta the promise I just made.*

# CHAPTER TWENTY-SEVEN

Johnny parked the car a short distance before they crested the top of the hill looking into the valley and onto Kaiser's shifter-war headquarters turned semi-legit marijuana operation. He'd already turned the headlights off half a mile back to lessen the risk of being seen and so far, they hadn't met anyone else on the nonexistent road.

He turned the engine off and everyone was silent.

"All right, Charlie. Hand me the bag."

"You got it." As chipper as ever now, his cousin snatched up the black messenger bag with their recently upgraded gear inside —the only thing Fiona had on hand to give to the bounty hunter before they'd left Coalition HQ. He hefted it toward the front seat and stopped. "Hey. Did you know there was a giant smiley face on the back of this?"

"Give it here." The bounty hunter yanked it from his laughing cousin and opened it. "Y'all still have those comms units from our failure at the park, yeah?"

Lisa tapped her ear. "Mine's already in."

"Hold on. One sec." Charlie slapped fervently at his front

pockets, then pressed himself against the back of the seat to feel his back pockets. "Uh-oh."

"Dammit, Charlie. Are you serious right now?"

"I thought I put it right—oh. Yeah. Here it is. Ha." He removed the earpiece and wiggled his eyebrows. "I knew I had it."

With a heavy sigh, Johnny put his unit into his ear and tapped it twice. "Y'all can hear me?"

"They're sitting right next to you, Johnny." Luther sniggered. "Yeah, one guy's half-shifter, but even I know Lisa can hear you."

"No one wants to hear you right now, bro."

Everyone ignored the hounds and Lisa nodded. "You're coming through clearly."

"Yeah, me too," Charlie confirmed

"All right." Johnny removed three black plastic boxes a little larger than his hand and gave one to each of them. "We each have four in there. This ain't gonna work if all of 'em ain't positioned and activated, understand?"

"Plant four bugs." The shifter dwarf grinned. "It's a piece of cake."

"Uh-huh. Between four and five feet off the ground—the best guess you can make. I'll take the front of the main house. Y'all get the grow houses. The entrance door is the best place if you can make it look inconspicuous."

"No problem."

"Stay in contact." He tightened his hand around his boxed set of bugs and looked out Lisa's window toward the crest. So far, there wasn't any movement or sound but they still had to get over the top of the hill and down again before they could do anything. "Last time we were here, the fellas Langley had workin' for him were mostly local. I don't think there are many bodies mannin' the place right now—"

"Definitely not." Charlie shook his head. "The seasonal workers don't come in for another three weeks at least. Remember?"

"Sure. But if you do see anyone…"

Lisa's lips twitched in and out of a smile that she tried to hold back. "Don't engage. This isn't my first time bugging a property, Johnny."

"Uh-huh. But we have a rookie on the team so I'm coverin' my bases."

Charlie frowned and turned to look at the hounds. "Who? Them?"

"What?"

"Oh, you meant me." The shifter dwarf snorted. "Trust me, 'coz. This isn't my first time either. A couple of years ago, I was running around with this MC out of Detroit. Okay, yeah, not exactly the kinda guys you'd wanna bring home or anything, but they needed some help with this other crew who were—"

"I don't wanna hear a damn thing about your business with a biker gang."

"MC, Johnny. They seriously do prefer that, you know. There's so much stigma that comes with being called a gang."

"Jesus Christ." Johnny switched off the overhead light that was set to stay on with an open door and slid out. He paused to peer into the car and whispered, "Leave the doors open. Stay quiet. As soon as you get these bugs where they need to be, y'all come right back here."

"Copy that." Lisa gave him a goofy salute.

He rolled his eyes, grateful for having grown his mustache long enough to hide the smirk he couldn't hold back on his own, and pointed at Charlie. "Got it?"

"I'm good to go."

"Then let's do it."

When all the two-legs exited the car, Rex and Luther crouched at the rear hatch until Johnny opened it. They landed silently in the browning grass and immediately got to work sniffing around.

"It smells like a whole horde of stinky shifters, Johnny," Rex whispered.

"And rabbits."

"Y'all keep it down from here on out too." He pointed at his ear. "This ain't the place to talk when there's nothin' but shifters."

"Yeah, yeah, Johnny. We got this."

"We'll be quiet. So, so quiet."

With a nod toward the top of the hill, he strode forward in a half-crouch.

*It helps that the moon ain't high or on this side of the valley. But if anyone's down there and chooses the right moment to look up, we could be detected.*

They moved as silently as possible and only when he approached the tree he'd almost rammed with an SUV during their first visit there did he realize that he could hear and see Lisa and the hounds but not his cousin.

*Dammit, if he went rogue on this one, I have no problem goin' back on my word about a damn motorcycle.*

"Charlie," he whispered. "Where did you—"

"I'm at the side of the house, 'coz, and moving in. What's wrong?"

The partners exchanged a surprised look in the darkness and he shrugged. "Nothin'. I didn't see you, is all. Keep goin'."

*The first time I gotta sneak around anywhere with him and I damn near forgot he's half-shifter now. Real fast and quiet. Well, all right.*

When they reached the front of the main house, he fully expected to see lights click on inside or at least some kind of motion-activated floodlight mounted over the front door. Nothing moved in the darkness and fortunately, all the lights stayed off.

*Either Kaiser ain't decided to set this place up with security or he ain't worried about someone tryin' to sneak in. Probably because of Agnes. It might be he has someone mannin' the place who can already see in the dark.*

The hounds didn't pick up any other scents, sounds, or movement, so he stepped cautiously toward the front of the house and nodded at Lisa.

She nodded in response and slipped around the far side to set her bugs up on the warehouses in the back.

*So far so good. But that ain't never been a good enough reason to assume nothin's gonna go wrong.*

Johnny reached the front of the main house and stepped more carefully across the narrow wooden porch in his thick black boots than he could remember stepping anywhere. When he was two feet from the front door, a twig snapped behind him.

*Damn.*

He waited for another five seconds and heard only the rustle of some small creature skittering into the sparse bushes that dotted the valley beside the house.

*Quit psychin' yourself out, Johnny. Get it done.*

The black box in his hand opened silently and he removed one of his newly created devices. It was an exact copy of the one he'd given Bronson to wear but with a few adjustments to pick up sound and movement from a stationary location.

The bounty hunter slipped the bug under the base of the doorknob mount, removed his hand slowly, and waited.

*Good. That'll hold just fine.*

He started down the porch to find another position above the boarded-up front window for a second bug when Lisa whispered over the comms. "Charlie, did you see that?"

"What?"

"I thought I saw...I don't know. Movement behind the house."

"It's probably only a critter."

"Right."

"Keep movin'," Johnny whispered but he stopped paying attention to the window and focused entirely on listening.

*It might be wildlife but it could be somethin' else.*

"Boys?"

The hounds didn't reply immediately, which was probably just as well.

*It means they ain't found somethin' we oughtta deal with. It's fine by me.*

He finished setting the bugs around the boarded window, the opposite wall of the house beside the gutter drain, and on the splintered railing around the porch. That done, he turned, stepped onto the grass, and scanned the darkness.

*If Lisa and Charlie are still quiet, we're good. Get up that hill and get outta here.*

"Wait," Lisa whispered.

"I'm all done," Charlie replied.

"No, I saw something. For real this time. It looked like— whoa!" Even her breathless whisper had enough surprise in it to make Johnny's pulse race.

That also probably had something to do with the crack that split the air and the crackling hum of electrical interference.

"Johnny." She no longer whispered. "We have company."

"Did you get a look?"

"No, but it's the...we saw...think..."

Static filled his ear as he hurried around the side of the house and tried to stay in the shadows. He gritted his teeth and tapped the comms unit. "Lisa. Lisa? You're breakin' up, darlin'."

Another loud crack and sizzling hum came from the back of the main house and he broke into a run. "Charlie? Can you hear me?"

There was no reply from his cousin.

A third and fourth crack and hum rose in quick succession and with the back corner of the house in sight, he immediately knew what it was. The brilliantly flickering glow of dark-red mixed with the electric hum of transformed magic made that very clear.

*Goddammit. Stick to the plan! How hard can it be?*

The bounty hunter raced around the back of the house and

almost barreled into Lisa. She gasped in surprise and stepped away from him with wide eyes. "Johnny, we're not alone."

"Yeah, I can see that."

The warehouses used to grow Kaiser's marijuana plants were covered in crackling red light. It snaked across the walls and roofs, snapped and sparked, and emitted a low, warning buzz. The heat of concentrated magic around each building intensified.

"I think someone had a different idea with the farm than we did," Lisa muttered.

"You heard that rebel say she'd rather burn the place down than let us come in here to bug it, right?"

"Who, Dee?"

"Yeah. That's exactly what she said."

"Johnny, they told us they would stay out of it."

"Uh-huh. When was the last time you saw Addison and her team do somethin' exactly the way they said they would?"

"Johnny!" Luther uttered a strangled bark and raced out from behind the grow warehouses. "We didn't do it, I swear."

"Over here! Johnny! I found her!" Rex's bark came from the other side of the row of warehouses. "Someone's—"

His sentence ended in a sharp yelp.

"Rex!" Luther raced across the grounds. "Johnny, we gotta help him!"

With a growl, the bounty hunter sprinted after his hound.

*I swear to everythin' I believe in, if that shifter with a serious attitude laid a hand on my hound, I ain't holdin' back even a little.*

Lisa was close behind him and almost on his heels. "Charlie?" She tapped her earpiece. "Charlie, can you hear me? He's not answering."

"Maybe he went back to the car."

They raced around the warehouse on the end to see Rex seated in the grass, his ears flat against his head and his left forepaw raised in front of his chest. He panted furiously and uttered a low whine.

"Whoa. Bro." Luther raced toward him and sniffed his brother. "What happened?"

"I don't know. Something came up out of the ground and… and bit me."

"Hold still." Johnny dropped to one knee in front of the hound and felt around the limply dangling paw. "What the— Damn chipmunks."

"A chipmunk did this?" Luther squealed and spun in a tight circle. "Where, Johnny? Tell me where, and I'll—"

"He stepped in a hole. Come on, boy. We gotta get outta here."

"Johnny, he said he saw someone." Lisa drew the pistol in her shoulder holster and scanned the hillside on the north end of the property. The blazing light from transformed magic that hissed and snapped around the warehouses was enough to light up anyone who got too close. Unfortunately, it also blinded them to anyone standing beyond the glow. "Rex, where did you—"

"Right there." The hound whined and stood, still favoring his paw. "Running toward the house."

"Where's Charlie?"

# CHAPTER TWENTY-EIGHT

As soon as the two partners looked at each other, the first warehouse at the end emitted a piercing shriek of crumbling, ripping metal. In the next moment, it exploded with a blazing light of intensifying red magic and the first flames as all the electrical wiring inside caught fire.

That was certainly enough light to see the figure in all black with a black beanie sprint away from the warehouses toward the front of the house.

"That's her." Johnny spun and searched the darkness. "Dammit. No way is there only one of 'em here. If Dee came here to blow the place up, the others are—"

The second warehouse in the line screeched and burst into flame like the first. A massive column of white smoke billowed from a hole in the warehouse ceiling.

"We need to get out of here," Lisa said. "Right now."

"Charlie!" The bounty hunter turned and cupped his mouth to shout over the crackle of magic that consumed the warehouses. "Charlie! Where the hell—"

A thick, roaring column of red light erupted from six feet beside the main house of the farm and blasted into the side of the building. It triggered a vicious shudder through the entire house and pieces of broken siding and wooden beams sprayed toward the hillside. Shingles toppled from the roof and the structure groaned before the same crackling red magic spread like a real fire across the exterior.

"Dammit, Charlie! Where—"

The back door to the main house burst open and pounded against the exterior wall. Two seconds later, the red snakes of sparking magic seemed to swallow the doorway, but Charlie was already racing toward them with something slung over his shoulder.

"Are you kidding me?" he shouted. "We told them to stay put and let us handle this."

"Yeah, that's what I said." The third warehouse exploded, and the shifter dwarf stopped short a split second before a ripped, dented metal panel landed where he'd been about to step next.

"Oh, come on!"

"Get to the car. Now!"

Johnny raced toward the side of the house, followed by his team as the fourth warehouse went up in smoke and flames with a deafening roar. Something crashed inside the main house and the windows at the back shattered and sprayed shards of glass two stories down. Flames licked around the window frames as the building groaned again.

"Johnny!" Luther howled wildly. "Johnny, help him. He'll get burned alive!"

"Go." Johnny pointed toward the front of the property and his teammates raced away without a word.

He dodged falling glass and pieces of wood from the burning farmhouse as he sprinted toward a limping Rex while Luther ran around his brother in wild circles.

"Help him, Johnny. Help him. Help!"

"Quit yellin' and get to the car." The bounty hunter scooped his injured hound up and tossed him halfway over his shoulder before he turned to run after the others.

"I know we said to not carry us, Johnny." Rex licked his master's ear and uttered another low whine. "But there are exceptions, right?"

"That's fine, Rex. But..." He slowed as he reached the front of the house because he saw now exactly what he'd hoped no one else would see when their positions were switched.

A lone figure stood at the top of the hill behind which they'd left the car. It was a woman, he could tell that much. But beyond the blaze of a burning farmhouse and all those warehouses, the only detail he could make out was the tight-fitting black clothes and the black beanie.

"When I'm done with you, you'll be—"

Something highly flammable exploded inside the house with a roar. The boards over the front windows cracked and toppled to the deck. Johnny staggered forward under the heat with the force of the explosion behind him and ignored Rex's panicked clawing at his back and chest.

"I gotcha, Rex." When he looked at the hill again, the woman's silhouette was gone. A moment later, Lisa and Charlie's forms bobbed quickly over the rise of the hill.

*That ain't good no matter how you spin it.*

He ran up the hill with one hound slung over his shoulder and the other racing ahead of him. His teammates disappeared and by the time he crested the hill, they were already in the car with their doors closed.

"We'll get you looked at in a while." Johnny lowered Rex gently into the back of the Kia Rio.

"I thought I was dead, Johnny."

Luther leapt into the back with his brother and sniffed him wildly. "I thought you were dead. Don't worry, bro. Those chipmunks are gonna pay."

The bounty hunter slammed the rear hatch shut and stalked

toward the open driver's door as he glared into the darkness. The blaze from Kaiser's burning farm now rose like a beacon behind the hill.

"Where did she go?" He yanked his door shut behind him and looked from Lisa to Charlie.

She shook her head. "I didn't see her."

"I was too busy running from all the explosions, 'coz. My bad."

"She was standin' right—" With a growl, he struggled with his back pocket to pull his cell phone out.

"Yeah, good idea." Lisa stared out his window at the glow beyond the hilltop. "California has enough fires on its own. We should call this in."

"I ain't callin' the fire in." He pressed Fiona's number and practically slapped his phone against his ear.

"Oh. Okay, then I'll do it." Lisa pulled her phone out but he was no longer paying attention.

*Fiona had better answer this time. I think she knows how much I ain't playin'.*

The line rang twice before the woman answered. "You know, you don't have to give me a play-by-play—"

"Why the hell did you let 'em out?" he snapped.

The woman laughed. "Well, this will be an interesting conversation."

"We went over this too many times for you to not get the damn picture, Fiona. Why did you—"

"Okay, I'll stop you right there, Johnny, because I have no idea what you're talking about."

With an overwhelming urge to get fresh air—even if it was tainted with smoke—he shoved the door open again and stepped out of the car. "Addison," he growled. "And the rest of her loyal crew."

"Um…" The Coalition delegate chuckled. "Normally, I'd ask if someone babbling nonsense has been drinking but I know that's not your thing, so—"

"We're at the farm, Fiona. And those kids came through to turn the place into a giant bonfire."

"Huh." The woman paused for a moment, then sucked in a sharp breath. "It must have been someone else, Johnny. Because I'm sitting here right now looking at all seven of them. And let me tell you, they look as confused as I feel."

"What?"

"Do you have bad reception or something?"

Johnny turned and scanned the dark valley again. "They're all there with you?"

"Yes. That's exactly what I said. And I was in the middle of giving them a scintillating lecture on the importance of—"

"Even Dee?"

Fiona paused, then shouted, "Which one of you goes by Dee? Yeah, Johnny. They're all here, even Dee. So unless you have some other—"

He snapped his phone shut to end the call and climbed into the car. "It wasn't them."

"Who—Addison?" Charlie leaned forward in the back seat. "Are you sure?"

"Fiona's with all of 'em."

Lisa sighed heavily. "Well, that's something of a relief. But that doesn't solve our immediate problem, does it?"

The bounty hunter dropped his phone into the center console's cupholder and turned the engine on. "Yeah. It's a big problem. What other transformed do we know who'd come in here alone with heavy firepower to burn this place to the ground the way the others wanted to?"

Her eyes widened. "Do you think it was Agnes?"

"It's the only thing that makes sense right now." He strapped himself in and the others followed suit quickly before he jerked the gearshift into drive and turned on the brights to get them out of there. "The only thing I don't get is why."

"She was pissed when Bronson met her at the park." Charlie's voice vibrated and wobbled as they raced across the uneven ground. "Maybe it did exactly what we wanted, right? If he told her he's half-transformed too, maybe she realized she's been fighting for the wrong side the whole time."

"I think it takes a little more than that to get someone like Agnes riled up this much."

"Or…" Lisa gripped the armrest of her door and looked at her partner with wide eyes. "Or she got to Langley and told him everything. Maybe they found out what we were trying to do—or guessed it."

"How would they do that, darlin'?"

"I don't know. But think about it. If they found out somehow, the best way to keep us from gathering evidence against Langley at his farm is to—"

"Get rid of the farm."

"Oh, man." Charlie groaned. "That's a ton of burning weed."

"Johnny, what if Agnes told Langley about Bronson? That he's working with us now?"

The bounty hunter gritted his teeth and scowled through the windshield. "Then our whole plan went up in flames exactly like the farm."

"Should I—"

"Yep."

Lisa retrieved her phone again and scrolled through her contacts list before she pressed to call Bronson. "Okay, it's ringing."

"This is—" Charlie sighed in frustration. "This is heavy right now."

"Quiet."

The car bumped across the dry valley and only settled slightly when Johnny brought them back onto the worn tire tracks that led to the main road.

The half-Light Elf lowered her phone into her lap and shook her head. "He's not answering."

"Then make sure y'all are buckled up. We're makin' an unannounced visit to the Harford estate."

Charlie laughed. "You can't simply drive up to a house like that."

"Watch me, 'coz. I have an open invitation from Jasper Harford himself." He floored the accelerator and cranked the wheel as they passed the massive boulder. The vehicle skidded on the dirt road and in the next moment, they raced south again and back toward San Francisco.

*This is when I get to drive like Charlie 'cause we're runnin' outta time.*

# CHAPTER TWENTY-NINE

Bronson groaned and tried to roll over where he lay but he couldn't move.

*No. Not again. I thought the kidnapping part was over.*

It took him a minute as he struggled with his immobilized arms and the pounding in his head—mostly from his jaw—before he remembered what had happened.

With a jolt, he tried again to sit before his eyes jerked open and he realized he was lying on his side and staring into his father's wide eyes.

Jasper lay on the floor as well, his wrists bound behind his back and his glasses removed. Someone had tied a makeshift gag around his head and shoved it into his mouth. The man didn't try to say anything but his heavy breathing through his nose and the fear in his eyes told his son everything he needed to know.

*It wasn't merely someone who did this. It was Langley.*

"Are you okay?" he whispered.

His father closed his eyes slowly and when he opened them, they shimmered with unshed tears.

"I hear talking." Langley's slow footsteps moved toward them from across the room. Both Harfords flinched when the heavy couch was shoved aside with a screech and rumpled the expensive area rug beneath it. The older shifter came into view and smiled at them like he'd stumbled upon two toddlers playing happily together in a sandbox. "To be honest, I wouldn't have hit you so hard if I'd known how long it would take you to come to."

Bronson glared at his uncle, who sat casually on the armrest of the couch and crossed one leg over the other. He didn't miss the loaded pistol in Langley's hand.

*That's why Dad's tied up without magic-blocking handcuffs. He doesn't have a gun. Neither of us does.*

"I guess I could blame myself for that," the man continued wistfully and gazed at the bookshelves around the fireplace.

"For punching me?" the young shifter snarled. "Yeah."

"For not hitting you often enough." Langley leaned over his lap and sneered at the Harfords. "I know that's usually a father's job—man of the house and all that. I guess you and I both failed him that way, Jasper. Didn't we?"

Jasper lay on his side facing his son and had no way to look at his late wife's brother and no way to respond.

With a sigh, the older shifter slid off the couch's armrest and lifted one foot to roll the man onto his back by the shoulder. He leveled the pistol at his head.

"Stop!" Bronson shouted. "Langley, you can't—"

"I asked him a question. Man to man. I expect an answer."

Jasper glared at his attacker and narrowed his eyes.

"That's good enough." Langley turned away and clasped his hands behind his back, the gun held as casually as if it were a pocket watch.

"What do you want?" the young man growled.

"I want what I've always wanted." His uncle paced slowly around the room and gazed at the crown molding around the private study and all the valuables passed down through generations of Harford shifters who had lived there. "I've simply realized—and quite recently, I might add—that I have to make a few changes in order to achieve that."

"So you broke into our house?"

"Hmm." Langley turned and tilted his head to study his nephew intently. "I came here to talk."

"You put a gag in my father's mouth."

"Yes. Because he talks too much. And I didn't come here to listen to Jasper Harford's infamous diatribes on honor and responsibility and the duty we have as shifters to elevate each and every one of us across the globe. Honestly, I reached the end of my patience with that nonsense shortly before your mother died."

"Then let him go." Bronson glanced at his dad. Jasper widened his eyes and shook his head. "I won't talk to you until he's off the property."

"I understand. You're surprised." The man resumed his pacing. "Angry, even. That's all well and good, Bronson, but your father isn't going anywhere. He's all you have left to lose, isn't he?"

"Langley—"

"Family…" The crazed shifter tipped his head back toward the ceiling and grinned before he sighed dreamily. "That's what you've always wanted—mother gone, father practically gone from your life too after pouring himself so fervently into his philanthropy. I've always been here for you. Or at the very least I've tried my best."

He swallowed and watched his uncle move slowly around the room.

*What is he trying to get at here? I seriously hope I didn't have to find an on-switch for the camera and audio to start working.*

"Family's important, yeah," he muttered.

Langley turned toward him and raised an eyebrow. "I'm glad you agree."

*Keep him talking. Whatever happens, if this is all being recorded, keep him talking.*

"You're family, Langley."

"Ah. Yes, but there's a difference. It's not quite the same, is it? No blood relation so no real strength in a bond that doesn't come from the same family tree. Still, I took you in and gave you a chance to prove to me that you wanted a better world as much as I did. And yeah, you threw me for a loop there with the whole Tyro act."

"Stop." He glanced at his father, whose small frown was enough to show him that Jasper was putting the pieces together all on his own. "I don't know—"

"And you're a terrible liar," Langley snapped. "One of the worst I've ever seen, honestly. It's amazing the media didn't chew you up and spit you out again when you went into mourning."

*Why is he bringing Addison into this? He can't know where she is or who she is.*

"You know, there's nothing I wanted more for you than to give you the life you deserve, Bronson."

"That's not your job." The young shifter's dangerous anger welled inside him and his breathing grew heavy. "It never has been. My life is—"

"Your life is a lie." The older shifter stormed across the study, withdrew his hands from behind his back, and waved the gun at the floor like a lunatic. "All of it. You don't deserve a single thing you think you're so entitled to, Bronson. And if I hadn't—" He swallowed and grimaced. "If I hadn't made a promise, I would have told you the truth a long time ago."

Bronson glanced at his father again but now, Jasper stared at the ceiling.

*There's no way he's giving up. He's pretending. He has to be.*

"Okay." He nodded at his uncle. "Now I have no idea what you're talking about."

"Of course you don't." Langley studied Jasper's face and

lowered slowly into a crouch in front of the older Harford. "I might have let you tell him, Jasper, but you always take so long to get anything done—"

"Hey." The young shifter struggled to rise, gritted his teeth against the dull pull of his arms behind his back again, and hauled himself into a seated position. His uncle smirked. "You said you wanted to talk to me. Not him."

"You…" The man chuckled and wagged the pistol at him. "You always have been so impatient. To grow, to take over the Harford Foundation." His smile vanished. "To ruin your life with that no one transformed girl."

His gut clenched into tight, hard knots. "Her name was Addison."

"Yes. Was being the operative word." Langley drew a deep breath through his nose, stood, and paced slowly in front of his captives. "But her name doesn't matter, Bronson. Yours does and I already let Helice take a name she didn't deserve. I wasn't about to let that happen a second time simply because you thought you had found the one." He snorted in disgust and turned to stalk across the study again. "So I did what I had to do. And I had—ha! I had no idea it would make you so willing to finally join me."

"What?" Bronson's mouth had gone completely dry and his bound hands tingled on the edge of numbness. But it wasn't from the rope or whatever had been used to tie him. "You—"

"I knew exactly what you were planning that night, yes. To propose. Honestly, Bronson, I was sure I'd taught you better than to stoop to such a disgusting level, but no. You were serious. And it was very convenient that I happened to have a meeting that needed to be scheduled. The docks are always a good place to start."

"You had her killed."

The corner of the older shifter's mouth twitched. "You're welcome."

"You bastard!" With a growl, he pulled his legs under him and managed to kneel before his uncle tsked and waved the gun in his face.

"I don't know what you think you'll do to me, Bronson. But your hands are quite literally tied. Mine are not."

The young shifter snarled and his chest heaved as he watched his uncle trail his fingers along the back of the leather couch.

*I could kill him now anyway. When was the last time he shifted, let alone for a fight?*

But then he remembered the black square on his watch and the whole reason he'd come home in the first place.

*Get him to talk. That's all you have to do.*

"Why?" he whispered. "Why would you—"

"Kill your girlfriend? If it isn't obvious by now, you need to open your eyes."

*If that right there isn't enough proof, I don't know what is.*

"Because you didn't want me to marry a transformed shifter? Langley, do you hear yourself? You're insane—"

"No." The man waved the gun in his face again. "I am not. I'm fighting for generations of shifters who will not be forced to suffer the same indignities. It merely takes a little work to get rid of the mongrels who shouldn't even exist—those who stand strongest against me, of course. You would have made the list too, dear nephew, but a promise is a promise."

"What?" When Bronson looked at his father again, the pain and remorse in Jasper's eyes almost broke him.

*He knows and he thinks I don't. As does Langley. Jesus, Mom, how many secrets did you make us promise to keep?*

"I know it's a little hard to wrap your head around," Langley continued. "So I'll spell it out. Helice was one of them, Bronson—your mother and my sister. I thought it would be fun growing up with a human in the house. And sure, it was for a while. But she got herself caught up in all the wrong messes, and when those—" He sucked in a sharp breath and bared his teeth. "Well, you know how transformed shifters were made back then. And judging by the look in your eyes now, boy, I'd say it's safe to assume you understand how transformed like you are made too."

"You had no right—"

"I have every right. I'm the one who cares about what happens to us. I'm the one who won't let them ruin everything the rest of us who were meant to be shifters worked so hard to create. And I'm the one who sacrificed more than enough to keep my promise to your mother to not tell you what you are because I can only assume she knew what I was planning." Langley scoffed. "Keeping promises to the dead doesn't do anyone any good. And it sure as shit doesn't keep a love-drunk idiot from breaking everything wide open by marrying one of them."

"Who I spend the rest of my life with doesn't have anything to do with you, Langley."

"Oh yes, it does. When the rest of the world sees that kind of peace and harmony between a transformed and the beloved Harford family, it would only open the doors for every natural-born shifter on this planet to do the same. You and I lead by example, Bronson. I couldn't let you lead this world in the wrong direction. Now, I'll steer you onto the right track again—by my side where you belong."

But you..." Bronson focused on the floor and couldn't believe he had it in him to continue to press the issue after everything he'd heard.

*Keep him talking. He's already said this much. It's not like he has anything else to lose as far as he knows.*

"I what?" His uncle sneered.

"You had no problem using them for your gain." He raised his eyebrows and met his uncle's gaze. "To do your dirty work for you."

"I didn't send you to do anything you weren't already willing to do yourself."

"I'm not talking about me. I'm talking about Agnes."

"Oh." Langley chuckled and licked his lips, clearly surprised by this turn of conversation. "You know, it's interesting that you should bring her up."

"She's a transformed too. Isn't she?"

"What?" The small smile that played on the man's lips was impossible to read. He was surprised but he looked like he was equally amused by it too.

"She is, Langley. Think about the red magic and how powerful she is. Agnes isn't a blood witch—"

Langley threw his head back and roared with laughter. "Of course she isn't. I honestly thought you were smarter than to listen to all the rumors around the farm. My God, Bronson! You've been fed everything on a silver platter except for an ability to think for yourself."

His courage faded. "You already knew?"

"I've known since the day I found her. She was three years old and your aunt Marissa, who was so happy to open her heart to everyone, couldn't stand the sight of her."

"What?"

"I know. It's a lot to sacrifice my family—even my son—for the greater good. They simply couldn't see the bigger picture so I let them leave and didn't make a fuss. Honestly, Agnes made a better prodigy than you ever could, but she doesn't come with your pedigree. The best part is she has no idea."

"You raised her to…what? To think she was a witch?"

"I didn't come here to talk about Agnes. I came to—"

The door to the study splintered and shards of wood streaked across the room in a blaze of crackling red light. A bloodcurdling scream filled the air and more red light streaked across the study and struck Langley in the chest.

With a grunt, he staggered back. The gun fell from his hand and clattered to the floor.

Agnes stood in the doorway, her hand outstretched toward him as she breathed heavily and snarled. "I've wanted to do that for a long time."

Bronson was too stunned to do anything but stare at her. She'd discarded the trench coat and her usual combat boots but had added a black beanie pulled down over her forehead to hide most of her red hair.

*How long was she standing out there?*

"Agnes." The older shifter cleared his throat. He grasped the back of the armchair beside him to try to steady himself when his legs shook violently after the blast of magic he'd taken to the chest. "I've tried to get in touch with you."

"Well, here I am." She spread her arms and stalked toward him, completely oblivious to the two Harford shifters tied up at the side of the room. "I came here to ask you a few questions."

"I'm a little busy at the moment." Langley darted a glance toward his nephew. "But feel free to stick around—"

"Because I heard a few things that made me think." Red light blazed around her hand when she stopped six inches from him. He leaned away from her and failed to maintain his cavalier expression. "So I did a little digging on my own."

"Now is not the time to—"

Her hand darted to his throat and cut his voice off in a choking wheeze. The red light of her magic cast eerie shadows across his features. "And do you know what I found?"

Langley's mouth opened and closed but he couldn't speak a single word.

"Yeah." Agnes broke into a slow grin as she studied his wide eyes and all the terror behind them. "You know. Because I heard you say it all in your own words, you son of a bitch."

"Agnes," Bronson muttered. "Wait."

"Thanks for the heads-up, Bronson. After this, we're even. Give me two minutes with this asshole and I'll tell whoever needs to hear it that your hands are clean. This'll be the last shifter I kill and then I'm done." The red light flared even brighter from her hand clenched tightly around Langley's throat.

The man uttered an agonized shriek even with his windpipe constricted.

In the next moment, chaos erupted.

Jasper roared through the gag around his mouth and the ropes binding his wrists snapped. He lunged to his feet and stormed across his study.

Agnes stretched toward him with more red light blazing from her fingertips.

Footsteps pounded down the hallway outside before Johnny, Lisa, and Charlie burst through the already shattered door. The low whine of the bounty hunter's borrowed and upgraded EBP transmitter filled the air as he leveled it at the woman's back. Lisa summoned a fireball in each hand. Charlie snarled and his eyes flashed silver as he prepared to shift and fight.

"Get your hands off the Harfords," Johnny shouted. "And we can all—"

Jasper stopped halfway across the room and turned to stare at his guests. He pulled the gag from his mouth and grinned. "Well. This is certainly an unexpected visit, Johnny."

The bounty hunter widened his eyes. "Uh…"

"Where's Bronson?" Lisa asked.

"Here." He stood from his knees and popped up from behind the couch. "Please tell me you heard all that."

"You mean the screamin'?" Johnny kept his weapon trained on Agnes' back as Langley choked and spluttered in her grip. "We thought it was you."

Jasper gestured toward Langley. "Fortunately, that is not the case."

"Agnes?" Lisa snuffed her fireballs out and stepped forward. "That's you, right?"

"It's all me," the woman replied through a quivering laugh. "Lies and everything."

"You oughtta put the shifter down now," Johnny added. "He ain't goin' anywhere."

"No." She sneered and leaned toward Langley before she uttered an insanely creepy giggle. "He sure isn't."

The light in her hand flared again.

"Watch it!" the bounty hunter shouted.

Jasper leapt back in surprise as Johnny pulled the trigger on the device and launched a shimmering spray of blue light and energy at the furious woman's back.

It caught her like Fiona's taser had caught Addison, jolted the woman, and canceled her magic a split second before it knocked her out. She didn't make a sound before she crumpled on top of Langley Appleman, who had suffered the same effect from the upgraded weapon.

The room fell incredibly silent.

The bounty hunter lifted his awesome new toy and slung it against his shoulder. "Damn, that felt good."

"I…" Jasper drew a deep breath through his nose. "I can't say I'm not grateful for the assistance, Johnny. But was it necessary to kill them both in my study?"

"They're not dead." Charlie hurried across the room to study the fallen shifters. "She'll wake with a hell of a headache tomorrow, and he'll… Well, hopefully, she crushed his vocal cords with that hold. Am I right?"

Lisa's mouth dropped open. "Charlie, that's not—"

"Kidding. I'm kidding. Mostly."

"Bronson." Jasper swept the armchair out of his way as he raced across the room and swept his startled son into his arms. "Are you all right?"

"Yeah, I'm fine, Dad. I'm only…uh… Listen, everything you heard—"

"It's okay." He pulled away to smile at his son. "It's okay."

"I'm sorry. I should have—"

"No, I don't want to hear any more tonight." The man released him and squeezed his shoulder gently before he turned to glare at the unconscious shifters. "I've heard enough. But we have more than enough time to go over whatever you want to discuss in the morning."

Bronson stared at him for a long moment, then nodded. "Okay."

"Johnny. Lisa." Jasper nodded at them. "And..."

"Charlie." The shifter dwarf nodded with a pert smile.

"Yes. How long will they be..."

"They ain't comin' to for another twenty hours. And that ain't a guess. I set the timer on that myself."

"Then that's sufficient time for a stiff drink. Would you all care to join us?"

Charlie laughed. "You're insanely calm given everything that happened."

"Well, it doesn't do anyone any good to lose their heads. Which I might if I don't pour myself that drink."

"Sure." Johnny chuckled. "We'd love to stay."

"Excellent."

As the man crossed his study to open the minibar beside his desk, Bronson sidled toward Johnny and Lisa and stared at the massive cannon propped on the dwarf's shoulder. "You did get that whole conversation recorded, right? Everything Langley said?"

"Yep." The bounty hunter cocked his head and sniffed. "I ain't heard it yet, though. Did he say anythin' good?"

"Oh, yeah. He said more than enough." Bronson rubbed his wrists as he scowled at Agnes and Langley on the floor. "So how did you know what was happening here?"

"We didn't...*know* know," Lisa replied. "But we do now."

"Oh, yeah." Charlie rubbed his head. "Without the trench coat, you can barely recognize her."

"Wait, Agnes told you Langley was here?"

"Nope. But she burned the farm down."

"Wait, what?"

Johnny placed a hand on the shifter's shoulder. "And we had a hunch."

"Another one in the bag." Charlie punched his opposite palm and whooped. "Case closed, criminals taken out—"

"Charlie."

"Yeah."

"Now ain't the time."

"I wouldn't exactly call this a nightcap." Jasper turned from the minibar with five glasses and a bottle of Johnny Walker Black on a tray. "But it's most certainly time I try your brand of whiskey."

The bounty hunter grinned and tossed the energy cannon on the floor before he spread his arms, making Lisa wince and Charlie leap nimbly away. "Aw, Jasper. Now that's how you let a fella know he's appreciated."

# CHAPTER THIRTY

*One week later*

Charlie stalked across the grass behind Johnny's cabin on the swamp and headed directly to the Adirondack chair facing the water's edge. "Lisa."

"Charlie." She put down her tablet and the book she'd been enjoying and turned in the chair to fix him with a calm smile.

"Where is he?"

"You know, I couldn't tell you."

"Aw, come on." The shifter dwarf scratched the side of his head and scanned the property. "He said today."

"I'm sure he'll show up when he wants to. You know Johnny."

"Uh-huh. I do. Which makes me think he was blowing smoke up my—hey." He walked around the chair and cast a shadow over her that blocked the sunshine she'd been thoroughly enjoying. "Did you see the news this morning?"

She slid her sunglasses down the bridge of her nose and raised an eyebrow. "You'll have to be a little more specific."

"Right." Charlie dropped into a crouch before he sat in front of her chair and stretched his legs out on the grass.

She snorted and pushed her sunglasses up over her eyes.

"I'm talking about the charity."

"There are many different charities, Charlie."

"The Harford Foundation. The new one they made. You know, the something-something for transformed—"

"Oh. You mean the Transformed Voices Association? That charity?"

He squinted at her and shook his head. "You were screwing with me, weren't you?"

Lisa grinned. "Yep."

"So you saw it? Yeah. Duh. You saw it. Whew. Those Harfords move fast with that stuff. Two weeks and they have an entirely new venture put together for shifters like us. I'm not exactly sure how that's gonna help but hey. Maybe I'll go down there and pay them a visit. See what they're doing."

"Well, if they managed to fund so many college educations for California students, I'm sure whatever they're doing for the transformed across the country is just as good."

"Huh." Charlie frowned at his outstretched legs. "I'm not sure I wanna go back to school."

She fought back a laugh and shook her head. "No one's trying to make you, Charlie."

"Good. Good. 'Cause I can't stay in one place for too long, you know? I gotta keep moving—meet new people, see new places, and get into new kinds of trouble." He slapped his thighs. "Dammit! Does he have to make me wait for this? We had a deal."

Lisa shifted in her chair to face him. "He's a dwarf of his word, Charlie. Give him a little time."

"Two weeks is forever." He cast her a sidelong glance, then sighed and sprawled on his back. "So. Have you heard from Addison or anyone else?"

"Not since Fiona told us they were heading to Michigan."

"Michigan." Charlie wrinkled his nose. "What's in Michigan? Okay, yeah, I have friends out there."

"The MC you mentioned?"

"Okay, fine. Not friends. More like acquaintances. But besides that, there's nothing but lakes—all the lakes."

She picked her tablet up and opened her book again. "Mm-hmm."

*Johnny had better hurry with this. I only have enough patience for one Walker dwarf and Charlie's about to use all of it.*

"Hey, do you think—"

A heavy thud followed by the clang of metal hitting metal came from behind Margo's giant hull in the yard. Two more thuds were followed a low, heavy scrape across wood. "Oh, hell."

"Wait a minute." Charlie bolted off the ground and stared across the yard. "That's Johnny."

"Oh." Lisa didn't move. "Look at that."

"What? Are you kidding me? He's been here the whole time?" The shifter dwarf glowered at her and trudged across the yard. "Johnny! I heard you, 'coz. Where are you?"

"Hey, Johnny. Hey." Luther crept around the side of the shed toward the sliding door and sniffed the edge. "I think he heard you."

"Yep." Rex caught sight of Charlie and sat directly in front of the shed door. "He heard you, Johnny. Want us to chase him away?"

"I can hear you too, you know." The shifter dwarf stopped and scanned the shed. "Johnny! I thought you were out doing something with fish traps."

"Dammit, Charlie. What kinda idiot sets a trap for fish? It's crab traps, all right? For crabs."

"Uh-huh." He folded his arms and glared at the shed door. "But you're not out there doing either of those things right now. Have you been avoiding me the whole time?"

With a grunt, Johnny slid the door of the shed open and poked his head out. "No. I ain't avoidin' you. Now go away."

"You are." He lunged forward and slid his hand through the

crack in the door before his cousin could shut it all the way. "Get out."

"Charlie, get your hands off my—"

"Right now. I've waited for this and you're gonna make me wait forever. Shit, even the dogs got their steaks the day we got back."

"Oh, yeah." Luther sniggered. "And they were delicious."

"Hey, Johnny." Rex stepped away from the shed to sniff along the outside of Margo. "Speaking of steaks—"

"I swear, Charlie, if you don't let go of this door right now, I ain't doin' a damn thing for you."

"Okay, fine!" The shifter dwarf heaved the sliding door aside and Johnny stumbled sideways inside the shed. His bucket of tools toppled beneath his feet with a clang. "Then tell me why you won't—" He gasped and his eyes grew incredibly wide. "No…"

"Well, now I gotta say, 'Yeah…'" Johnny grumbled with a heavy dose of sarcasm. "'Cause you ruined the damn surprise."

"What surprise, Johnny?" Rex and Luther tried to sneak past Charlie to see into the shed.

"A surprise for us?"

"We love surprises, Johnny."

"Unless it's a chipmunk hole in a fire. You're not hiding that in there, right?"

"Y'all git." The bounty hunter shooed them away. "I gave y'all one job and you couldn't even keep him away for another few hours."

"Why would you keep me away from this?" Charlie spread his arms wide like he was about to throw himself forward into the shed and wrap his arms around the custom motorcycle propped inside. "She's…"

Johnny rubbed his hands on a rag, sniffed, and stepped out of the shed. "She ain't finished. But you couldn't keep your nose outta my business long enough to—"

"She's perfect. Holy shit, 'coz." The shifter dwarf thumped his cousin on the chest and made him scowl harder. "I didn't know you could build bikes."

"I can build damn near anythin'."

"Yeah, but this... Ha! Here I was getting all pissed off 'cause you wouldn't take me to the dealership. But you..." Charlie sniffed and pursed his lips, which made him look like a mohawked toddler in leather about to burst into tears. "You built me one."

"Don't do that."

"Come here."

"Naw, Charlie. I ain't— Don't do that."

He wrapped his cousin in a massive hug and completely ignored Johnny's grunts and frantic squirming to escape.

Lisa rounded the side of Margo and stopped when she saw the Walker dwarves in their strange embrace. Or maybe Johnny in Charlie's. "This is touching, guys. Truly."

"Lisa!"

The bounty hunter shoved his cousin away and rolled his shoulders back before he straightened his black t-shirt. "Hug me like that—"

"Did you know about this?" Charlie pointed at the gleaming chrome of his new motorcycle. "You did, didn't you? Man, and I thought you guys were acting so weird because you wanted me to get lost and didn't know how to tell me without breaking my heart."

"Yeah, that ain't what happened," Johnny said flatly. But his sarcasm went right over his cousin's head and when Lisa fixed him with a "be nice" look, he shrugged.

*It's the truth. Except now he can get his ass on the road and we can get back to our lives. Alone. As soon as I finish this bike.*

"Oh, man, Johnny." Charlie leaned into the shed and burst out laughing. "I can't wait to see what she can do."

"Sure you can. 'Cause she ain't finished."

"Yeah, yeah. Okay. I get it." The shifter dwarf turned and raised his hands to concede the point. "I can be patient. Mostly. Probably. You know what, I'll try."

"That's good enough."

"You guys—" Charlie shook his head and wagged a finger at them. "You guys went above and beyond, you know? Like way more than you had to. I...thanks."

"No problem at all," Lisa said happily.

Johnny snorted. "It wasn't only for him. We got a couple of thousand transformed shifters out there turnin' things around with help. It wouldn't be happenin' if he hadn't arrived and told us about the whole situation in the first place. And no." He pointed at his cousin. "That ain't an invitation to break into my house and nap on my couch anytime you damn well please."

"Yeah, I get it. It's cool." Charlie folded his arms and studied the brand-new motorcycle. "I was saying thanks for me, though."

The bounty hunter snorted and regarded his cousin with a small frown. "For what?"

"You know. Everything." After a quick shrug, the biker dwarf's sly, crooked smile returned. "Yeah. We had our moments. But you didn't kick me to the curb, Johnny. It...it means a lot."

"Yeah." He swallowed and didn't even have to be prompted by a gaze from his partner that he could feel on his face. "That's what family's for, ain't it?"

"Damn straight. And you built me a bike. Ha!" Charlie sidled up to his cousin and smacked his shoulder with the back of his hand. "So...when she's finished. Do you, uh...you wanna go for a ride?"

Lisa laughed and clapped a hand quickly over her mouth.

Johnny looked from his biker cousin to the motorcycle glinting inside the shed. He leaned toward him without looking at him and muttered, "Not on your damn life."

"Yeah, I didn't think so."

Get sneak peeks, exclusive giveaways, behind the scenes content, and more. PLUS you'll be notified of special **one day only fan pricing** on new releases.

Sign up today to get free stories.

## AUTHOR NOTES - MARTHA CARR
### AUGUST 18, 2021

Life is a little complicated right now – more than usual. I have 3rd stage melanoma and I'm going in for chemo once a month in Houston at MD Anderson. The sweet pittie, Leela, has terminal cancer and she's getting a lot of different prescriptions to make her comfortable. And there's that Delta thing and I'm sitting in a hot spot in Austin.

Not my first time being surrounded by events I can't control, but every time it takes a lot of work to just let go. That's right, surrender all of it and stop worrying.

I'm a big fan of that serenity prayer, which says in short form to recognize what I can change, do something about it, what I can't – and for that last part let that go.

There's a payoff for me too. I stop thinking that overworking, overmanaging, over-volunteering is necessary for my part of the world to keep running. For everyone I care about to be okay. It turns out that the universe is requesting a much more manageable amount of contribution from me. A kind of spiritual arrogance where I put myself at the center holding things up.

In fact, it has happened that when I do less, more good has actually opened up for me. Go figure.

Like a spiritual magic trick instead and the best kind.

If I'm not spending time trying to figure out how to help, how to make things better, how to get more done by myself, that leaves chunks of time to ponder doing something else. Like – something fun. Suddenly hobbies are possible. Time opens up to sit still on my back deck watching the flowers grow. Reading a good book just because. And the more I let myself try those things, the more fun things I think up to do. Kayaking on the lake, learning to ride a bike again. Yeah, you heard me, learning to ride a bike. Turns out that old cliché is wrong – at least with me.

Even better is the payoff I didn't expect. When things didn't crash to the ground without me driving the bus, and weirdly even got better, I felt more like I was a part of the universe. I was snugly fit somewhere in the middle as just a piece of everything. I was never meant to try and take on so much. What a relief.

I am just a passenger on the bus and I don't need to know where I'm headed. I didn't anyway, only raising my anxiety and probably my meddling. I was able to give myself permission to hang back, do less and still know I'd done my part. Go enjoy the rest of life.

And that's exactly what I'm setting out to do. Maybe a little later than most, but all we have is the day we're in so – it's never too late. Next week I'll be sitting among the redwoods listening to the sea far below. More adventures to follow.

Thank you for not only reading this book, but this entire series and these author notes as well.

I spoke with Martha a couple of days ago on her vacation (I received some nice pictures) and she is enjoying herself. What she isn't doing is ignoring work.

I'm not sure she knows what 'vacation' means. Or, more likely, she knows the books might go slightly off track if she allows me to make the decisions.

Hehehe… Could you imagine what trouble I could get into with Carte Blanche cover choices?

Hmmm… "I know that the dragon was blue for seven books… But I'm feeling kinda gray today. Let's make him gray with undertones of pink."

She'd get over it. Eventually.

I mean, I'd hear about that sh#t for months. It wouldn't stop her from going on another vacation, but you know she would have secret handshake meetings with Grace. Instructions so when I would say something in the main channel with the artists, and Grace would go behind my back and put in a direct message to the artist(s) like Moonchild or Mihaela:

"I know Mike suggests we go with a gray dragon. What he meant was to leave it alone. Get his approval for the gray, make the action the same, but give a blue dragon to Kelly at the last second. We won't tell him."

I think in time, I'd be helping Martha. You see, it would let her realize that by truly letting go and allowing the universe just to be, book sales would take care of themselves.

Probably by you, the loyal readers, asking Martha in direct chats, 'Did you let Mike play with the covers again?' Followed by, 'Didn't Grace cover for you?'

Hehehehe… (Did you see the pun, did you??)

Go ahead Martha, go on another vacation. I double dare you!

And get better too. I have many years of harassment - all in good fun, or at least my fun - planned. So, take vacations, don't worry about covers, leave the details of other peoples lives to them and relax.

I got this™*!

Anyway, stay safe and sane out there, and I look forward to talking to you in the next book!

Ad Aeternitatem,
Michael Anderle

*I'm joking about the TM on "I got this!" – It IS actually a trademark of a few different companies related to jewelry, toys and other items. Geez, if you can TM "I Got This!" what can't you TM?

**Solve a murder, save her mother, and stop the apocalypse?**

What would you do when elves ask you to investigate a prince's murder and you didn't even know elves, or magic, was real?

Meet Leira Berens, Austin homicide detective who's good at what she does – track down the bad guys and lock them away.

Which is why the elves want her to solve this murder – fast. It's not just about tracking down the killer and bringing them to justice. It's about saving the world!

If you're looking for a heroine who prefers fighting to flirting, check out The Leira Chronicles today!

**<u>AVAILABLE ON AMAZON AND IN KINDLE UNLIMITED!</u>**

# CONNECT WITH THE AUTHORS

**Martha Carr Social**
Website:
http://www.marthacarr.com
Facebook:
https://www.facebook.com/groups/MarthaCarrFans/

**Michael Anderle**

Website: http://lmbpn.com

Email List: http://lmbpn.com/email/

https://www.facebook.com/LMBPNPublishing

https://twitter.com/MichaelAnderle

https://www.instagram.com/lmbpn_publishing/

https://www.bookbub.com/authors/michael-anderle

Made in the USA
Las Vegas, NV
29 September 2021

31369425R00157